# BONE
# TRUTH

# BONE TRUTH

## A NOVEL BY ANNE FINGER

COFFEE HOUSE PRESS :: MINNEAPOLIS

Cover design by Allan Kornblum

Back cover photograph by Peter Reiss

"Deep Purple": By Mitchell Parish and Peter DeRose. Copyright © 1934, 1939 (Renewed) EMI Robbins Catalog, Inc. International Copyright Secured. Made in USA. All Rights Reserved. Used by Permission of CPP/Belwin, Inc., Miami, FL 33014

"Joe Hill": Words by Alfred Hayes, Music by Earl Robinson. © 1938 MCA Music Publishing Inc., a division of MCA Inc. Copyright Renewed. International Copyright Secured. All Rights Reserved. Used by Permission.

The publishers would like to thank the following funders for assistance that helped make this book possible: Dayton Hudson Foundation on behalf of Dayton's and Target Stores; The General Mills Foundation; The National Endowment for the Arts, a federal agency; The Jerome Foundation; The Lannan Foundation; The Andrew W. Mellon Foundation; The Beverly J. and John A. Rollwagen Fund of the Minneapolis Foundation; Star Tribune/Cowles Media Company; and The McKnight Foundation. This activity is made possible in part by a grant provided by the Minnesota State Arts Board, through an appropriation by the Minnesota State Legislature. Major new marketing initiatives have been made possible by the Lila Wallace–Reader's Digest Literary Publishers Marketing Development Program, funded through a grant to the Council of Literary Magazines and Presses.

Coffee House Press books are available to the trade through our primary distributor, Consortium Book Sales & Distribution, 1045 Westgate Drive, Saint Paul, MN 55114. Our books are also available through all major library distributors and jobbers, and through most small press distributors, including Bookpeople, Inland, and Small Press Distribution. For personal orders, catalogs or other information, write to:

Coffee House Press

27 North Fourth Street, Suite 400, Minneapolis, MN 55401

Library of Congress CIP Data:
Finger, Anne.
    Bone truth : a novel / by Anne Finger.
        p.    cm.
    ISBN 1-56689-028-4 (paperback : acid-free)
    1. Adult child abuse victims—United States—Fiction. 2. Fathers and daughters—United States—Fiction. 3. Women photographers—United States—Fiction. I. Title.
PS3556.I4677B66    1994
    813'.54—dc20                                      94-12602
                                                           CIP

10      9      8      7      6      5      4      3      2      1

*Dedicated to the memory of Laura Lenart*

*1967–1990*

# I

"I have the results from your test," she says. "And you are pregnant."

The prickle of artificial upholstery fabric against my bare elbows. My cane and purse on the floor next to the chair. The woman, who introduced herself to me a minute ago ("Hi, I'm Sherry. I'm one of the counselors here—"), sitting opposite me in a blond wood and brown fabric chair. The poster on the wall opposite, a bear balancing on a gaily painted circus ball, the word CYRK beneath it.

"Have you thought about what you're going to do?" she asks, leaning toward me. Her body language says, I'm open, I'm nonjudgmental, you can share with me.

I consider saying, No, Sherry, I have never given it a moment's consideration. The subject of offspring has not crossed my mind before. Nope. No. Never.

I stiffen in my chair. I concede, "I've thought about it."

"Yes?" she asks, an indeterminate, open-ended "yes."

I wonder how she spells her name. Maybe it's Sherri or even Cheri. Whatever else I might say about my parents, at least they never went in for frothy names, the cute. At least we were all named after stalwart saints.

She is looking at me, waiting for me to say something, and so I say, "I'm uncertain."

"Uncertain?" she repeats.

"Uncertain."

Ease up on her, Etters. You hate all this empathy, all this

"Hi, I'm Sherry and I care about your feelings," but what do you want—Prussian efficiency?

"I suppose you have more to think about than a lot of people."

"Yes." How did she sense that? No, she doesn't sense it. She's talking, obliquely, about my disability. I feel my stubbornness surge, my old sense of *Don't tell me I can't*. The last thing that I need is to get carried away by rebelliousness.

"It's not so much that. It's . . . other things."

"Other things? . . . Are you married?"

"No." I want to get out of the Women's Medical Center. I want to be someplace, any place, else. I keep answering Sherry's questions. I give her the date of my last menstrual period, just over four weeks ago; yes, I do have some time to think this through. I listen to her while she tells me how safe abortion is before twelve weeks; I don't interrupt her to say I know all this, you don't have to tell me.

I am giddy as I walk down the stone front steps of the clinic. Giddy, what a wonderful word. I see ice skaters on a frozen pond, almost falling over backward, laughing as they do, but catching themselves and skating on. Giddy. A baby is growing inside me. A baby. Inside of me.

No, not a baby, a fetus. Not even a fetus. Maybe not even an embryo yet. Maybe it's still just a zygote, a collection of cells that look like thick soap bubbles when seen under a microscope. I'll go to the library and take out a book on fetal development; I'll take out one on exercise during pregnancy and one on nutrition. I'm going to eat tofu and kelp and cabbage and carrots and bee pollen and—

What am I thinking of? This is crazy. Matt and I are so new. Too new. How could we have made a baby? Don't they get made face-to-face, in the missionary position? Don't they grow out of acts of love or familiar boredom, under thick blankets?

I guess not. Not always.

I wish I still worked. Worked at the law firm, that is. Work-Work I used to call it, to distinguish it from Real Work, my art. I could use something mindless, almost physical, sitting in front of the blank screen, processing words. "Lessor hereby warrants to Lessee that there are no prior covenants or restrictions, except those which may be herein expressed, and that . . ."

I trudge up Geary Street, a gentle slope as the steep streets of San Francisco go, but still enough to make me have to stop and rest every block or so, to stop my lungs' gentle asthmatic song. I find a phone booth and call Ann Marie. Four days ago, she'd played the role of the Archangel Gabriel, as we were sitting by the deep end of the Nickel Pool in the Mission.

She handed me the sunscreen and said, "Get my back, will you? I want to make sure I live long enough to get Alzheimer's." As I leaned towards her, she said, "Jesus, your boobs are enormous . . . You're not—pregnant?"

I looked up. The first thing I saw were the words painted on the turquoise tiles at the edge of the deep end of the pool. I read them out loud: *"Agua profundo."*

*"Agua profundo,"* she agreed.

Now, a giddy girl standing in a phone booth on the corner of Geary and Bush, says, "I'm pregnant," into the black plastic receiver. I say it while the phone is ringing and then I say it to Ann Marie's answering "Hello."

"Do you want to come over? I don't have a client until noon."

Ann Marie dangles her crutches from her arms as she hugs me.

"I'm happy," I say. "I feel crazy, but I'm happy."

Then I start crying. She hands me Kleenex and gets me a mineral water with lemon and rubs my back.

"Have you told Matt?"

"I didn't want to tell him over the phone. . . . I'm not ready for this."

Ten minutes after I get there, I leave. Ann Marie lends me a pair of sunglasses, to hide my red eyes.

At Lucca's, an Italian deli at the edge of the Mission, I stand in a long line to order my sandwich. But when I get to the front, I still haven't decided what I want. The problem isn't that nothing appeals to me, it's that I want everything: I want tuna on sourdough with hot peppers and Swiss cheese; I want copa and provolone with oil and vinegar; I want Cheddar and Swiss on whole wheat. I want to eat foods that will soothe me and foods that will sear me and wake up my mouth.

When I get to the front, I say, "I don't think I'm going to get anything after all," and leave. The minute I get outside, I know exactly what I want: the tuna. But I'm too embarrassed to go back in.

I drive up to Twin Peaks to look out over the city. Since it's a weekday the tourists aren't too bad: there's only one charter bus parked in the lot. I stand there for a few minutes, looking out over the ocean and the Bay, the Golden Gate and Bay bridges. Mission Blue butterflies live on the slopes of this hill and nowhere else in the world. An endangered species. Every time I come up here, I look for them, but I've yet to see one.

I drive to my studio. Just because I'm pregnant, just because my life has been tossed into the air, that doesn't mean that I'm not still going to be a serious artist, that I'm not going to put in at least six hours today.

A manila envelope is taped to my door. I pull it free. The number five flashes on my answering machine—when it displays zero I feel depressed, however momentarily. A few calls from my students; some books I've ordered have arrived at Modern Times. No call from my mother. No news is good news. My father is in the hospital, dying of cirrhosis of the liver.

When Clara, my oldest sister, called me three months ago to tell me they had diagnosed his problem, I looked cirrhosis up in medical textbooks. *Cirrhosis of the liver, usually caused by excessive alcohol consumption, a fatal disease. . . . Bands of fibrosis (internal scarring) break up the normal structure of the liver. The surviving cells multiply to form islands of living cells separated by dead tissue . . . no system of the body is spared in the syndrome . . . the therapy is nondramatic, nonspecific, supportive. . . .*

A chart in one book detailed what would happen to him. *State of Consciousness*, read the heading of the first column: he will decline through hypersomnia, insomnia, or inversion of sleep pattern through somnolence to semi-stupor and then unconsciousness. The next column, *Intellectual Function*, mapped the journey down from subtly impaired computations and shortened attention span through loss of time, down through amnesia for past events, then loss of place; loss of self. Under *Personality-Behavior* the list reads: exaggeration of normal behavior; euphoria or depression; decreased inhibitions; bizarre behavior; paranoia or anger; ending with "rage" and then "none." He has already taken the first step down.

I open the manila envelope that was taped to my door, take out contact sheets from Cyndi. When this last batch of photos is printed, I'll be ready for my exhibit, which opens in a few weeks.

I pore over one contact sheet with a magnifying glass, staring at women's bodies. I move my black cropping cards. My exhibit is photographs of disabled women, naked.

In *Roget's Thesaurus*, I look up the word *disabled*. It's under the heading for *Impotence*.

*Impotence, powerlessness . . . inability, incapability, incapacity, incompetence, inadequacy, insufficiency, inefficiency, unfitness, imbecility; disability, disablement, disqualification. 5. emasculation, demasculinization, effeminization; castration. 6. impotent, incapable, incompetent; flash in the pan, blank cartridge, dud [slang]; eunuch. VERBS. 9. disable, disenable, incapacitate; cripple, becripple, maim, lame, hamstring, hock; bugger [slang], queer, queer the works [slang].*

I read these words out loud to myself; I think about recording them on tape, playing them in the background as part of the exhibit. But I'm not sure, maybe this would detract from the impact of the photographs.

I only last about two hours at my studio.

I go to 24th Street in Noe Valley and buy a pair of lilac socks, a pair of earrings, a Häagen-Dazs ice-cream bar—even though there's a boycott of Häagen-Dazs because the owner gives money to right-wing causes—a Guatemalan blouse and a bunch of lilies. I spend over a hundred dollars. I never do things like that. I only buy things on sale and even then I usually think and think and think. Is this me, doing these things?

I drive back home to Bernal Heights and sit, just sit, staring out the window.

An hour or so later, Matt calls to say that Sean, his co-worker with AIDS, had another one of those little strokes, what are they called?—not TIAS, we agree, but neither of us can think of the right initials—and so Matt's working his shift for him. A double, it means he'll make almost $500 for sixteen hours' work. He drops his voice: is it OK if he comes by a little after midnight?

"Sure," I say. I haven't told him anything: not that my clockwork period was late, not that I went yesterday morning for a test. I'm considering saying, Matt, I have to talk to you about something. But I don't. Let him work his double; I'll tell him later. Still, he catches the note of hesitancy in my voice, asks, "Is everything okay?"

"Yeah," I say, "I'm just distracted. I'm thinking about my exhibit."

Three evenings a week Matt is a word processor at a law firm. Working three shifts a week, he can almost support himself. The trick is to pick up extra shifts on holidays and double shifts, where you make time-and-a-half, and then, after twelve hours, double-time. Marx said that the proletarianization of labor would spread. The word-processing room does look like a factory: rows of terminals, getting typed on twenty-four hours a day, seven days a week. Closed only on Thanksgiving and Christmas.

Until a year ago, I processed words at a law firm too, the swing shift, just like him, though I made enough money from my art that I only had to work one shift a week. When I arrived in the building at four-thirty in the afternoon, the place was laced up straight: partners in thousand-dollar silk suits, secretaries dressed for success. As the night wore on, the associates shed their coats and ties; the word processors and proofreaders and paralegals shed their shoes and socks. We walked barefoot through the thick carpets, rearranged the paintings on the wall (good art, relentlessly inoffensive), ordered Chinese food and charged it to Drexel Burnham Lambert, their biggest client. When things were slow, Kirk and George and Roger, three gay men who worked in proofreading, would form a chorus line and lip-synch old Ronettes and Supremes songs.

Most of us on the swing shift—late afternoon until midnight—were artists, actors, writers, some almost successful, working one or two shifts a week, a few people who were paying off a loan on a new car or were were strung out on Saks Fifth Avenue. The people who worked the graveyard shift—midnight to eight-thirty in the morning—tended to be truly strange, without the social lubrication to work a daylight job, some teetering perilously close to psychosis.

Four months ago, Matt moved into the studio down the hall from me. He bugged the shit out of me—a kid, a couple of years out of art college, tramping up and down the stairs in his motorcycle boots, loud conversations and music always coming from his studio. It wasn't just the noise: it was the jeans, the leather jacket, the motorcycle boots, the whole artist-as-bad-boy trip that got to me. And the friends crowding into his studio. I don't let people into my studio, don't want them sniffing around, asking me what it is I'm working on. I distrust show-offs.

"Can you hold the elevator?" he called to me one day, and came tramp-tramp-tramping down the hall in his heavy boots. I was about to say something to him about the noise, was trying to put the words together, firm but not bitchy, when he said:

"You're Elizabeth Etters, aren't you? . . . Matt Roth."

We shook hands. "I like your work. I like it a lot."

"Thank you," I said.

"My mother liked your work. Theresa Gagliardi."

"Oh, sure. . . ." She was an artist, a feminist. "I was sorry to hear that she died."

"Yeah," he said. "My mom was a swell lady."

*Swell lady?*

"What kind of work do you do?" I asked as the elevator lumbered to a stop.

"I'm a photographer," he said, stepping forward and pulling the webbed strap that raised the gate. "And I do word processing."

A few days later, he knocked on my door. "I'm having a show," he said, handing me a postcard announcement.

"Okay," I said. I'm brusque—my studio attitude. Don't interrupt me; don't break my concentration. I didn't want to seem too crabby, so I looked up at him and smiled.

His eyes, hazel irises ringed with black, staring straight back, startled me. The attraction I felt was sharp, nothing diffuse and feminine, a pure pulse of lust.

"I'll try and make it," I said.

"I hope you can."

On the card was a photograph of an empty stretch of two-lane road, somewhere in the Southwest, the straight white line dividing the highway faded almost to invisibility, sparse sage alongside the road; on one side, broken barbed wire stretched between rails.

At odd moments during the day I played that encounter back. Was I being crazy, I thought, reading meanings into superficial banalities, into his "I hope you can"? How can I be a woman, a solid, rooted-to-the-ground feminist, and still feel ga-ga over boys, tongue-tied and ditzy, sixteen years old again? (Except when I was sixteen I didn't have boyfriends, wasn't ditzy and tongue-tied. I was serious: serious about ending the war, serious about ending oppression, too busy to giggle, to be bothered with boys.)

I daydreamed lustful daydreams: inviting him in for a glass of wine, giving him a coy smile, pulling him close to me, unzipping his jacket, unzipping his jeans. Skip the romance. Except of course there's AIDS. We have to have a Serious Conversation these days before we screw; we have to wrap ourselves in latex. Except of course I'm too scared to lunge at him, scared of making a fool out of myself, scared of being rejected.

Here I was, lusting after a man who was short. At first, when I ricocheted away from Danny, my ex-husband, I saw men who were grad students in electrical engineering, aspiring Buddhists, men who bored me but didn't frighten me. Tall, they had to be tall—not short, like Danny, like Daddy. I counted my attraction to Matt as a good sign, a sign that I was breaking the spells of the past.

I went to his opening.

The empty road.

An unmade bed in a cheap hotel room; an iron bedstead, a sink in the corner, tattered curtains with sunlight pouring in through them.

Ocean Beach on a gray day, a two-foot wave rolling wearily for the lonely shore, the tide line of pebbles, plastic bags, seaweed, beer cans.

He grinned when he saw me. We talked. I was hoping he would ask me out for a drink after the opening. I could have asked him. But I made the first step, going there. Maybe he's intimidated by me, I thought, and sometimes, when you're disabled, you have to everything but hit people over the head: Here I am, I'm a woman, I'm sexual, look!

"It's okay," I said, after he had been talking with me for a few minutes, "don't hang around with me, go talk to the important people."

"If you'll go out for a drink with me afterward."

"Sure," I said.

Ten minutes later I snaked through the crowd to him. "Come by my studio and pick me up when you're through. I want to get some work done."

Almost two hours later he knocked on the door. "No," I said, "I don't have my car. I took the bus."

Could I manage on his motorcycle, with the cane and everything? He was forthright. I liked that about him.

The cane wouldn't be a problem; did he have an extra helmet?

No, he didn't wear a helmet; if he had a bad accident, he'd rather die then end up a vegetable.

I wondered if I should say: "Some of my best friends have brain damage." I decided not to. I didn't think we would have gotten into an argument; but there would have been a residue of awkwardness throughout the evening. And I wanted to sit behind him; I wanted to wrap my arms around his waist.

I climbed on behind him. He wasn't going that fast, but it felt fast. I felt sexual again. For years, sex meant sex with Jeremy, the man I lived with for five years: sex tied up with love, and later love and anger, familiarity, and, finally, obligation. We knew each other so well. We knew what we liked; we knew what we needed.

This was something different. The tension was sharp: nothing muddy, no desire bleeding into depression. This was pure, I was scared.

The waitress asked what I wanted to drink. I told her I needed a minute to think it over. I hardly ever drink, so when I do it's an Occasion. A margarita, I decided. I'm like a kid, I like sweet drinks, drinks that taste like ice cream sodas, not hard liquor.

"I'm twenty-four," he said.

"Thirty-three."

"I just thought we should get that out of the way."

We talked: about the Museum School in Boston, where we had both gone; about the difficulty of heating our studios. He asked me questions. I answered them. How long have I lived here? Seven years. I came to California to go to Cal Arts. Where am I from? Originally, Massachusetts—Western Mass and then Boston. I told him about my parents being old leftists, about my father being blacklisted and how we tried to live off the land. I was funny, charming, telling my story of the city slickers on the farm.

"Then after Boston, London," I said.

"London, why London?" he asked.

"I went to school there. And then I married an English man. It didn't last long. And then I lived with someone for five years. We just broke up, six months ago."

"Oh," he said. Thirty seconds of silence, while those words sank. I bet he was thinking, When she first got married, I was nine years old. Then: So when did you go to the Museum School?

After I left my husband. Then I got a fellowship to Cal Arts.

Matt told me he liked Southern California, which I'd never heard anyone else in San Francisco say, ever. "Do you like Valencia?" I asked, naming the barren desert where Cal Arts is. "San Francisco feels like my home now," I said.

My single friends say that after a while it gets to be a rap that you've got down pat: the history of your family, your marriages / major relationships, the places you've lived, your political / philosophical / spiritual attitudes and values.

Then I started asking him open-ended questions. He grew up here in San Francisco. His mother was a North Beach person. His father was, too; now his father works for an advertising agency. He's an art director. His mother was Italian; his father Jewish. The fights were terrible, but the food was great. Matt went east to go to art school so that he wouldn't be his mother's son. And then he came back here. My spiel took half an hour; his took ten minutes. I liked his eyes, I liked the timbre of his voice. When we got outside, I liked the way his mouth felt against mine; I liked the easy way he moved his hands against me.

I lie awake in bed waiting for him to come home. In this almost bare room. The windows are unshaded, curtainless, and the light from the moon, the light from the stars, the odd flickering lights from my neighbors' televisions, the few electric lights still lit at midnight, the street lights, all make the air gray. The plain shapes of my bureau, my electric air-cleaner, the single halogen lamp at my bedside are darker gray.

No curtains. No shades. No carpet. No throw rugs, India dhurries. No bookcases. No newspapers, no worn clothes tossed cavalierly on the floor. I used to imitate Frida Kahlo; I had a bedroom that was a work of rich, messy, busy, anti-Classical art: prints friends had made thumbtacked to the wall, carnival masks, objects full of memories, souvenirs from places I've been, places I've only dreamed of going.

That was back in the old days, before I had chronic asthma. When it first got really bad, the doctor told me that if I didn't want to spend the rest of my life on steroids I'd have to strip everything from the place where I slept, leave no place to collect dust, wipe a bare floor with a damp mop once a day. He showed me a picture, taken through an electron microscope, of a crablike monster: a dust mite. What I'm really allergic to is the "fecal matter," as he put it, of this creature that lives on the sloughed-off cells of human flesh.

I purged my familiar objects, packing away my Mexican Day of the Dead papier-mâché skeleton wearing a floppy black hat, blowing her saxophone; my Guatemalan trouble dolls; my framed Japanese postage stamp; my remarkably authentic-looking Greek fake-icon (six hundred drachmas, a little less than a dollar) that Ann Marie bought for me when we were on Santorini: mother and child, to which I have attached with Krazy Glue a plastic dime-store baby.

I used to worship Frida Kahlo. Now I worship Matt's dead mother.

The first time I went to his studio, our second date, he showed me a painting of hers, which hung above his couch: a pure black circular brushstroke on rice paper.

"It's beautiful," I said.

"She got into Zen Buddhism before she died. All she did was eat grapefruit and brown rice and meditate and paint hundreds of those paintings. The exact same thing. The circle on rice paper. And then sometimes she'd do this ritual burning of them. Once we went up to Twin Peaks on a windy day with a couple hundred of them, and she let them go. She'd do this thing with peeling the membranes between the grapefruit sections perfectly, so each section would come out whole. I mean, I really loved my mother, but, at the end, she was pretty woo-woo."

A watershed: three years ago, when my asthma got so bad that I had to give up painting; the paint fumes made me sick.

If I have this baby, it will be the ultimate divide in my life: time will be measured Before Child, After Child.

It could all so easily unravel, this skein of luck and cleverness, small miracles, that holds my life together, enabling me to live as an artist, a political person. There's my grant from the Arts Council to teach at the San Francisco Independent Living Center. The recipe Isaiah gave me, his grandmother's kosher Cuban black beans and rice, complete protein, full of fiber and vitamins C and A, which costs twenty cents a serving, and I eat two or three nights a week. The shopping skills of my student Carl, a former museum curator, who got multiple sclerosis. His wife divorced him, he didn't have the stamina for work anymore, he maxed out on his health insurance, and from solid, trendy middle-class he plummeted down to a rented room, taking the bus instead of driving a Saab. No more trips to Italy/Greece/some undiscovered island off the coast of Venezuela. But the guy's got taste. He makes a religion out of shopping the thrift stores. Carl finds me linen tunics, men's black velvet smoking jackets, hides them under the used sheets, takes me to the Salvation Army with him after class to try them on.

Matt's taught me another Salvation Army trick, taught to him by a textile-artist ex-girlfriend. You can buy things that are well-cut but have horrendous prints or colors and strip them with sodium hypochlorite, dye them black or, if you're feeling adventurous, gray or teal.

And the biggest miracle of all, this one-bedroom rent-controlled apartment. My friend Lydia had lived here for years. She was moving out; I was breaking up with Jeremy and needed a place to live. The only catch was that the rent-control ordinance in San Francisco allows for "vacancy decontrol": the landlady could raise the rent as much as she wanted when Lydia moved.

"Pretend to be me," Lydia said.

"Pretend to be you?"

"She hardly ever comes over here. When there's something wrong, she shines it on or she sends a plumber or an electrician over. Anyhow, we all look alike to them," Lydia said.

"Lydia, we both walk with canes. The similarity ends there. You're half a foot taller than me. We'll never get away with it," I said.

"We all look alike to them."

Every month I went to the bank and bought a money order, signed it with Lydia's name, mailed it off. And one day when I limped down to get the mail, a landladyish-looking woman was standing there; she said, "Hello, Lydia," and I said, "Hello, Mrs. DeSantini."

Matt opens the bedroom door at one in the morning.

I'm not asleep, but I pretend to be. I pretend to be asleep while he sits down on the corner of the bed and undresses. I pretend to be asleep while he crawls into bed and starts circling my nipple with the tip of his index finger. I know that if I say anything to him, I will say everything to him, and I want one last time between the two of us when everything is pure and untrammeled, when we are just two honest bodies in the night.

The dark shapes of my bureau, of my wardrobe, of him above me. A car pulls into the driveway next door—its headlights move shadows of the windowpanes across my wall. In the light, I see Matt's face: he looks so young. When I work too hard, I get circles under my eyes, my face gets puffy, and I look as if I've crossed over the line into middle age. When he works hard, he looks softer, more vulnerable, younger.

We fall asleep together, we fall asleep in silence.

A long night, deep sleep, sleep without dreams.

I wake up in the morning wondering how much a box of Pampers costs. No, we won't use Pampers: cloth diapers, it'll be cloth diapers. How many will we need? I'll get—*we'll* get?—a washing machine? . . . I wonder how much that costs. $200? $500? I couldn't possibly schlepp buckets of dirty diapers to the laundromat.

Getting by is in my blood. My mother did it. She lived with the five of us on luck and ground beef on sale and promises and what a woman could earn. In the fifties, the decade that was called prosperous, my mother and "aunt" Louise remembered recipes from the Depression. Lima bean casseroles and baked beans and chili and lentil soup and split pea soup and if you take butter and whip it with ice water, it'll go twice as far. Will that work with margarine? There's a bakery outlet over on Pine Street. You can get day-old bread there for a nickel a loaf. Go down to the welfare office, you can get government surplus food there, even if you're working. The government surplus food comes in five- and ten-pound cans: peanut butter and powdered milk, honey and white gloppy shortening. The cans have black-and-white labels that read: GOVERNMENT SURPLUS. NOT TO BE RESOLD.

Health insurance. In a few months, I won't be covered anymore under the extension on the insurance I had when I worked at the law firm. I'm uninsurable. I'll have to go back to work so I can get health insurance, or else go on ssi, so I can get Medi-Cal: live in utter poverty, like half my disabled friends do. A twenty-cent phone call a luxury. Buying a book an impossibility.

But I could manage to skate by.

The bumper sticker on my car says, Reproductive Freedom for All Women. When I was sixteen, seventeen, in 1967, '68, my mother's friends, the women I babysat for, a bit high on Manhattans or maybe just on the promises of that time, would tell me about their own marriages, how they'd slid into them through accidental pregnancies or, if they were good girls, girls who didn't have sex before marriage, out of lust. A few times I heard stories of illegal abortions. I felt an odd adolescent mix of contempt and pity and sure superiority for those women, the certainty that my own life would be so much better than theirs. We had birth control pills. Soon abortion would be legal. There wasn't any more rigid division into "nice girls" and "bad girls." I thought this would make us free. I thought freedom would make us happy. Now I know freedom just makes you unhappy in a better way.

Now I get to choose. Lucky me. I get to draw up some balance sheet in my mind, list in one column "Reasons for Having a Child," in another, "Reasons for Not Having a Child." On the plus side, I have all my wild selfish reasons: that I want to know what it feels like, to have another person grow inside of me; that I want to feel the wrack of labor sweeping through me; that I want the experience of motherhood as fodder for my art.

And on the negative side? Just the past, that's all.

If I do this, I'll really be the odd one out. Me and my four childless sisters. I'm the one who doesn't have money stashed away for retirement, the one who doesn't drive a well-main-tained car that gets good gas mileage. (My sister Jenny doesn't own a car; she thinks driving is a crime against nature, pedals her ten-speed to campus, always wearing her helmet strapped under her chin.) The aunts always said of me, "What a pretty face!" and asked me, like they asked the boys, "What are you going to be when you grow up?" If I do it, this will be the ultimate act of refusal: I won't be a brain, split off from an ignored body, floating, a disembodied Cheshire-cat's head above them, wearing a crippled supplicant's smile.

I get up. I close the bedroom door carefully behind me. I pad around the apartment. I pour myself half a cup of coffee. I sit in my big chair. After a while, through the door, I hear Matt sigh, the bed sighing a bit in its turn as he gets up, his footsteps, the door creaking open, louder footsteps as he shuffles to the bathroom. I meet him in the kitchen. I hand him a cup of coffee.

"I'm pregnant," I say.

He takes the cup of coffee, sips it.

"What do you want to do?"

"I don't know," I say.

The air between us is suddenly brittle.

"I had a test the day before yesterday."

He puts his arm around my shoulder. "My dad was twenty-four when I was born."

"How symmetrical," I half-laugh. "Maybe."

He holds me. "I've got to get back to Hutchinson, Rubin. It was part of the deal, with me getting the double. I'd work this day shift no one else wanted."

I start crying. "We can talk later. I'll be okay."

"Yeah," he says. He strokes my hair against the nape of my neck. He rubs my shoulders. "It'll be okay. Want me to call in sick?"

"No," I say, "I'm all right."

Then I'm alone. I go and sit in my bare bedroom, my knees drawn up to my chest.

When I was with Jeremy—perfect cool Jeremy, who was (almost always) gentle and good, who went to four meetings a week and spent the other evenings reading *The Nation, Left Business Observer, The Guardian, Radical Teacher,* novels by Nadine Gordimer, books about economic development in Africa, U.S. population-control policies in South America—my companion Jeremy, we had made a decision not to have children.

It wasn't so much my personal history. Or, as they say in the legal documents I used to process, that question was never reached. We watched our friends have kids. Saw the near impossibility of juggling it all—political commitment, eight hours of work a day, caring for children. And something else, too: the way that everyone believed, setting out, that they could shape their own children—give them nothing to read but nonsexist, interracial books from Old Wives Tales, send them to progressive day care—and then find out that you can't remake the world in one family. The kids want G.I. Joe and Smurfs. The girls want to wear make-up and the boys want to play with guns. And the parents? Well, they become parents.

That longing, for the tiny body flopped against mine, for the swell of pregnancy, was like all those longings I had that would never be fulfilled: the longing to dress in beautiful clothes, the longing to travel everywhere: to the Caribbean, the Aegean islands, Thailand, Burma. Nothing was wrong with the desire itself, but the cost of it was too much.

Hormones of pregnancy. Half an hour ago, wasn't I high, as happy as I've ever been, dizzy with hope? And now I'm mournful and low. Half an hour ago, I was sure that this was right, as sure as I now am that it's wrong to go on with this pregnancy.

My embryo. No bigger than my thumbnail, you've already thrown my life into chaos. Growing faster than any cancer could, doubling, tripling every day.

When I was twenty, I had a nervous breakdown, spent three years being crazy, staggering through life. A *wunderkind* who seemed so mature, so wise beyond her years and then cracked at adulthood, fired at too high a heat.

And then, when I was twenty-three, I said, *I won't live anymore in the house of the daughter. I don't want anymore to be the one who came from my father, who was born to prove that he wasn't a ghost dressed in the skin and bone of a man.* I said, No more.

I folded up my past and put it away. I knew it was there; I knew what was there. I took off that skin of shame and hatred and folded it up, sealed the trunk shut.

Now, it's not so much that I return to it; it returns to me.

# 2

My father, Jake, is the apple of his mother and father's eyes. The reddest, shiniest apple you ever saw. His mother is too indulgent with him, his father says. His father thinks that he is just indulgent enough. (There is a girl, too, Jake's sister, Eloise.)

For Jake's mother, it is not a life without hardship: there is the smell of cheap hair pomade from the maids' rooms, and the maids' coarse speech, which Jake picks up; the trashmen cutting catty-corner across the back lawn even though Jake's mother has called their supervisor twice already; the occasional parties to which she is not invited; and the newcomers who are insufficiently deferential.

But I forget, he is not Jake then, he is still Jacques, the name his mother has given him.

Jacques' father is a lawyer. He has never had grease under his fingernails, nor blood on his hands. He merely works for men who do. The men with new money and big problems come into his office, an office where the leather chairs creak out, "We know the rules," when you sit down in them, and the oiled wooden walls whisper, "We know how things are done."

Jacques builds bridges and skyscrapers out of the Erector set in his bedroom. His father keeps buying him more of the round cartons filled with thin aluminum girders and screws, and the metal city in Jacques' room, the metal city of towers and spanning bridges, the unpeopled city, grows and grows and grows.

Jacques wants to be an engineer. The father responds, "Ha.

Ah," making a sound somewhere between a laugh and a sigh. But Jacques won't change his mind.

Jacques flies through school. Done with high school at sixteen! There is a picture of him, taken the day he leaves Detroit for Cambridge. He stands on the steps to the train, leaning out, waving. His mother told him to pose that way—I could tell—he looks embarrassed.

The summer before he starts his senior year at MIT, he wants to go to San Francisco, to see the Golden Gate Bridge being built. Of course, it will be a family trip; they are that kind of family. His father has a client who is a friend of the engineer. (His mother is petulant. She wanted to go to Mexico—after all, Jacques is going to go to Europe the summer after he graduates from college.)

The bridge is almost finished. Jacques watches as the suspended roadway is being hung. It is breathtaking, the way the men move together. An amazing feat: like watching the pyramids being built. His parents leave him there, having their driver take them round to see the sights. The engineer talks to Jacques like an equal; the two men walk outside of the construction shack so that the older man can show a massive rivet to him. They are standing on the bluff when they hear a strange sound.

It is metal groaning. The moving scaffold has torn loose from the underbelly of the bridge. Men fall and land in the safety net, but the scaffold rips through it. From the shore, it looks beautiful for a fraction of a second, the net a huge flag waving as it carries the men downwards. A flailing man reaches across impossible space for the arm of another man tumbling through space.

It all falls away: the house on Lake Shore Drive, the gardens, the teas at the Hotel Cadillac, next summer's trip to Europe, the easy future laid out in front of him, plummeting into the Bay, sweeping out through the Golden Gate, gone forever.

The engineer turns ashen white. For five minutes he stands, his hands holding the railing, looking out over the lonely towers rising from the cold, cold water. Then he gets busy. He telephones the papers, telling them about the fund being established for the families of the dead workmen. He goes around personally, offering his condolences, sitting with stunned widows, his eyes filling with tears. He launches an immediate investigation, but still, the next day, the newspaper headlines read:

TWELVE DEAD AS SCAFFOLDING COLLAPSES!
Lax Safety Procedures, Union Charges.

Jacques reads the papers, over and over again. His parents quarrel while they wait for him to come down to dinner at the Mark Hopkins, his mother sipping her wine, his father drinking Scotch. His mother says of course her Jacques is upset, he is very sensitive, she's always known it.

Back home, Jacques locks himself in his room, and reads— Upton Sinclair, Emma Goldman's *Living My Life*, Maxim Gorky. At a bookshop, he buys a five-cent edition of the *Communist Manifesto*. In *The Daily Worker* he reads of the Ethiopians battling the fascists at Makale, of Angel Herndon, a "heroic young Negro worker . . . condemned to slow death on the barbarous chain gang." Dust settles on his model of the city of the future. He looks in the phone book, finds the Communist Party, dials the number and says, "I want to join."

My father does sail for Europe the summer after he graduates from college. He does sail across the Atlantic, on the *Normandie*, but he does not travel first class. He is only pretending to be the person he is meant to become, only pretending to be a college boy travelling to France for a summer's holiday. He tells the men he is travelling with about the beautiful cities that will be built after the revolution; how the world will hum when the forces of production have been harnessed for the good of the people.

"None of that," my mother likes to say. "None of that mattered." She is referring to her childhood in the town of Mechanic Falls, Maine. What matters is the day she arrived in Cambridge, Massachusetts.

"On one side of the street, there was a bookstore. And on the other side of the street there was another bookstore. I thought I had died and gone to heaven—two bookstores."

In the late thirties, my mother and my father—she an undergraduate at Radcliffe, he a grad student at MIT—both live in Cambridge, but they do not meet. I imagine them sometimes riding the same trolley, my mother sitting, my father hanging onto the strap; she walks through the space he walked through fifteen minutes before.

One day my mother stops to listen to a gawky boy standing on a wooden box and shouting about fascism; shouting about the Jews of Germany; shouting about the Republic of Spain, betrayed by the world; shouting about the Soviet Union, where the people have taken charge of their destiny.

My mother listens. A young woman working the crowd sells her a copy of *The Daily Worker*. The date is December 21, 1937. I remember the date because I will be born exactly thirteen years later. My mother will show it to me when I am helping her pack her things when we move back from Springfield. She will show it to me and then say, "Remember, some people don't understand."

LYNCH MOB STORMS TENNESSEE TOWN. CHICAGO COLISEUM FORCED TO PERMIT LENIN MEMORIAL. HANDS OFF THE USSR. IN THE HOME: In many cases when girls and women first enter the movement, they feel they must cut entirely loose from

their old associations, their old life. They develop
a very casual manner of dressing. They put away
lipstick, powder, and rouge. They put on a beret,
a skirt, a careless blouse or jacket and comb their
hair straight back in the morning. . . .

My mother keeps that copy of *The Daily Worker* for twenty
years, until she burns it on an April day in 1957, when, not
knowing that the worst is over, fearing that the worst is yet to
come, she piles her black-covered notebooks, old newspapers
and magazines, the books with the cream-colored covers and
the cameos of Lenin or Marx on the cover, into the incinerator in back of our house in Jefferson and sets them on fire with
the fluid we use for starting the backyard barbeque.

My father looks rugged and handsome, his face unshaven.
The boy from Grosse Pointe, formerly Jacques, now Jake,
poses with the Spanish peasants who eat meat twice a year.
My father's blond, blond hair and clear blue eyes make everyone think that he is one of the German anti-fascists who have
formed the Ernest Thaelmann Brigade. But my father isn't
expatriated to Dachau; he makes it back to a house in Grosse
Pointe, where a Black woman's arms fling around his neck.
"Praise God," she cries, weeping on his shoulder, then steps
back, wipes her eyes, and says, "Excuse me, Mr. Etters." The
house where he had grown up now seems more foreign to
him than anything in Spain ever had: the elms, the servants,
the cultivated lawns and gardens, the thick-carpeted hush.

"Thank God that foolishness is over," his father says. His
mother wants to know if he dressed for dinner in Spain. "But
you were an officer," she said, "surely the officers dressed for
dinner." His mother had heard that the Republicans were
anti-Catholic, and so she allowed herself some measure of
sympathy for them. Ignorant medieval religion, worshippers
of stone idols.

Upstairs, the radio croons: "When the deep purple falls,

over sleepy garden walls, and the clouds begin to twinkle in
the ni-i-i-ght. In the mist of a memory . . . " His sister tries to
get Jake to dance with her, swaying against him, but in a
shocked tone of voice, he says, "Cut it out, Eloise! You're my
sister!"

In December, my mother buys her copy of *The Daily Worker*;
in January, she joins a demonstration; in February, a study
group; and in May of her freshman year, she joins the Young
Communist League. Eleanor goes home for the summer to
Mechanic Falls as if she were going back to another planet.
She goes back to work as a salesgirl at her father's friend's
store, having to remind herself, as old Mr. Kenyon put his
arm on her shoulder, that he is her class enemy, an exploiter
of labor. I am a worker, she thinks, arranging the silk scarves
in a display on the glass-topped counter. *I am a worker.*

But she is still her parents' daughter, still helpful to the old
ladies who come into Kenyon's to buy stockings and under-
clothes, still distant with the daughters of millhands who
work in the stock room, who act as if they don't know they
have a historic mission as members of the working class.

Chafing and bored: bridge parties and ice cubes clinking in
tall glasses, the slowness with which her mother does everything, the superfine sugar poured into the pitcher of lemon
juice and water and then stirred and stirred and stirred, the
time spent considering whether to make timbales or Duchess
potatoes, slowly turning the pages in Fannie Farmer's *Boston
Cooking School Cookbook.*

Don't slam the door. Don't run. Don't leap up from the
dinner table the minute you're done eating. Come and sit
with us. Why are you always up in your room with your nose
stuck in a book? Eleanor, you need more sleep. You're still
growing.

I am still growing, but not in the way you think.

Her friends in Cambridge send her the books she asks for.

*Capital* she reads in one hungry week, then goes back and takes extensive notes, writing always in her neat handwriting, the blue-black ink against the white paper, filling the notebooks she will later burn in the backyard incinerator.

Back in Cambridge, my mother bakes cakes for bake sales, runs off leaflets, and at a party at an apartment on Prospect Street, dances with the ruggedly handsome man who has come back from Spain with a scar that winds around his left leg and a reputation as a hero.

They dance to "Deep Purple," a dance of frivolity in the midst of lives of serious purpose, not frivolity in the midst of frivolity. She lets him go much further (she has only the language that the daughters of millworkers use to describe it) than she has ever let anyone go before: his hand up her skirt, feeling her through her cotton underpants, pushing his hand away when he tries to work his fingers inside the elastic band.

They get engaged in 1942. The wedding will be in the Episcopal Church, it makes everyone happy (everyone but them). The wedding is a big do for Eleanor's parents: their brainy, bookish daughter has done well for herself, a good catch, the son of a fine family, handsome to boot. Awkward, too-skinny Eleanor is marrying money. The girls who shunned her in high school suddenly start calling, angling for an invitation. Her mother and father have been saving their sugar rations for months, but still the wedding cake is small.

Her parents are thrilled about the marriage, his resigned. At least she isn't their image of a Communist woman: a big-breasted harridan, a believer in free love who might sleep with the chauffeur or spit on the carpet. This Eleanor is so polite.

Eleanor and Jake sell their wedding presents, silent butlers and etched champagne glasses, to a genteel second-hand shop in Cambridge.

❈

At twenty-four, my mother does not know that she will give birth to a race of daughters as she wheels my sister Clara in a ridiculously large baby carriage, making the circuit of her block in Cambridgeport, selling *The Daily Worker*. My father is off fighting the fascists again.

She types the minutes for the Workers' Committee for a Second Front, runs off leaflets on the cranky mimeograph machine (she is the only one who can get it to work). When they ask her to give a speech, she does, although she doesn't sleep at all the night before, she is that nervous. So many of the men are gone that my mother becomes the Boston correspondent for *The Daily Worker*.

My mother keeps a map on the wall of her living room. Green pushpins are the U.S. and British Armies, red pushpins are the Red Army.

My mother's diaries are gone now. Did she burn them the same day she burned her books? I think it must have been later, because I remember reading them once. "Hard day," she would write in telegraphic shorthand. Some entries only consist of the word "Tired." Sometimes she names a city that is being liberated, or one where a battle is raging.

> Clara walked today: let go of the couch without realizing what she had done, and stumbled along, five or six steps, before she figured it out and plopped down onto floor. Left her at Edwina's and went to Sofie's. 122nd day of L. [Leningrad] siege. Really heartbreaking story in the paper today—most of the children are dead. Sofie read it out loud to us. She said we were to feature it in our talks with people. I started crying while she was speaking, and then she said, 'The daughters of the bourgeoisie weep over the horrors of the world. It is not because we are hard that we don't weep: instead of crying out and bemoaning, we see that our task is to do away with these horrors.' I felt really awful, small.

Went out selling with Louise, who is very nice, I really have a different impression of her than I had at first. She said I wasn't the only one crying, several girls were, and that she didn't think Sofie's remarks were directed particularly at me. (I had thought they were.) Louise laughed and said, 'See, you haven't yet lost that middle-class tendency to think the world revolves around you.'

My father comes back from fighting the fascists. My mother grows more and more girl-children in her belly, walks picket lines with swollen feet, takes in typing late at night while my father finishes his PhD dissertation, is so happy the day they get a second-hand washing machine with a wringer on the top that she cries. On Mondays, they have Boston baked beans, spaghetti on Tuesdays, "meatless meat loaf" made with rice and cheese on Wednesdays, chicken the first Sunday of every month.

On page six of The Daily Worker of August 7, 1948, is a photograph of my mother, pushing that impossibly large baby carriage, Rose and Clara peeping out over the edge; she carries a sign that reads, Red Meat—Not Red Hunt. The picket line is made up of women; it must have been billed as "Mother's March Against Witch Hunts . . ." and every woman is not just a mother, but a mother of a young child, a child in a stroller or a baby carriage.

Is it that day she realized, falling asleep in the car on the way back from the picket line, her face warm against the glass, that she was pregnant with me?

We were all named after saints. Clara after Clara Zetkin, author of On the Woman Question; Rose after Rosa Luxemburg; me after Elizabeth Gurley Flynn, the "union maid who never was afraid"; Helen after Helen Keller; and Jenny after Marx's wife.

❁

From Cambridge my family moves to Jefferson, in western Massachusetts, where I will be born. My father leaves early in the morning and comes home late at night. He teaches mechanical engineering.

One day when I am three years old, I fall down in the living room and can't get up. My mother dials the doctor and she answers his questions: Yes, she has a fever; yes, this morning she complained her legs were aching; yes, yes, yes. By dinner time that night, I can't even lift my head. The next morning, my father goes to work and my mother takes me to the place where they tell her what she already knows. Polio.

A yellow notice with black lettering is put on the door, QUARANTINE.

The first night in the hospital, my mother is about to leave. I start screaming, "'Joe Hill,' Mommy! 'Joe Hill!'" demanding that she sing me the song that she sang me every night to put me to sleep.

All day long, my mother's face has been clouded with fear: fear for my life, fear that my sisters will also become ill, maybe even fear for herself. Suddenly, as I scream "'Joe Hill,' Mommy! 'Joe Hill!'" the fear becomes sharp and immediate.

She is shrouded behind a mask and a long blue gown. I can only see her eyes. She leans towards my ear and whispers the words to the song. Her mouth is right against my ear, but still, I can barely hear her sing:

*I dreamt I saw Joe Hill last night*
*Alive as you or me*
*Said I to Joe, "You're ten years dead."*
*"I never died," said he.*
*"I never died," said he.*

*"The copper bosses killed you Joe,*
*"They shot you Joe," says I.*
*"Takes more than guns to kill a man,*

*"I never died," said he.*
*"I never died," said he.*

*From San Diego up to Maine*
*In every mine and mill*
*Where workingmen defend their rights*
*It's there you'll find Joe Hill*
*It's there you'll find Joe Hill.*

Every night in the hospital she will whisper that song to me.

When I am twelve or thirteen I will finally understand why it was she whispered. Maybe nobody at the hospital had heard of Joe Hill, maybe nobody knew that he was one of the early Wobbly leaders, a union organizer and songwriter, executed by firing squad in Utah in 1915, on a charge of murder. Maybe nobody knew that, but even if they didn't, the words "copper bosses" and "where workingmen defend their rights," would have tipped them off to the fact that this was a subversive song.

What would have happened if my mother had been suspected of heresy? Would she have been declared an unfit mother? Would they have tried to stop her from seeing me? In that world turned topsy-turvy, anything was possible.

More and more, my mother stops conversation by saying:
"The walls have ears."
"Jake, they're too young."
Sometimes my mother doesn't say anything, just holds up a hand like a cop stopping traffic.

Our house is upside down. The other fathers who teach at the college have living rooms and studies lined with bookshelves. Our books are all upstairs, out of sight.

Once, visiting Boston when I am five years old, I see Molly on the street. Molly, who used to give me presents on my birthday and Christmas, Molly who would always bake us special cookies, Molly who taught us Yiddish songs.

"Molly!" I call. She glances over, and then her face freezes, and she keeps on walking.

"Molly!" I call. "Molly! Molly!" while my mother tries to hush me.

"She doesn't want to know us," my mother says. "Be quiet. I'll explain it to you later."

She never does.

An overheard conversation:

"She lost her job? His mother?"

"Yes."

"For what? For being his mother? That's a crime, to be someone's mother?"

There is the Soviet Union, the country my parents talk about, land of great poets and writers, land where people burst into song, where fields of flowers bloom and no one goes hungry or jobless or without medical care.

And then there is the country called Russia that I learn about in school, a country where everything is gray, where no one ever smiles, spies and assassins lurk behind every tree, whole families live in one room; the country that has promised to bury us.

A map of the world hangs at the front of Miss Langston's second-grade class. I knew that my beloved Soviet Union, where children frolicked in fields of flowers, occupied that same physical space as gloomy hate-filled Russia: for there on the red blob that spread from Asia through Europe is the word written in black, *Russia*, with *Union of Soviet Socialist Republics* in parentheses underneath. I understand that my Soviet Union is a shadow state, living somehow in the same geographic space as the hated Russia.

I go to camp at Children's World, where I learn that the peoples of the world want peace, hear about the civil rights movement and the oppression of Negroes in the South. We

sing "all men are brothers" (and when my best camp friend
Rachel sings "all women are sisters," it makes us giggle so
hard she and I get sent to the camp directors office for a talk).
I can't wait to get back to school to tell my teacher—when
she starts frightening us with talk about the atom bomb—that
the peoples of the world love peace and it is only the imperial-
ist warmongers who threaten us.

How's Jake? That question is no longer chit-chat. "How's
Jake?" they ask, and the unspoken part is, "holding up?"
   And then one day he is simply gone. My father is on the run
from the fascists.
   How's Jake?
   There are two answers now:
   He's moved out of state. Any further questions brought
more of a suggestion that they had separated.
   Or: a glance to the left and the right, and that gesture—my
mother's hand close to her side, and a downward motion
made with her fingers. Sometimes the words "gone under?"
are whispered back by the questioner, but more often there is
just a nod so slight it can hardly be seen.
   We leave the farmhouse with sloping floors in Jefferson.
Someone else moves in, they are renting it from us, and we
move to Springfield, to an apartment. The landlord looks at
me, not really at me, at my braces and crutches. "It's three
flights up, you know."
   "It's all right," my mother says. "She can do it. The exercise
will be good for her."
   In Springfield, all the rules are different. We are strange: we
don't have a television, and my father is "away." Mrs. Kennedy, who lives next door, brings over a friend of hers, a
housepainter, well-scrubbed with slicked-back hair, who
keeps smiling at my mother.
   My mother gets a job as a secretary at a cardboard box
manufacturing plant. Her boss loves her. She knows how to

do everything, not just typing but bookkeeping and reorganizing the filing system, and once when the adding machine broke down she even fixed that herself. "Where'd you learn to work so hard?" he asks her, and she smiles, "Wouldn't you like to know?"

She isn't afraid of angry customers. She sizes them up and then puts on a half-joking, half-flirting voice, or acts grim and efficient. Her boss gives her flowers and calls her Honey, and gives her a raise twice in one year. My mother understands devotion. We are happy when she gets her raises, but she doesn't lose the opportunity to instruct: the raise had come out of the profit that the bosses made from her labor, and was only a fraction of what they stole from her every day.

"That Eleanor," her boss says, shaking his head in pleased amazement. "And she's got five kids. All on her own."

She isn't afraid of angry customers or even of pleasing the boss. She is only afraid of men in hats and trenchcoats. Once I hear her heels click-clack, click-clack, up the stairs, and then she shuts the door quickly behind her. "They're down there," she says. She sits down on the couch, grabs a pillow and presses it against her belly, and begins to cry—really cry, rocking herself back and forth. "They're down there. Talking to Mr. Moses."

I can see the scene. My mother's frantic rocking, the dust motes from the green polyester-satin pillow dancing in the light, my mother's voice distorted with crying, her words that were whispered but sounded like a scream, "Oh, Jesus, Jesus, Jesus, Jesus. Jesus Christ."

They're downstairs. The Nazis, the FBI. What would happen to us if they took our mother away? Would they take us too? Leave us behind?

We hear the footsteps coming up the stairs. They stop on the first floor. We have stopped breathing. They knock on that door. We hear voices, but cannot sort out words. There are two of them. My mother is still crying, but not out loud.

Her body is shaking, her sobs are silent. I want to cry for her, but we, all of us, stand in the doorway between the living room and Rose and Clara's bedroom, silent and watching.

The footsteps are on the second floor landing. Two knocks on two doors, no answer. The third floor—we're next. My mother puts her index finger to her lip, "We're not home," she mouths.

A knock on the door. We do not answer. They do not go away. We wait. Finally, a card is slipped under the door. We listen. Their footsteps retreat down the stairs. My mother picks up the card. She cups her hands in front of her face, with one quick movement she wipes away tears, wipes away what has just happened. "Oh, it's nothing," she says. She picks up the card off the floor and puts it in the pocket of her apron.

An hour later she calls Louise. She's just made some peach cobbler, would Louise and Bernie like to come over for desert. Seven? Seven, then.

There's no peach cobbler.

But Bernie gives us money for ice cream, and the five of us troop down to the corner.

"Who knows?" Louise says, kissing my mother good night at the front door. "Maybe they really were just selling life insurance."

Later, I find the card tucked in a safe place in my mother's desk.

O'Malley and Roberts,
Life Insurance
648 Sycamore Street, Springfield 6, Massachusetts
UNion 2-4527

The Rosenbergs are dead, and men have come in hats and trenchcoats carrying a card that says *Life Insurance*. I try to put it together, were they for us or against us? Life insurance. Is it a veiled threat? Come over to us and save your life? Or just the opposite, we'll protect you? The uniform is that of the enemy, but hadn't Bernie gotten away from the Nazis by dressing up like one? Look at that phone number, is there a message in that? UNion. Unions are good, they are places where you are safe.

Mama, you are always so tired. Supermarkets close at six, and on Saturday you shop, loading bags of groceries into the car. You teach us to iron, you teach Clara how to make dinner, but still. I remember you lugging those bags of groceries up the three flights of stairs, the trips to the laundromat that were almost expeditions, all of us and a week's worth of laundry in tow. And in *The Daily Worker*, now *The Worker*, the exhortations to valor, the working class showing it would no longer tolerate the attacks of the ruling class, the divisions fomented for the purpose of isolating democratic elements within the society.

No wonder I hate New Age "affirmations" so much.

Late at night, she types papers for college students on the old Remington. Coming out of the bedroom I share with the little kids, I watch her sitting in a pool of light, a Winston curling smoke in an ashtray next to her, and hear the steady beat of her fingers against the keys. When she gets a dissertation to type, it's as if we have won the lottery.

Even that isn't enough, so on three-by-five white index cards she writes "Mature lady will do ironing—50 cents per hour." Even then I know it is a ridiculously small amount; hamburger is sixty-five cents a pound.

We would drive in the old Ford station wagon to deliver the stacks of starched white shirts, going to back doors. Clara and Rose start helping with the ironing, they get to keep half of what they earn, the other half has to go to the family. "We hang together or we hang separately," my mother says. The image in my mind is immediate—derived, I think, from a Hieronymus Bosch painting—six lifeless bodies hanging from gibbets against a hellish sunset.

❀

A jumble of memories. Waking up one morning in the apartment in Springfield, the smell of sex heavy in the front room. I couldn't have been more than seven, eight maybe, but I know what it is. Has my father been there?

The landlord saying to my mother, "Look, lady, I don't want any trouble." Lady, lady, it is always lady. To this day, the word makes me jump.

Another apartment, this one on the second floor. My mother works all day, comes home at night to type and iron. Still, there isn't enough. I overhear her on the phone one day to Bernie and Louise, she doesn't have the rent. She apologizes and apologizes and apologizes for having to borrow from them. When they bring it over, they say to her, "Couldn't we give you something every month? . . . It's not a personal favor, don't think of it that way . . ."

A man's voice in the night. Bernie talking to Louise. Where is my mother? She had a meeting, Louise says. It is one in the morning. Louise sings me a song in German and puts me back to bed.

That summer, we are hot and cranky and my mother can't afford the two dollars a week per child for the city-run day camp. Then, a boy in the playground pulls out his penis and shows it to my sister Helen. Helen has no qualms about telling my mother, she is only scared to tell my mother that it had been a Negro boy. Even Clara didn't believe her. "You're lying, Helen. A Negro would never do a thing like that."

My mother calls my father's parents. We have never met them. My mother says it's because they live a long way away. Yes, my mother says, we could come and visit. She calls my grandmother a few days later, to tell her when the bus will be arriving in Detroit. I can hear her end of the conversation, "We'll manage . . . they're good girls, they'll do fine . . . No, you don't need to do that." Two days later, airplane tickets arrive. We dance around the house in a conga line—we have just seen one a few weeks before on *I Love Lucy* at Mrs.

Kennedy's house—singing, "We're going on an airplane. We're going on an airplane."

For weeks before our visit, my mother coaches us. Our grandparents are very old people, set in their ways. We must not lie or pretend to be other than who we are; but we must try not to offend them. My grandparents have servants; most of them are Negroes. We are to address them as Mr. or Mrs. and their last names, no matter what. We are not to make any extra work for them. We must be careful to pick up our clothes and wash the ring out of the bathtub; otherwise, they would have to do it. We are always, always, always to say "please" and "thank you" to them.

My mother makes us dresses to wear. The pattern is McCall's "Easy," and they were to be identical seersucker dresses, the material given by a comrade in Boston who ran a wholesale fabric business.

"The nap," my mother cried, her head on the table. "I forgot about the nap." The cloth had been free; but she'd bought the notions, the thread, the zippers, the hooks and eyes, the fake lace and ribbon for the collars, and the money for that had set us back.

Still, she went ahead and finished them, and we wore them, though Clara cried, "We look like clowns!"

"Oh, no," my mother said, when we were seated in the first-class section of the plane.

At the Detroit airport, my grandmother's black chauffeur held the door open for us. I said, "Thank you," and, not knowing his last name, "Mister."

Five ragamuffins, in identical dresses with unmatched nap, stand and receive dry kisses. Our grandfather is resting, Grandma explains. She studies us, putting names to faces. "Who were they named after?"

My mother takes a deep breath: "Rosa Luxemburg, Elizabeth Gurley Flynn, Clara Zetkin, Jenny Marx, Helen Keller."

"And whose idea was that?"

My mother does not answer.

The house is vast and lonely. My grandmother has white hair and dark purple clothes; she smells of spring lilacs. Her lip is arched in permanent disapproval. Nothing satisfies: the coffee is always too weak or too strong; the maids overwhelm with their cheap dime-store scent, or smell too strongly of themselves; her once-portly husband has grown frail; her only son is a failure.

"The milk tastes funny," Jenny announces.

My mother hushes her, takes a sip.

"They're used to Starlac," she explains.

"Starlac," my grandmother says. "Starlac, what's that?"

"Powdered milk."

"Powdered milk," my grandmother repeats. "Do they think that had anything to do with the girl getting polio?"

Our grandmother takes us to the dressmaker, where we are told we can have anything that we want. "We can choose any one thing?" Clara asks tentatively. No, Grandma corrects, not just one thing, whatever we want. We flip through the pattern books. We choose party dresses with frills and sashes, beachwear outfits, pedal pushers. We are princesses. The dressmaker says softly to my grandmother that she could take care of buying us some new underwear, too.

We are so excited when we get back to my grandmother's house that we can't stop laughing. My grandfather looks over his glasses at us and says, "Children should be seen and not heard."

We laugh even harder.

"Why are these children laughing?" he demands of my mother.

With a shock we realize that he means it.

"But, Grandpa," Clara protests, "that isn't fair."

My grandfather turns bright red.

"Girls," my mother says, "remember what I told you . . ."

My grandmother keeps pressing money into my hand, slipping it into my pockets, whispering to me to buy myself some toys. I know it is because of my crutches and braces. When I get home, I have $120. I give it to my mother.

After that, my grandfather sends us a check every month.

When my father returns we go back to the house in Jefferson. He can't teach anymore. Instead, he has a big case, filled with—is it office supplies? He opens it up and says grandly: "These are the finest products American capitalism has to offer. An electric pencil sharpener? Who could live without one? It will be obsolete in three years. My job, which will someday become unnecessary, is to sell you these products which you do not need, so that I can purchase food and shelter for my family, which they do need."

But a week later, the fun has worn off, and two weeks later, the sound of his car in the driveway sends us scurrying up the stairs.

Student, soldier, student, worker in a defense plant; soldier, teaching assistant, assistant professor of engineering. Salesman, office supplies; salesman, mimeograph supplies; salesman, men's ties.

Using a friend's name and social security number he works for a while as a machinist. A red-blooded American finds out and tells the boss. "You ought to thank me for not having you arrested," the boss says after he has fired him. He waits to be thanked. He means it. My father thanks him.

It is 1960, it is 1961, it is 1962. The eyes of one-time friends still avert, from force of habit, but then they soften, they smile. You can measure the change in the times by measuring the force of the slap on the back, the generosity of the splash of good Scotch in the glass, the sway of the head as they say, "It is a shame . . . selling office products."

On March 22, 1965, a letter comes in the mail for my father. In red ink in the upper-left-hand corner, it says, "Department of Mechanical Engineering, Building 36, Massachusetts Institute of Technology . . . " MIT is offering my father a job. We whoop and holler, we run through the house, up and down the stairs, I clack my crutches over my head. My mother and father call Bernie and Louise, both sets of grandparents; the word goes out: our phone rings and rings and rings. Over and over again, my father says into the receiver, "Yes . . . and it represents so much . . . things are changing . . ." My father wants to take us all out for a fancy dinner, but he only has five dollars in his wallet; my mother, three. There are no credit cards then, no automatic teller machines. But my mother pools everything we girls have, even Jenny's penny collection, and sneaks out the back door to buy a bottle of champagne. Clara makes popcorn, we all get an inch of champagne in mismatched glasses.

We move to a big, big house on River Street in Cambridge.

In the yellowing photograph cut from the newspaper, we look like one of those Catholic families that march in the St. Patrick's Day Parade, all seven of us, Dad on one side, Mom on the other, the kids in order of age neatly in between. We are marching behind a banner that reads, Another Family for Peace in Viet Nam. I wanted it to say, Another Family for N.L.F. Victory, but my father put his foot down, hectoring me with quotes from Lenin's *Left-Wing Communism: An Infantile Disorder*.

# 3

The airports—they're what I hate most. The fluorescent lights and the crowds of squalling families and morose businessmen. The souvenir shops selling their Mickey Mouse telephones and stuffed Big Birds. In Boston, they sell miniature lobster traps and baked bean pots; in Dallas/Fort Worth, where I changed planes when I was flying back to Boston after my father first got sick, they sell plastic cattle horns and ten-gallon hats. Those underpaid women, who sell me overpriced spinach-and-cheese croissant sandwiches and Perriers, who mutter the phrases they are required to say, "Good morning. How may I help you?" and force the requisite smile.

On my way to Boston. Waiting in line at the check-in counter, waiting to board the plane, then the plane has to wait. The captain says—I suppose it's meant to be reassuring—"We're number five for take-off now, folks." Waiting for the seat belt sign to go off so I can get up and pee. I'm seven weeks: it feels like I have to go every fifteen minutes. Waiting for the beverage cart, the food cart. Waiting to deplane.

I'm annoyed at everyone: the mother who shushes her child when he says, "Mommy, how come that lady walks that way?"; the people around me who are reading Tom Clancy or Danielle Steel or USA Today. This mood is not mine, not really; when I get like this, I can feel my father staring out from behind my eyes.

The airports, the telephones! My mother's disembodied voice coming out of the lightweight plastic receiver. All those steely phone calls that followed that first one from Clara, reporting that such and such a number—the result of a medical test—was up or down, and that was a good sign, a bad sign, a neutral sign. Those people who sit next to me on planes. Why don't I ever just lie, say that I work for the General Accounting Office and am on my way to a conference about systems analysis, or that I'm a dog breeder, flying to Boston to pick up a champion Shar-Pei who will be mated with a West Coast champion Shar-Pei? I always tell the truth, and the people who sit next to me always sympathize, offer elaborate details of their own medical histories. They tell of a cousin who made a miraculous recovery, fouling all the doctors' dire predictions. I should pray to St. Jude, an all-fruit diet would cure him.

But when I saw my father in the hospital bed for the first time I knew he was beyond the help of St. Jude and the fruitarians; he was beyond all help. My father looked pregnant. I have read about this, how the bile the liver is no longer able to process gets trapped in the abdominal cavity. Bile, the bitter fluid that is meant to break down what has been taken in so it can be digested.

My father is dying, but I have come to be with my mother. She is "taking this hard." Our family has never gone in for clichés and evasions, we've always prided ourselves on being blunt, but now we seem to find a ritual comfort in saying, over and over again, "She's taking it hard," "When the time comes," "There's nothing more that can be done."

I am sitting alone next to my father's bed at Mass General. Mass General is what everyone calls Massachusetts General Hospital. The nickname is so masculine and efficient. It sounds like a military maneuver. I like the names of Catholic hospitals: Mary's Help, Providence. Although of course we would never go to a Catholic hospital.

My mother is meeting with a realtor this afternoon, talking about selling the house. She wants to get rid of it. She wants to move into a condo. My mother in a condo, in a place with white walls and beige carpeting? Soon someone who appreciates the lines of our old house in Cambridgeport will buy it. They will sand the floors, strip paint from woodwork, peel the grungy wallpaper from the halls and kitchen. They will paint the living room white, the kitchen pearl gray. The house will be filled with light. There will no longer be stacks of newspapers, magazines, important papers piled in the hallways, the corners of the dining room, the kitchen. The oriental rugs my father inherited from his father, the Wedgewood cups set on Woolworth's saucers, the piano my mother bought at a rummage sale to benefit the Negro Women's Council, that has sat, untuned and unplayed, in the hallway for more than two decades—those things will all be gone.

My father looks fragile in his blue nightgown—I suppose they are called nightshirts when men wear them—his pasty white legs showing. The hair on them is sparse now. When I was a child I hated the thick hair that covered him, his legs, his chest, his arms. He is so small now. He cannot hurt me anymore.

I get up and wander to the window. His room is on the ninth floor. Through the slats of the venetian blinds, I stare out over Storrow Drive, past the Charles, to the city of Cambridge. I stare out at a map of my past. There's the apartment building where Alice's family lived, where I first dropped acid one weekend when her parents were away. There's Harvard Square. I can't see it, quite, but I know the Blue Parrot is there, where I used to sit with Lisa, stretching a cup of coffee out for a whole afternoon, snickering at the people around us for being pretentious. There's the restaurant—God, how could I have forgotten the name of it?—where the waitresses went out on strike in the mid-seventies. I picketed there with

them for an hour or so every evening for months. I trace the
routes of anti-war marches, the streets I walked home from
school on.

I could work with this. I could do it like one of those posters
they sell to tourists in San Francisco, an illustrated map:
windy Lombard Street banked with flowers leading down to
Fisherman's Wharf, illustrated with crab-sellers and fishing
boats tied up in the harbor. A decorated map of my own life.
Or perhaps something less whimsical. I like the effect that
these slats of the blinds have, breaking this view up into
planes. Except that I can't paint anymore. I could draw it,
after putting on my dust mask, careful not to breathe in the
chalky powder from the pencils.

I am always scavenging images for my art. I am a vulture,
circling over my dying father, getting ready to pick at his
flesh, knowing that his death will be material.

My father sleeps. I stare out the window. I read.

My father's body is rotting; inside me, there is a body growing. Now it looks like a polliwog, pure white, soft as jelly.
Curled, so it appears to have an oversized head. Stumps that
will, or will not, grow into arms and legs; two bulges on either side that may become eyes.

Seven weeks. The thing growing in my belly is a question
mark. There is an answer: yes or no. Halfway measures are
not allowed. You either have a child or you don't have a child.
There is no such thing as a semi-mother, not now, not in this
world.

I could fold, throw my cards down on the table, lie back
and put my feet in the stirrups: the machine will make a soft
burr as it gets switched on, a soft-voiced woman will murmur, "Relax, relax."

Seven weeks. Soon I will have to come up with an answer
to this question. I will have to decide whether or not to have
a child, to be a mother. To have, to be. I *have* a gray pair of
pants; I *have* a new winter coat; I have a child. I am hungry, I
am thirsty, I am a mother.

I go to the pay phone down the hall, to call Matt. Even though my father's asleep, even though when he's awake he's pretty ga-ga, I don't want talk in front of him. The phone rings four times. I should hang up—I'm going to get the machine. But I want to hear his voice, even if it's only his voice on tape saying, "You know what this is, you know what to do."

"It's me," I say. "Nothing. Nothing important. I'll call you later."

I punch in Ann Marie's number. First I get her home machine, then I get her office machine. "In case of an emergency . . ." her recorded voice says.

"It's me. I'm in Boston. Don't try to call me. I'll call you later."

I go back to my father's hospital room and sit by his bed.

Eight weeks ago, a flu epidemic swept through the word-processing department at Hutchinson, Rubin. Sally from proofreading did a ritual incantation to protect Sean, Matt prayed for him, and me, I sent positive energy. Sean stayed home, and didn't come down with flu. Matt covered for him and a lot of other people who were out, and ended up making over a thousand dollars in a week.

A thousand dollars. Matt wanted us to go on a trip, to visit a friend of his in New Mexico, take some pictures along the way. Come on, he said, cancel your workshops for a week. Or get a guest artist. Come on, we'll have a good time. We weren't going to split expenses; it was going to be his treat. He borrowed his father's car, a Volvo (of course). His father tried to lend us his credit card, too, but I put my foot down. I'm thirty-three, I'm past the age when you can borrow a grown-up's credit card.

We drove across the Golden Gate Bridge, even though it was in the wrong direction; Matt wanted to go past the Marin headlands. Behind us was the cliff on which my father stood, the day the scaffolding collapsed. Was it foggy that day, Daddy, or bright California blue? We were driving across what was once empty space. Someday, the bridge will be no more—in a hundred years, a thousand? Even those stern cliffs that supported us, the swiftly flowing water beneath, someday those too will be gone.

We escaped from the chill of a San Francisco summer; escaped into the heat of the central valley. We rolled up the windows, put the air conditioner on. We listened to Jimmy Cliff singing, "You can get it if you really want . . . but you must try, try and try, try and try . . ." We listened to Martha and the Vandellas singing "Dancing in the Streets," U-2, The Clash. We headed for Vegas.

In Vegas, we did things we never do: played the slots, ordered from room service and ate breakfast in bed (eggs, toast, and hash browns for Matt, Caesar salad for me), made love and didn't bother with condoms.

As we drove across the desert, Matt stopped the car to take pictures of a cyclone fence with a sign on it that said, Property of U.S. Army, No Trespassing. The fence ran on for as far as we could see, the sign repeated every twenty yards or so.

The desert on either side of us: on one side sand and scrub; on the other, sand and scrub behind the cyclone fence.

After a while, the motion of the car lulled me to sleep—me, who can never take a nap. I leaned my face first against the cool glass, then laid my head against Matt's thigh. A damp circle of sweat grew where my face was pressed against his jeans. His muscles tightened as he moved his foot from the accelerator to the brake and then back again. His fingers idly stroked my hair.

We drove through the Arizona desert, crossed into New Mexico. In the fifties, this was the place where my mother feared she might end up, in a concentration camp. The desolateness of this place could be either beautiful or terrifying, a place of infinite possibilities.

If I'd been out here with Jeremy, we would have gone to Ludlow, Colorado, to see the monument to the massacre of striking miners. We would have taken WPA guides out of the library and learned about the history of class conflicts in the Southwest.

Matt and I talked. He told me that the first thing he remembers is being carried on his mother's hip up and down the hills of North Beach, the smells of espresso coming out of those narrow dark cafés. Did I know why a cappuccino is called a cappuccino? Because the steamed milk rises in a point so it looks like the hood of a Capuchin monk. When you do it right. None of those pseudo-cafés in Noe Valley or on Union Street do it right, not like in North Beach.

His mother used to carry him on her hip; she really took the starving artist trip seriously. She couldn't afford a baby carriage. When he was older, three or four, she still carried him when they went to art supply stores because he loved the pretty colors, the feel of the paintbrushes, and she couldn't bear to tell him, "No, no. Don't touch. Don't touch." She had always complained that it ruined her back.

I pictured her, that woman I talked with a few times, knew to smile and say hello to at gallery openings; pictured her when she was twenty years younger than when I had seen her. In the early sixties, she would have worn skinny black pants, a white Mexican wedding blouse with red embroidery that her mother-in-law had brought back from Acapulco; later, maybe, she dressed all in black, with big silver jewelry. I pictured Matt, a fat-fisted three year old, reaching out to touch the tubes of cerulean blue or Quaker red, burnt umber, while she jiggled him up and down, maybe singing him songs in mangled Italian that she half-remembered from her childhood or civil rights songs that her friend Sheila had taught her.

He said that's why he became an artist. All those colors, the smells of art studios.

"But you're a photographer. And in black and white."

"Well," he said, "I'm rebelling."

I told him about my mother's fear of being sent to a concentration camp out here. He laughed: "That was pretty paranoid." "No, it wasn't; it had happened to the Japanese. It had only been twenty years before that it had all started happening in Germany. And that was the most politically developed country in western Europe, the one with the strongest working-class tradition." I was using my mother's language.

My mother comes back to the hospital. It's ridiculous, she reports, what the realtor wants to ask. It's way too much money. The house just isn't worth it.

There must be some pithy quote from Lenin I could say that would bring a smile to her face: maybe the line about the capitalists haggling over who's going to sell the rope that will be used to hang them. But no, that's not quite right; and now the moment has passed.

"Are you sure you want to sell the house so soon?" I ask.

"What do I need all the space for?" she shoots back.

Killing time. The people in my family never were any good at it. We never went in for card games, crossword puzzles, trying to outdo the contestants on *Jeopardy*. So for a few minutes we sit, just sit, you and I, facing each other. Your lined face, hands that are beginning to wrinkle. You wear one piece of jewelry, your wedding band. Your salt-and-pepper hair; your feet planted firmly on the floor. I'm not like you. I adorn myself. Three earrings in my right ear, two in my left. ("What does that mean?" you asked me, the first time I came back to Boston with these extra holes in my ears. "It doesn't mean anything," I said. "But why do you have three in one ear, two in the other?" "I just do," I said. "Why?" you kept asking. "Okay. Okay. I'm protesting symmetry. I'm seeking the overthrow of the Greek ideal. I want people to confront the fact that our notions of what's beautiful are derived from an aesthetic that originated in a slave-owning culture that repressed

women. It's a call for an end to Eurocentrism." My mother
nodded her head. "But do you think people will understand
that—that they'll get that from your earrings?" "Don't
worry," I said, "I'm writing a leaflet I'm going to hand out,
called, 'Why I Dress the Way I Do.'")

"I don't suppose there's anything good on TV, is there?"
I hand her the section of the paper with the TV listings. She
scans them. "I didn't think there would be," she says. We try
to do *The New York Times* crossword puzzle, but we're not
much good at it.

My father wakes up. She moves to stand next to him. She
tells him it's afternoon. He falls back asleep.

"I could read to you," I say.

"Oh, that would be nice," she says. For the first time that
day, she comes close to smiling.

I read aloud to her from the book I have in my purse, Alice
Munro's *Lives of Girls and Women*. My mother used to read to
me when I was in the hospital: *The Story of Ferdinand* when I
was first hospitalized with polio and later, when I was older,
going back for surgery, *The Wizard of Oz, Little Women*.

She enjoys hearing this, I know she does, the richness of the
prose, Munro's keen eye. But I know she wishes I had a more
serious book than this story of a girl coming of age in rural
Ontario; something by Nadine Gordimer, maybe.

I am reading to her about a relationship that is "just physical." I like reading this out loud to her, the words heavy and
solid in the air between us. Someone else says what we could
never say. We never talked about sex. My mother was too
progressive not to give us the rough outline, but she told it
like a biology teacher, ready to move on to the distinctions
among phylum, genus, and species. Talking about sex
("dwelling on that side of things") was silly, a waste of time.

My mother falls asleep sitting up while I am reading to her.

❀

"None of it mattered," my mother always said.

Mama, you were born Eleanor Ann McKenzie, on August 19, 1921, in Mechanic Falls, Maine. You grew up in that grim town. Your parents were what passed for society there. Your mother with her bridge-party afternoons and your father with his green eyeshade and creosote cuffs, at his desk by six-thirty in the morning, there till six-thirty at night. He used to say, "A penny saved is a penny earned." He used to say, "Early to bed and early to rise makes a man healthy, wealthy, and wise." He used to say, "The devil has work for idle hands." He used to say, "Genius is one percent inspiration and ninety-nine percent perspiration." He said those things over and over and over again. A penny saved is a penny earned. Early to bed and early to rise. The devil has work for idle hands. I remember Christmas and Thanksgiving dinners; how he would set his water glass down always in the same place, precisely equidistant from top of spoon and side of knife. The enforced idleness of Sundays and holidays made him nervous, so he used to walk: ten, fifteen, twenty miles. He would look at his watch when we finished dinner, and then an exact hour later, having given his food the requisite time to digest, he would stand by the coat closet in the hallway, and put on—always in this order—a scarf, which he always called a muffler, a coat, hat, boots, gloves (I remember the way he tugged on each calfskin finger until it was tight against his flesh), and then walk: to West Paris and South Paris, to Norway, Lisbon, Lisbon Falls. He liked to say, "Well last week I went to Paris. I think this week I'll go to Lisbon."

I remember, Mama, the way you held up your hand, palm facing outward, fingers pressed one against each other. "None of it," you always said, "none of it mattered."

Mama, I know too much about families. I can't believe that your life was a blank slate, that you stepped out of that house with its upholstered furniture and thick carpets and iced tea clinking in glasses straight into the hurricane of the Left. I

asked you once how, in the space of months, you transformed from Sunday school teacher and high school valedictorian, into the comrade who sold *The Daily Worker* on the
streetcorners of Cambridge. You looked at me, through your
thick glasses with their dark thick rims, and said, "Because I
saw that it was wrong. For some people to have so much
while others had nothing."

I can see you, wearing a ruffled dress with a sash tied in the
back, ten years old, sitting on a hard pew in the Episcopal
Church; the man who will become my grandfather on one
end, my grandmother on the other, my Aunt Katherine next
to your father; your brother, Lloyd, who will never become
my uncle, who will be killed in the war, sitting next to your
mother; you in the middle. You listen. You believe what they
tell you. *Take all you have and give it to the poor. It is easier for a
camel to pass through the eye of a needle than for a rich man to enter
the kingdom of heaven.*

You were always so straightforward, so literal. It used to
drive me nuts sometimes when we argued: "Marx said . . ." as
if you were quoting scripture. (And I would shout back, "So
what?" and you would say, "How can you call yourself a
Marxist and say 'so what?'" And I would say, "Sure I can be a
Marxist and say 'so what?' It's not a Bible, Mom. He wasn't
outside of history.")

But I see now in your literalness a sort of . . . devotion. Forgive me these words, smacking of Christianity: steadfastness,
devotion. Language is fossilized history—the past in which
we struggle to speak the present. I see in the face of the puzzled girl wearing the ruffled dress with the big sash—whose
eyes peer at the minister in his perch high above the congregation—a refusal to gloss those words, *Take all you have and
give it to the poor.* A refusal to see any complexity in them, only
their bare and simple truth.

It was your literalness that saved you.

What would I think of you, if I met you, if we were strangers? If someone said, "My Aunt Eleanor's in town, from Boston. She used to be in the CP. She's an interesting person—a bit of a Sherman tank, but I think you might like her. Why don't you come have lunch with us?"

Where would we meet? At Greens at Fort Mason, a special treat? No, more likely we would stand in line at La Cumbre, clear a table, take sips of guava nectar from aluminum cans, unfold the paper wrapper down over the stout *carne asada* burritos. You would say, "Now these are good. What are they called, tamales?" and your niece and I would smile over your head, and say, "No, burritos."

"Burritos," you would say. "I'm going to write that down." And you'd pull a little notebook out of your purse. "When you get to be my age, you forget everything. Now what is it that makes this a burrito?" You would take notes while we defined burritos, differentiated among them and tacos, tamales; and tried to figure out for ourselves, so we could explain it to you, what it is that makes an enchilada an enchilada.

While you turned to study the mural on the wall, the Aztec man holding the unconscious or perhaps dead maiden in his arms, I would study you. Your coarse gray hair, peppered with black, pulled straight back, the blue polyester slacks and black pullover turtleneck, dotted with old stains.

My friend, your niece, says, "Elizabeth has an exhibit opening in a few days."

"You're an artist? A painter?"

"No. Multimedia."

"Multimedia," you repeat, suspiciously. "Now explain that to me."

And so I would tell about how I had taken photographs of naked disabled women. I'm a bit embarrassed, annoyed at my friend for having brought it up, as I see your back stiffen.

"Now why don't you say 'nude'? I thought that was the artistic word."

"That's just why I don't use it—"

"And, now, the point of all this is—what?"

I use big words like "embodiment" and "non-essentialist" as I explain my art to you.

"Uh-huh, uh-huh," you say. You tell me about an exhibit you've just seen of art about the Rosenbergs.

"Oh, yes," I say, "I've heard of that."

"I'll send you the catalog," you say, and take out your notebook again, and pass it to me to write my address.

"I read a wonderful book about Ethel Rosenberg, a few months ago. By Ilene Phillipson. Have you read it?"

"No. I've heard of it, and I don't care to read it."

A door slams shut between the two of us. To you, Phillipson's book would be dangerous, nonpolitical. I loved it for its unorthodoxy: the portrait of Ethel Rosenberg singing Puccini's aria *Un bel di, vedremo,* in the holding cell in the basement of the courthouse after she and Julius had been sentenced to death. An overindulgent mother who didn't want the cruelties of her childhood visited on her sons. She was no plaster-of-paris saint. I love the book for the very reason you hate it. I see your anger rising, and as a peace token, I offer: "It made me understand that period in a way I never had before."

But you have no patience with these young people who "understand" the lives of their elders. You glare at me, and tell me your story: during the McCarthy years—although you don't really like to call them that, because it wasn't just one man, long before McCarthy came on the scene there were HUAC investigations and the Truman Loyalty Boards—anyhow, your husband had gone underground. You want me to know that it wasn't my generation that had invented going underground, these Weather-whatevers, playing at being revolutionaries, building their bombs, when real revolution was about the organization of the masses— When you take a bite of your burrito, you do it in mid-sentence, and hold up one finger while you chew, a signal to us to wait, you have more to say.

You tell me about how you'd had to leave your farmhouse with sloping floors in western Massachusetts and move to Springfield; work as a secretary, support five kids on your own, take in typing and ironing.

Your niece and I murmur "how terrible" and "yes, yes" at appropriate moments.

You go on, about your husband coming back, being blacklisted. You want us to know how easy we've had it, how lucky we are.

While you were talking, I would notice something watery behind your eyes, the slight tremor of your hands: the gin, although I wouldn't be able to name it.

Here's something, you tell me, I should do one of my "multimedia things" about: those years. If I want to do art about women, women's lives, here's something that needs to be done.

*Poor old fossil,* I would think, as we said goodbye, and then feel guilty for thinking it. After all, who might you have been in other times, other circumstances? Why was it that I got to born in this time and you had to be born in that?

But who is this "I" who would meet you? How could there be a me who wasn't your daughter?

Brood. A hen squatting on her eggs, coddling them to life with the dull warmth of her body is a brood hen. I brood. Usually I'm efficient, always busy: I do the ironing while I watch TV, knit in meetings; now I'm sitting here, on this Danish modern, high-fifties sofa in my parents' living room, sitting and staring into space.

The hormones of pregnancy are a drug that exaggerates everything. I have been back here a hundred times since I left at seventeen, back to this rambling old house on River Street. But this time it's different. This time, when I walk through the rooms, I see the things that happened here. Here is the door between the living room and the kitchen, the door against which my father pounded my head and pounded my head, screaming over and over again, "Bitch! I'll kill you! I'll kill you!" Here is the living room couch on which he pinned me, crouching about me on his knees, his hands around my neck, choking me. Here are the stairs, the stairs carpeted in blue, the carved mahogany banister of an old New England house; Jenny said he kicked me down those stairs once. Don't I remember? Don't I remember running to the neighbors in our bare feet in the January snow? No, I don't remember. (And I wonder what else I don't remember.)

Here is the kitchen stove. Once he turned the burner on high, that one right there, the right front burner, and held my hand above it. When the burner glared red, he tried to push my hand onto it. I was sixteen. It was the one time I fought back, pushed back against the force of his hand. But I wanted it, too. I wanted him to push my hand against the burner and hold it there, wanted the blisters to rise up in the shape of the rings of the stove, because there it would be, written on my flesh: proof of what went on inside those walls. When my arm started to give way and inch down, and I kicked him in the balls, kicked him with my strong leg and so fell down, then scrambled to my feet and out the door while he, doubled over in pain, called out, "You bitch! You goddamn fucking bitch!" was I rebelling for the first time? Or was I still protecting him, keeping him from marking me so that everyone would at last know what he did to me?

The phone rings. It's Matt. Why should it give me such pleasure to hear him say my name? But it does: "Elizabeth," he says in his deep voice, his bland accentless California speech, "It's Matt."

"I know it's you," I say, laughing and almost crying.

"How's everything going?"

"I'm okay," I say. "How are you?"

"Okay," he says.

"Just talk. I just want to hear you talk."

So you tell me that Sean's come back to work; that you've had nothing but down-time, and you've been getting paid for reading. Today you made $12.75 an hour reading *One Hundred Years of Solitude*. You miss me. You've been to the movies three times since I've been gone. This is what I want to hear, ordinary conversation. As we are saying goodbye, you tell me that Phyllis called. She wants me to call her as soon as I can.

I sound so cheerful and upbeat. "Phyllis, hi, it's Elizabeth Etters. How was your trip?"

"Elizabeth," she sounds relieved to hear from me. "I'm so glad you called. . . . My trip was rough," she says slowly. "It was very rough. . . . Can you hang on for just a second?"

Phyllis is a midwife. Last time I saw her, she was getting ready to go to Nicaragua, to learn about women's health care there. While I hold on the phone, waiting for her to come back, I wonder what might have gone wrong. Did she drink water straight from a creek and come down with an intractable case of parasites? Did she get raped?

When she comes back, she says, "I have some friends over. I just needed to let them know—"

"Do you want to talk later?"

"No. I really want to talk to you."

"What happened?"

"I'm so glad you called. I need to talk to somebody who's grounded, politically. I just got back yesterday," she says. "I can't tell you how bizarre this is, the indoor plumbing and the electricity and all the food in the stores. I feel dizzy.

"That's not what I called to talk to you about." She sighs, "It was supposed to be this tour where we went and talked to Nicaraguan midwives and heard about vaccination drives and infant mortality being turned around and then came back and said how wonderful everything was. I mean, that part of it was wonderful. But then, we went to the hospital in Managua— You know, abortion isn't legal there."

"Yeah. I know."

"Elizabeth, there were all these women there, dying. Of illegal abortions. They were scared to come in to the hospital. They were scared to come in, and it was hard for them to get there, to leave their other children. By the time they got there, most of them had such terrible infections. And antibiotics are so hard to get. . . . Are you still there?"

"Yes. I'm still here."

"You weren't saying anything."

"I was just listening."

"I've got cultural shock. I've got political shock. Two weeks ago I was getting on the plane, with my sunscreen and my salt pills, and a week ago I was sitting in this village eating beans and tortillas with a woman who was telling me about losing her first three children in infancy before the revolution, and then three days ago, I was in the hospital in Managua with this woman, Patricia, who . . . Elizabeth, she died."

Phyllis's voice cracks; she sobs.

"Oh, dear," I say, aware, as soon as the words are out of my mouth, of how ridiculous they sound.

I picture her crying. I don't know her that well; I've never seen her cry. But I can imagine how she would look, imagine that she wouldn't hold back at all, that her face would get red and her nose would run, and she'd wipe it with the back of her hand.

"I stayed with her. Their hospitals aren't like ours, usually your family stays with you, they really do the nursing. She didn't have anyone with her, so I took care of her."

"Phyllis," I say.

I hear odd, half-choking sounds, then a cough.

"There's a point to all this. I mean, to my telling you all this. There's this program already scheduled, at the Women's Building. For us—you know, I went with Cathy, Cathy Ferguson, do you know her?"

"No."

"For us to report back. Anyhow, we want—we want to report on everything, you know. We wanted to know if you would be the moderator."

"Well," I say slowly. "It doesn't sound like it would be a whole lot of fun."

Then: "I'm sorry. I didn't mean to be glib."

"It's okay. We thought of you because we think it might be rough, and that you could handle it. That you'd be good at keeping the balance."

"Keeping the balance," I echo. I check my calendar. "Yes, I can do it. The only possible hitch is that my father is sick. I'm not even in the Bay Area now, I'm on the East Coast."

Phyllis is all apologies.

"It's all right," I say. "Really, it's all right."

"Take care," we say to each other. Take care.

There were no sleepwalkers in our family. In the big house on River Street, night was a solid black thing into which we plunged, straight down. We were never restless; we never woke at three A.M. to pad down the stairs in bare feet; no muted sound from an insomniac's television ever came muffled up through the floorboards. Night was night; day was day, bright and purposeful. When we woke up, our dreams were gone, forgotten.

Now I wake up four or five times a night to pee. Up and down, in and out of sleep, all night long, wavering in and out of consciousness.

I must be the only artist in all of California who doesn't remember her dreams. Make that the past tense. Now, with this constant in and out of sleep, I remember swimming underwater, swimming and swimming and swimming and never needing to come up for air. The water pure and pale: not the chlorinated sharp burn of a pool or the murky thickness of ocean water. Climbing out of bed, half-asleep, padding down the hallway, my bare butt sticking out beneath my San Francisco Mime Troupe T-shirt.

I crawl back in bed, close my eyes.

I must fall asleep almost immediately, because when I wake up, all I can remember is that I've dreamt of fish, hundreds of them, identical, bright red, swimming together in vast schools.

All the next day, Phyllis's phone call is with me. As I wheel my shopping cart through the unfamiliar aisles of the Star Market, doing my mother's shopping for her, or sit by my father's bed, I think of Patricia, and find my eyes welling with tears. Has she become some stand-in for my father, a way I can transfer sorrow? Or is it just easier to weep for an abstraction, "Patricia," a woman whose face, whose life, I can only imagine, rather than the contradictory, dirty father wheezing next to me?

For years, I've heard activists come back from Nicaragua and say that although abortion was still illegal there, Nicaraguan woman didn't want them anyway. It wasn't part of their culture. And I knew I couldn't assume that what's on the agenda for North American feminists is on the agenda for Nicaraguan women. And now this.

I know better than to look for salvation on a foreign shore. I know that change comes hard. That revolutions are messy, full of contradictions. I have to remember that ten years ago, under Somoza, Patricia would be just as dead.

Still.

At three-thirty in the afternoon, the hospital cafeteria is almost deserted. I am eating yogurt; my mother is eating a banana. My mother wears her uniform: stained polyester pants and an acrylic sweater. How odd, for all our talk of materialism, how things, objects, were supposed to mean nothing to us.

I can tell by the way my mother is arranging her face that she is getting ready to say something.

"We really appreciate it that you came all this way to be

with your father. I know he would like it if you . . . said something to him."

"Said something to him?"

"Something," my mother struggles for the words, "something appropriate."

"Something appropriate?"

I've never lied. I've just never told the truth. At Christmas, I send him generic gifts: a Swiss Army knife, Anti-Monopoly. On his birthday, I send a card, "Happy Birthday—Elizabeth." Dash, the thin line I substitute for the word *love*. Dash: to run fast, to run away.

"To let him know—" my mother is saying.

I swallow; I swallow hard. My throat swells. Am I having an allergic reaction? No, it's lies clogging my throat.

My mother thinks I'm getting choked up over him. She slips her hand over mine. I pull mine back.

"It isn't that," I manage to say. "I don't care. I mean, I only care in a general way." I look straight at her. "I never loved him."

"I don't know what's the matter with you. I don't know how you can say such a terrible thing."

"It's true."

"Your father's a good man. He—he risked his life in Spain. Half the men he fought with died. I don't know if you can begin to imagine that—" She says these words to me as if she hasn't said them a hundred times before, as if she hasn't spent her life explaining my father to me. Then another war, she says, then the witch hunts, how he had to go underground, being blacklisted.

"Mom, he abused me."

"You make it sound like he beat you, like we locked you in a closet."

"He did beat me. Sometimes I thought he was going to kill me."

"He never came close to *killing* you," my mother says. "He had a very hard life. You were very . . . rebellious."

We stare at each other.

I hear myself say, "I'm pregnant." Did I say this to hurt you? To try to get through to you? To short-circuit our old argument? All of the above?

Tears gather in her eyes. "What are you going to do?"

"I don't know."

"Who is it? The father?"

"A man I've been seeing. Matt."

"A man you've been seeing," she repeats, coming down so heavy on the word *seeing* that I smile. "Well," she says, and sighs.

"Is that all your going to say? Just 'Well'?"

"What do you want me to say?"

I shrug. "Tell me what you think."

"It would be nice if one of you did. Have a child. I understand. You girls, you're all busy with your careers—"

"It's more than that."

"You can't let go of it, can you? You can't let go of it for a minute. Can't you just—put the past behind you. Get on with your life?"

"No," I say, my voice rising, "no, I can't just put the past behind me."

"Keep your voice down," she hisses. I could be five years old again. "I can't change the past."

"Ma, I'm scared to have a child."

For a few minutes we are silent. I spoon my yogurt steadily into my mouth.

Finally, she says, "You know, I think that my generation was lucky. There was always an enemy outside—Hitler, McCarthy. We didn't have time to sit around and—"

"Think?"

If we weren't in this cafeteria, she probably would slap my face. "You think it's so easy. You sit there on your high horse and look down on us. I'm not ashamed. I'm not ashamed of anything I did. And I don't mean that I didn't make mistakes.

We made mistakes. And when we found out it was—it was terrible. You can't know how terrible. But we took what we knew and we acted on it. We acted. It's because of us that there's social security. It's because of us that there's unemployment insurance. We were the first to see that Hitler wasn't a joke. I'm supposed to pound my chest and wail over what we didn't see?"

"Ma, I'm trying to talk about having a child. Could we for once leave Adolf Hitler out of it." I wanted to break the conversation; I wanted her—not to laugh, but maybe to smile. Instead she glares at me.

"I can't talk to you. Have a child. Don't have a child. Do what you want."

"Ma. I'm sorry. I didn't mean to get in a fight with you." She's old. Her husband is dying. I'm a bitch.

"I just want to say one more thing. We gave ourselves to the movement. We lost ourselves in it. We ceased to be individuals. You can't understand that, can you?"

"Ma, I understand it. I just don't think that it was always such a great thing."

"Then you don't understand it," she says. "You want to talk to me, but then you don't want to listen to what I have to say."

"You always say the same things."

"That's what I have to say. The things I always say."

# 4

Daddy, that story, of you growing up in the house with the oaks and the broad lawns in front, and rejecting your moneyed life, of my mother growing up in her narrow New England town, of each of you joining the Party, of the hard days in Springfield, of your being blacklisted: that's our official history.

But Daddy, there's more. The things that didn't matter, the things we don't speak of, the things we dreamed about. I need that other history: what existed on the edges, what seeped away.

I am four years old. My father has gone away. We are still living in Jefferson. My mother is outside. She is working in the garden.

I go into their bedroom. I am not supposed to be here.

His brown bureau is there. It used to belong to his grandfather. The wood is dark. A fine strip of golden wood forms a square inside the square of each drawer front.

(Now I can imagine how this golden square on the front of the bureau was made: a strip of pale veneer pressed into a faint groove in the darker mahogany. Then, I didn't know how anything had come to be. Things simply were. My father's bureau. The trees in our front yard. My self.)

It's the top drawer that I want. The one where he keeps his underpants and socks, his undershirts, the things that sit against his flesh. I open the drawer. His smell mixes with the sharp scent of the cedar lining. His smell is dirty. Dirty in both senses of the word: sweaty and sexual.

I am four years old. How do I know the meanings of these smells? Why do I feel this sense of shame? But I do.

I finger his maroon and brown socks, his white cotton boxer shorts and white ribbed undershirts. They are forlorn and empty, so very thin.

He has left these things behind. Someday he will come back.

I know I am being bad. I know if my mother comes in and finds me here, she will say sharply, "What are you doing?" and I won't be able to answer.

Why do I want to touch these ugly things so much?

I close the drawer.

Daddy, where did you go when you left?

I know it all, all the facts, I've read them in books. Members of the Communist Party were being prosecuted under the Smith Act for failure to register as agents of a foreign government. The first level of the Party leadership was in jail; the second level on trial; men who two years ago you would have trusted with your life, now sold you out for a card that read Get Out of Jail Free. Fascism is almost here, the Party thought, and sent cadre with leadership potential underground.

I know all that now. At the time I only knew that I woke up one morning, and the shadow I had known as my father was gone.

Daddy, where are you?

Living in a lonely boarding house in a mill town in Pennsylvania, or a factory town in upstate New York; breakfast off a hot plate, a meat loaf sandwich for lunch, cold beans for supper? Do you work in a lumberyard, repair televisions, go door-to-door selling life insurance, vacuum cleaners, Fuller Brush? Do you work in a shoe factory, a candy factory, a steel mill, a jewelry factory?

I see you walking with slumped shoulders down a gritty street where boys play kick the can and girls jump rope and chant, "My mother/and your mother/were out hanging/clothes./My mother/punched your mother/right in the/nose./What color blood came out?" You do not smile at them as you walk past. You leer at the landlady or the landlady's daughter, you climb the stairs, your room is on the third floor, it's a dollar a week cheaper that way.

I think it's you that I'm seeing, but then I realize what I see is gray and white. It's a television image, a man being led up a flight of stairs by a dumpy landlady, a row of doors with numbers on each of them. "New in town?" she asks. "Yeah," the stranger grunts. "The rent's ten dollars a week. In advance," she says.

Daddy, the place where you are supposed to be has been taken over by shadows of shadows. It's the fifties, but not *Leave It to Beaver* or *Ozzie and Harriet*. It's the flip side, a *Twilight Zone* episode that features the lonely stranger just come into town, the man with a shadowy past. (Maybe the writer knew it all too well, maybe he wrote under a made-up name, maybe he'd sat, trembling but resolute, under the hot hot television lights and said, "I wish to invoke my Fifth Amendment privilege against self-incrimination . . ." Maybe he had known those shadowy men who trudged up staircases in lonely boarding houses.)

The next scene is always of the woman next door, listening to swing playing on a scratchy record player, wearing a slip in the thick afternoon heat. She's blond, a bit of a floozy, works as a secretary or a waitress; not a teacher, not a nurse.

But in the real world she's not Janet Leigh, so maybe her skin is acne-scarred or a dark line runs from belly to pubic hair, the sign of having borne a child.

How did the two of them meet? Did he pound on the wall and shout, "Turn it down?" and then did she knock on his door and say, "What's the matter, mister? You don't like jazz?"

Then the gray man made of tiny dots—the shadow who lives in my memory—is with her. I can picture it all, the tape keeps running, although I don't want it to. You're on her and hot, lust and hatred, fast, fast, you bore in. You feel guilty afterwards, and take her out to dinner to make up for it. Maybe I've got it all wrong. Maybe it isn't the woman in the room next door, the cocktail waitress with the mottled blue veins on her legs and sharp smell from her armpits. Maybe it's the woman comrade who sits next to you at the lunch counter and says, "Did the Dodgers win?"

You scarcely glance at her. You nod your head and say, "Koufax is a great pitcher." You leave your folded newspaper on the counter, the manila envelope inside.

You see her again at the meeting held in the motel room or the drafty living room of a summer house in winter. You whisper an arrangement to meet later—a breach of security. For once you broke the rules.

You never were any good at living without women.

Jake, you sit alone in your room. Your shoulders slump, but then again you've got the weight of the world on them. You dreamed of being a leader of men. Now here you are, in the upper level of leadership at a critical historic juncture.

Jake, fifteen years ago, fifteen minutes ago, you were lying awake in your bunk on the *Normandie* bound for Le Havre, you were spinning dreams of mighty rivers being harnessed to the will of men, cities that would run like clocks, and instead of the chaos of capitalism there would be rationality, order. Men would work three or four hours a day. The world, a well-tuned engine, would hum. It wasn't just inevitable, it was close; you could reach out your hand and almost touch it.

Now, over and over, you repeat to yourself what Marx said about the revolution being a mole, burrowing underground, burrowing, rising up when least expected.

Again and again you remember a story told by Lenin's companion, Krupskaya: In 1916, Lenin is an exile among exiles in Zurich, a man who drinks weak tea from a cracked cup, who calls meetings at the café Zum Adler to which hardly anyone comes. Krupskaya watches one day from the window as you corner the editor of a local socialist newspaper on the street, trying to impress on him the inevitability of world revolution. As you lean towards him, he leans away. He pretends to be in a hurry to catch a streetcar, while you, in desperation, grab his overcoat.

Comrade Lenin, soon you will no longer be an exile with a piercing gaze haranguing acquaintances on Zurich street corners. Soon, Comrade, you will be dancing in the Russian snow.

Soon it will be January 17, 1918. The Soviet government will have been in power for seventy-two days, twenty-four hours longer than the Paris Commune. You will rush outside, drunk with joy, and spread your arms and twirl yourself dizzy. Fat snowflakes will land on your bald pate and melt. Vladimir Ilych Lenin, you whose face will shortly stare down from the walls of post offices and school principals' offices, you will be laughing and twirling and shouting in the snow. Seventy-two days! Your Soviet Union has outlasted the Paris Commune by twenty-four hours!

This story is heady wine, Jake. Have another glass.

In Jefferson, my best friend's name is Debbie. Her parents are "sympathetic," the word my mother uses. I understand that the word has nothing to do with "sympathy," which is something I want no part of (my mother has told me that too). To be "sympathetic" means to read *The New York Times*; to say, very carefully, "Negro"; to not go to church.

Sometimes in the summer Debbie's mother or my mother packs us a lunch and we hike out to the abandoned apple orchard past the creek next to her house or up to the old elm on the ridge of the long hill behind our house. We hunt for fossils. Nearly every rock we pick up has one; we only bring back perfect sea clams, palm fronds.

We play a game called upchuck. While we are eating, one of us starts to sing to the other, "Great green gobs of greasy grimy gopher guts . . . why don't you try some soon. . . ." Or else, "The worms crawl in, the worms crawl out, the worms play pinochle on your snout. They eat your eyes, they eat your nose, they eat the crud between your toes. . . ." The first one to throw up loses. I always lose. The problem is my imagination. My mother always says I have too much of it.

I love the drowsy state of riding in the car as we drive from Jefferson to Springfield every week for my physical therapy, the two of us, my mother and me, alone together. One January morning, we hit a patch of ice, and slide. My mother steers frantically, while the green station wagon glides, with a will of its own, off the road, straight into the cow pasture, where it twirls around three times, a stout green ballerina, and stops. We sit for a minute, stunned, silent, then both burst out laughing.

On the back of the bathroom door, there is a blue-and-white sheet of paper. There's a thumbtack in three of its corners, a tiny hole in the fourth with a rust-red imprint of a thumbtack. There's a blue band across the top with big white markings, and smaller blue markings underneath. I ask my mother what it is; she says, "It's nothing."

Daddy, soon I will have forgotten you: you will be a word that my mother uses, "your father," "when your father comes back"; she speaks of you with the same tone of voice she uses to talk about the Negroes of South Africa, the Chinese peasants. Soon it will seem as if you have never existed, as if only women live in our world.

I am looking for my parents in the library.

I thread the microfilm into the machine. "Can you show me how to focus this?" I ask the librarian. She turns the knob. The image gets clearer, but not clear. I take out my glasses. I need them now for reading. My father started needing glasses too when he was about my age.

On November 30, 1937, the price of *The Daily Worker* was three cents. The weather forecast for the New York area was rain, colder temperatures. The banner headline read HOPKINS SEEKS TO END CASH RELIEF. To the left of that, a smaller headline: DEAD GIRLS LINKED WITH SUICIDE PAIR.

> . . . . bodies found on a mountainside near Altoona, Pa., . . . dead children linked with an unemployed couple that died in a suicide . . . restaurant proprietor . . . declared she remembered them by a conversation she had with one of the little girls who told her that the family was broke and jobless and often went hungry. . . . city pathologist . . . children slowly suffocated by gentle pressure on the throat as they slept . . . bodies found on a carefully-made bed of pine boughs and blankets. . . . The five dead persons numbered in the long and ever-growing list of working-class victims of capitalist chaos and crisis, of mass hunger and misery in the midst of plenty and cynical denial of adequate relief to the unemployed and their starving families.

Daddy, did you read those very same words I am reading now, sitting in your dorm room at MIT, the cold rain outside moving in from New York? You must have looked at these same *Little Lefty* comics, with svelte young Miss Goodheart and lumpy old Mrs. Meany; read how Patsy the Strategist kept Little Lefty and his friends from beating up the head of the school board after he fired Miss Goodheart: "Let's use your heads! Tonight we round up all the kids!! And their parents at our free food-fighters club and make this a real fight—how 'bout it?"

I look for my parents' wedding in the *Times*. There she is. I print the page; the microfilm reader prints out a negative: the background is black, the lettering white. My mother is a bride in black, her gown and veil are widow's weeds. In front of her she holds a bouquet of cinder roses; her white lips pull back in a grimace.

Mama, I read *The Worker* from the fifties, trying to find a clue to the texture of your days, but there's only relentless upbeat preaching. Every issue, there's a cartoon of a woman who looks like a Barbie doll (although Barbie dolls don't yet exist) holding a sign that reads, Defend Democratic Rights. This was for public consumption. Privately, the Party thought fascism was coming. You must have thought so, too. The Nixon-McCarren Act passed in the early fifties, with its provisions for rounding up subversives, detaining them for the duration of a "national emergency"; ramshackle wooden structures were built in the wastes of Arizona and New Mexico. You told me once that you didn't get a good night's sleep all those years. An off-hand remark. Did you have nightmares, Mama, about concentration camps? Were you afraid that we might have to be sent away from you, to grow up as good Americans? That we might go with you?

Was there anyone you could talk to? Louise? Could you have said to her, "I don't know how much more of this I can take!" or, "Last night, again, another nightmare . . . ?" No, to you, to her, that would have been wallowing in self-pity. More likely she would have noticed your puffy eyes, the dark circles under them, and maybe have said, "Another hard night?" Perhaps have laid her hand on your arm.

In Springfield, every siren woke me up every night for months. Was it the anxiety that you breathed out, Mama, and I breathed in? Or was it just that I hadn't yet learned what not to hear?

And you, Daddy, when you lived in those lonely boarding houses—day in, day out at your dull jobs, your real life a distant secret—did you think you could hone yourself down to a gray man who does what's expected of him, who can scarcely

recall the womanish passions that set him on this path he dutifully follows? A subversive version of the man in the gray
flannel suit, an atom moving among other atoms, a straw in
the winds of history?

The Worker, February 15, 1956: Khrushchev's Report to the
Soviet Communist Party Congress is a speech full of glorious
achievements. "As I looked down," the reporter writes, "I
could see many men and women who bore visible marks of
their sacrifices—an empty sleeve, war scars—as well as the
proud medals of victory. . . . " There is not a word about
Khrushchev's denunciation of Stalin.

In the same issue, a review of The Tender Trap with Debbie
Reynolds and Frank Sinatra. "Behind the slick jokes and the
skillfully managed fun lies a serious problem: how can everybody be happy in a competitive society in which women out-
number men and in which a woman without a husband is
taught to regard herself as some kind of failure. . . ."

Daddy, in the spring of 1956 did you see the headlines in news
boxes, MR. K SAYS: STALIN A MURDERER, as you walked to
work? Were you sleeping in a cheap motel? Did the headlines
stare back at you as you sat in the coffee shop eating breakfast? Did you say to yourself, "Lies, lies, lies, lies"?

I can see the The New York Times, with TEXT OF
KHRUSHCHEV SECRET SPEECH on the front page, lying for days
on the sideboard, unopened, unmoved.

And then, a month after the Congress, after the text of the
Khrushchev speech has been printed in the Times, The Worker
says that "a review" is currently being conducted of Stalin's
leadership.

Finally, Daddy, did you go to the library to read the text in
the Times?

> Comrades! . . . After Stalin's death the Central
> Committee of the party began to implement a

policy of explaining concisely and consistently that it is impermissible and foreign to the spirit of Marxism-Leninism to elevate one person, to transform him into a superman possessing supernatural characteristics akin to those of a god. Such a man supposedly knows everything, thinks for everyone, can do anything, is infallible in his behavior. Such a belief about a man, and specifically about Stalin, was cultivated among us for many years. . . .

Did you read of the false accusations, the confessions forced by beatings, the men who had given their lives to the revolution and were then accused of treason, plots, sabotage? (But Daddy, Khrushchev never says the word "I." He never talks about how he rose to power in the Stalin years.)

Did you make a photocopy of the speech, folding the awkward newspaper pages, dropping your coins in the slot? No, I forget, there weren't Xerox machines then. Maybe you made notes, copied whole portions out by hand.

Daddy, I remember clearly things that could not have happened. I remember that copy of *The New York Times*, TEXT OF KHRUSHCHEV SECRET SPEECH, lying on the sideboard in the dining room of our house in Jefferson. But I was only five years old in 1956; I couldn't have read that. And when I was five we lived in Springfield.

Yet I remember that *Times* lying on the sideboard unmoved for days.

My father's father dies and my mother tells me that everybody dies.

"Are you going to die?"

"Yes," my mother says, "but not for a long, long time. Not until after you are all grown up." My mother tells me that she used to be a baby; that my grandmother and grandfather used to be babies; that everybody used to be a baby. She has told me this before. I don't believe her.

My mother tells me that it only looks like the moon is following us when we drive in the car. Really, the moon stays in one place. It looks this way to everybody.

I think, The moon doesn't follow anyone else, but it does follow me.

One day, we come home from school, it is when we are living in Springfield, and he is sitting in the living room. My mother says, "Come and give your father a kiss." I don't remember him. I want him to go away.

At dinner, he stands at the head of the table. He puts on a special voice. He says, "There are a lot of things we wish we could explain to you. I've been away, but now I'm back. There are people in this country who don't believe in freedom, and it's because of them I've been away and lost my job. But we don't feel sorry for ourselves . . ."

We move back to the house in Jefferson. We are going to grow our own food; it won't matter that my father can't work. My mother plants a vegetable garden in the side yard, weeds down on her knees, ties the Kentucky Wonders to the bean poles, hoes between the rows; she wears gardening gloves and a big straw hat.

I go into the bathroom and the blue-and-white sheet is still pinned to the back of the door. I can read now. The big white letters say: "In Case of Poisoning . . ." Underneath: "induce vomiting . . . give milk . . . summon medical assistance immediately . . ."

Back in my old bed, the cracks and rough patches of the ceiling still make themselves into faces and animals, and the bare branches and twigs of the maple trees in winter do the same. But it takes longer than it used to for the faces to appear.

My mother doesn't know that the worst is over. She thinks the worst is yet to come. I come home from school early one day, the nurse brings me, I am sick. My mother is standing at the incinerator, a can of lighter fluid on the ground next to her. (I could not have seen it that day, but now in my mind I see it clearly, the blue-and-white can with the picture of the man in the chef's hat turning over a thick piece of steak on a barbecue grill.) My mother looks up at us, shocked, her hair uncombed, her eyes red and her face streaked with tears. She looks like a witch; I wish she wasn't my mother.

She walks down and meets the nurse. My hand is passed from the nurse's to my mother's. Nothing is said about the cardboard boxes next to the incinerator. My mother doesn't have to say to me, Go in the house. I walk up to my bedroom, in our upside-down house, the house where the books are not displayed in the living room or study, but are hidden upstairs. Only now the shelves are half-empty. Marx has been thrown into the fire, and Engels and Lenin and Stalin, along with André Malraux and Earl Browder, Rosa Luxemburg, and a hundred other, lesser lives. More books, more lighter fluid. The flames leap.

I hate you. I want us to have a TV; I want you to wear make-up; I want to be like everyone else.

A line of poetry from Sylvia Plath: "By the roots of my hair some god got hold of me." She didn't mean that line at all the way that it reads to me—she was talking about electroshock therapy. The god that got hold of me was the god of the Left.

Mama, every night you sang to me your promise of eternal life in the love of the people, "Says I to Joe, 'You're ten years dead'/'I never died,' says he." Daddy, you explained the world to me: the workers put the food on our table, they made the plates, they made the table; they made Yankee Stadium and the Empire State Building. It was because of capitalism that Negroes were shot in the back in South Africa, because of capitalism that Rosa Parks had to sit at the back of the bus in Alabama, that you had to go away. I believed it the way I believed that the earth was round, that summer followed spring, that the sun rose in the east and set in the west. Labor creates all wealth; the people will make history.

One day, when we are living in Jefferson, we come home from school and the green station wagon isn't parked in the driveway. A note on the kitchen table in my mother's handwriting: "Had to go to Springfield. Everything's OK. I'll be home before five. Oranges in the fruit bowl for snack." (Where were you, Daddy? Off selling office supplies, mimeograph supplies, neckties?)

We have a TV now, but we are almost never allowed to watch it. That afternoon, we watch *Adventures in Paradise*, Popeye cartoons. We are drunk on the forbidden. It is half past five. How late is she going to be? Are we really going to get to watch all those shows we've only heard about at school: *Dr. Kildare, Gunsmoke?*

It is six, six-thirty, seven. Where is she? We watch the news; we watch *What's My Line?* Her car turns into the driveway. I am suddenly furious. Where has she been? Rose leaps up and turns off the television; we know enough to scatter.

My mother comes through the white front door. She crouches down, holds out her arms to us, as if we were all little kids again. Her skirt is woven of thick threads of blue, flecked with purple and pale yellow—a bit Bohemian, someone must have given it to her. (I think of things that I have bought—placemats, a throw for my couch, curtains—that have that same rough weave and those same colors, and I realize that I bought them because they remind me of that skirt, that day.)

She kneels next to us and says, "Something ter—" She breaks off in the middle of the word. "Yesterday, in South Africa, a terrible thing happened. There was a strike by Negro workers, and the South African police came to break up the strike. The police shot forty-seven men in the back. Twenty-five of them died."

My mother's eyes fill with tears.

"Why did they do that?" says Rose. "Why did they have to kill them? Why couldn't they have used . . . tear gas, or—?"

"Because, Rose, they want to frighten people. They want other Negroes to be scared to strike, to be scared to fight back. . . . I have an important job for you girls to do. Will you help me?"

We eat hot dogs on Wonder Bread folded in half, with carrots and celery sticks. There, in fifteen minutes we're done with dinner. My mother sponges the crumbs off the table. Then she sets piles of mimeographed letters, boxes of envelopes on the table.

Helen starts: she picks up a small stack of mimeographed letters, folds the stack in thirds, passes it to Jenny, who pulls the letters apart, running her finger along the creases, making them sharp. I put the folded sheets into envelopes. Clara and my mother copy addresses off long lists. Rose stamps a return address in the upper-left-hand corner, puts a purple three-cent stamp opposite it.

"Dear Friend," the letter begins, "I am sure you were as shocked and outraged as we were to read the terrible news of the massacre of Negro strikers at Sharpeville in South Africa. . . ." There were addresses where letters and telegrams could be sent, a rally to be attended.

Mama, I remember everything: the purple three-cent stamps with the Statue of Liberty on them, the sharp paper cut on the inside of my left index finger from the envelopes, the solidity of those words, *brotherhood, massacre*.

It was after that that Nelson Mandela went on trial. He wasn't an international figure then. Regular broadcasting wasn't interrupted with news of his imprisonment.

One day my father goes off in the green station wagon. When he comes home he gets to the end of the driveway and he keeps driving. He drives up to the empty chicken coop. He unloads the bales of straw. He goes into the woodshed to get the wire-cutters and he cuts through the wire.

He tells us to get in the car, me and Helen.

"Dibs on the window," I say.

"You can't put dibs on the window," Helen says, "you have to run for the window." And she does.

"But that's no fair," I cry, galloping after her, swinging myself along on my crutches.

Helen puts her hand on the window and dances, "I got the window. I got the window."

"It's no fair," I protest.

"Shut up," my father says. "Get in the car."

I sit in the middle. I squeeze as close to Helen as I can.

"Move over," she says, kicking me in the shin.

When we go down the hill next to the Carpenters', the shotgun shell rolls out from under the seat. It's been there since October, since my father spent five goddamn dollars on a hunting license and didn't get a single goddamn deer. My mother tells us not to touch it. My father says, "Don't worry, it's spent."

It rolls back under the seat.

"Move over!" Helen says, and pushes her thigh against mine.

My father drives us to a place we have never been before. "Come on," he says. We go with him, into the building made of white concrete blocks.

There is a man there. He bends down. "Would you girls like to see where chickens come from?" The man is old. His face is stubbly and a big brown mole is on his left cheek. I hate grown-ups; I hate the way they smell.

We look up at our father. He says, "Go on." We follow the man back. Our father does not come with us. The hallway is dark and narrow. A *peep-peep-peep* sound comes from ahead. We come to the room. There are wooden boxes with light bulbs burning above them. The man pulls out one of the boxes. He puts on dirty white gardening gloves and starts pulling yellow chicks out of the wooden box. He counts as he puts the chicks in a flat cardboard box. He puts a lid on it. It is special, it has holes cut in it. "For air," he says.

This is where chickens come from, from these drawers.

He carries the box out flat, in both his arms, and sets it on the counter. My father takes his brown leather wallet out of his back pocket and gives the man some money.

He carries the box out to the car the same way the man did. He sets it in the way-back.

As we go down the hill by the Carpenters' place, the red shotgun shell rolls out from under the seat.

The chicks live in the straw in the henhouse. It smells bad in there now. After a while their feathers start to get dark and they turn big and ugly. In the morning now, it is Rose's job to go out and collect eggs. She puts them in an old carton. Sometimes they have bits of straw and yellowy chicken shit on them. My mother washes them off before she breaks them open.

We have to put the eggshells in with the paper trash, not with the garbage. We feed the garbage to the hens. My father says if the hens taste eggshells, they will like the way they taste and eat their own eggs.

When the hens stop laying, my father chops off their heads. Jenny and I sit on the side porch and pluck the feathers. He says it's just a little blood. He says, "Don't be babies."

My father slaughters the pigs. They squeal and squeal and squeal. He peels off the skins like little jackets. He says carcasses. They hang in the woodshed. We don't want to go outside, because we have to walk past them. A day later he takes them down. He brings them into the kitchen. We hear the sound of the knife hitting against the counter; he boils water; he burns himself and says, "Jesus Christ, Jesus Fucking Christ Almighty!" He wears old clothes spattered with blood.

Some Party members, when they finished reading Khrushchev's report on Stalin, lay down in darkened rooms. Some sobbed. Some said to themselves, This a sign of our strength, that we can stare without blinders at the past. My father got drunk.

When my father came home, he came home with a bottle of gin. He poured it out, one shot glass for each of them each night. The gin was clear. At the end of that first year, my father and mother have poured out a bottle a week, and still we scarcely notice it. It only sloshes a little bit about our feet as we tiptoe through the house.

At the end of two years, the first floor of the house is sunken. We have grown used to everything being muffled, to the odd near-silence, to the strange distortions of objects seen underwater. We have grown used to the effort it takes to push ourselves through the weight of liquid, to the fact that everything—promises, memories—floats away unless clutched tightly against us.

Every Friday, my father stops at the liquor store and buys a bottle of gin (later two, then three) and pours them out, jigger by jigger, glass by glass. The gin rises up the stairs. We barricade ourselves in our bedrooms, but it creeps through the gaps between the floorboards and the doors. It rises as steam up out of the heating vents, and then condenses on the ceiling, plopping down in fat droplets on our sleeping heads, disturbing our dreams.

My father drinks like the son of an attorney and my mother drinks like the daughter of a banker. They drink in measured doses; they drink deliberately; they drink.

Mama, you don't sing to me sleep anymore. You don't sing "Joe Hill" to me anymore, your promise of eternal life in the love of the people. You tell me that I'm too old.

Years later, when I am trying to understand you, I will read everything I can about the Communist Party of the thirties, forties, fifties. I will read one book by an American Communist who lived in Moscow, in a building for members of the Comintern, during the late thirties, the years of the purge trials. Every now and again, one of her neighbors would simply be gone. She said they all gathered, comrades from Australia and England, Canada, Ireland, Wales, Africa, India, the Philippines, gathered at night in their rooms to drink wine, to eat cheese and bread and tinned fish, to dance to Edith Piaf, and to talk about everything, everything except the disappearances, the trials.

Mama, I only knew that the phone didn't ring and ring the way it used to, that you weren't going off to meetings any more, that there weren't any more Sunday trips to Springfield to visit my "aunts" and "uncles"; that Bernie and Louise only called once or twice a year now. You still went to demonstrations every now and then; sometimes you sent money to good causes. But it was just going through the motions; easier than admitting that you'd given up.

I never even saw you drunk, only saw you, slowly and methodically, lifting those glasses of gin to your lips and dutifully swallowing the clear, searing liquid.

# 5

I'm flying home from Boston. The plane descends, coming out of the clear sky down into the clouds, then breaking out of the clouds to show a world in perfect miniature: toy houses, toy cars, toy freeways, dots of turquoise that are backyard swimming pools, the soft rolling hills, the blue of ocean and bay.

The plane descends; the pressure in my head builds into a stab of pain. I rub my forehead. I press my fingers against my eye sockets. Nothing helps. Is my head going to crack open? I couldn't be having a stroke, could I?

No, not a stroke. This is something else, just sinuses. It's because I'm swollen, every cell in my body is holding water, holding on.

Once I took a friend to the hospital when she was having a miscarriage. The doctor asked her how she felt and she touched her breasts and said, "I don't feel pregnant anymore. My breasts have gone down." It was only a few hours since she'd started to bleed. If I do it, if I have the abortion, then it will all reverse so quickly, the cells will let go, the hormones will stop pouring themselves into every crack of my body, I will no longer be swollen, wobbly-jointed, exhausted.

Now I understand something that my friend Allison tried to tell me: how pregnancy is will-less, it goes on with its own rhythms and powers, while abortion is an act of the self against the power of the body. I know you're not supposed to think that way, the self against the body. Still, I do.

Undecided. Not a box I ever check. I always know what I want. It's part of the pattern of adult daughters of alcoholics, that we leap. Shall I leap into motherhood or leap away? The clock is ticking. These phrases that repeat in my head. *Leap into, leap away. The clock is ticking. Eight weeks.*

Matt is standing right there when I get off the plane. I don't have to scan the waiting area looking for him, wander off toward the baggage claim hoping I'll run into him along the way. He is right there. He holds me and doesn't let go. He strokes my hair against the nape of my neck. I am comforted and turned on, both at once. He is so good to me. I shouldn't doubt him so much.

He doesn't care, or maybe he doesn't even notice, that people are staring at us, staring at this woman who has emerged in an airport wheelchair from the airplane and has now risen to her feet, and is being embraced by this leather-jacketed man.

I'm the one who lets go.

"How you doing?" he asks.

I wobble my hand in the air.

"You look great," he says. His tone of voice tells me: I know this is a strange thing to say.

"It's because I've been crying. It makes my eyes more blue." I haven't been crying about my father, not about the pregnancy. I've just been crying.

He pushes the wheelchair. This is only the second time I've used one at an airport. I'm just pretending, I tell myself. I remember sitting behind the steering wheel of the big green station wagon parked in the driveway of the house in Jefferson; holding the steering wheel, checking over my shoulder before I changed imaginary lanes. The first few times I drove a car, I felt as if I were still that little kid, pretending. I wonder if Matt feels awkward, pushing me, getting stared at. I want to rest my hand on top of his. I try, but I can't reach back that far.

It's when we are in the car, pulling onto the freeway, that he asks again, "How are you?"

"God, this is so hard."

"I know," he says.

He doesn't know, I think. Not really. You don't know how it feels to me. I stare out the window.

He says, "I mean, I guess the thing with the baby makes it harder—"

"It's not a baby. It's an embryo."

"Right. Whatever." He's angry now, too, staring straight ahead.

After a few minutes, I say, "I'm not being pedantic. It—"

"You?" Matt says. "Pedantic?"

"Don't. I can't take it right now."

He throws up his hands, hits them against the steering wheel, breathes out, "Shit!"

"Let's not fight in the car. It scares me."

"What do you think I'm going to do? Hit the accelerator and rear-end that semi?"

That's exactly what I think. That he'll lose it, that his anger will press down through the soles of his feet against the gas pedal, twist his hands just enough to swerve us into the other lane.

"What do you think I'm going to do?" This is probably a genuine question. But I'm not sure. Maybe he is about to laugh and floor it, calling out "Huh, what do you think I'm going to do?" while I cower in the passenger seat—

"Matt, I'm scared."

He presses his foot against the accelerator. He puts on the blinker and look over his right shoulder. He moves the car into the next lane. "It's okay." He puts his hand on my leg. I jump. "I'm just getting off the freeway."

"Why are we getting off the freeway?"

"So we can talk. So we can talk and you won't be scared."

We pull into the parking lot of a McDonald's. He puts his arms around me.

"Don't," he says, "don't do this to me. Don't drag all this baggage from your past with you. I am not your goddamn father, okay? I'm me. Let me be there for you."

"I'm sorry."

"I love you. Have I ever done anything to hurt you? Have I?"

I'm about to say, "Of course you have . . . " But I think back, and I can think of times I've been hurt by him, but I can't come up with a single thing he's done to hurt me.

"No. But I was scared. What should I do? Be scared and not say anything?"

"No. I don't want you to be scared and not say anything."

"I'm sorry," I say again.

"Yeah," he says. "I'm sorry, too."

It's hopeless. We're too new to have a child together. But I wanted someone who wasn't abusive and wasn't a wimp, someone who could push back against me.

We're too new and I'm too crazy. I think I've broken the spells of the past, think I've worked through coming from an abusive family, but I haven't, not really. The way I still flinch, instinctively. They tell me having a child cracks you open, leaves you raw. I'm afraid that all I've done is bury the pain, covered it over with understanding—that it's all still there, whole, ready to rise.

This isn't fair to any of us: not him, not me, not the baby who could grow out of this embryo. I'm going to call the clinic as soon as we get home, make an appointment.

When we get back to my place, we lie down together. He wants to make love; I want to sleep. I lie curled against him, satisfied by the press of his body against mine.

I wake up: two hours have gone by. Matt's sitting next to me, pillows propped behind him, reading.

"If we have the baby, do you want to live together?" I ask. He sets his book down.

"I didn't even know you were awake. . . . It'd be pretty hard to manage—if we didn't. Do you want to?"

"You know, it was so nice, getting this place when Jeremy and I split up . . . I mean, just the idea that I could move the sofa without asking anybody . . ."

"Maybe we should decide about the baby, first."

"Typical masculine linear thinking," I say. Then add: "That was a joke."

"Yeah?" says Matt, raising an eyebrow, smiling.

We make love. I don't want to, not really, not at first. My breasts ache. My body doesn't feel like me anymore. I'm tired, turned inwards, queasy. Until a few weeks ago, sex was still great. Now my focus has shifted. Ann Marie says it'll get better, once I get through the first trimeseter: I'll feel sexual again, ripe and connected. Well, she says, that's how she felt.

Connected, that's what I want. Everything's happening the way it's supposed to, he's touching me and I'm getting turned on, but it's at a distance. Okay, I tell myself, just let it happen, sex isn't always going to be wonderful.

I come—if feels automatic, like a switch has been flicked— he comes; I burst into tears. We pull apart. He brings in a roll of toilet paper from the bathroom, for me to blow my nose, wipe my eyes.

"I can't believe I have to deal with all this now," I say.

"What about you? What do you want to do?"

"About the . . . embryo?"

I nod.

"I want you to be happy."

For thirty seconds or so I'm angry. I think, Don't dump this all on me. Then I realize he means it. He wants me to be happy. Pardon the cliché, but my blood runs cold. It really does feel as if there's ice water in my veins. He wants me to be happy.

Daddy, it's absence, contempt, that feel safe to me. When I was a child, you were the thundering ogre who lived in the clouds at the top of the beanstalk, you were the troll who lived under the bridge, waiting to devour the three billy goats gruff.

Will these charming princes always pale in comparison to you, my giant? When Matt says, "I want you to be happy," I snap into contempt for him. I think: *You're weak*. It's no good. I'm still my father's daughter, still a prisoner of my childhood. If I have a child, it will all recur, predictable. Daddy, when I'm in the airport and I get stressed, nothing big, just the glaring fluorescent lights and over-priced knickknacks in the gift shops, I can feel you staring out from behind my eyes. Daddy, will I find you living in my hands, too? Will I someday slam my daughter's head against the wall, repeating, after you, "Bitch! Bitch! Bitch!"

My cold, efficient sisters are right: stop. Stop here. Let this line die out. They're right. Right to go off to Zimbabwe, right to finish their doctorates before they're twenty-five, right to live their solitary lives in the cold glaring light of the mind.

I get up. I have things to do. Messages on the answering machine. Noe Valley Community Foods calls to say that the henna I've special-ordered has come in. A message from the Arts Council. Mail to be sorted through. Bills and flyers about demonstrations. Sit next to the wastebasket and toss two-thirds of it out.

I magnet three flyers to the refrigerator: two about demonstrations (I might actually get to one of them) and another that tells of the arrest of a trade unionist in El Salvador, an address where letters urging that he be freed be sent, the last line reading, "We have found that international pressure can make a very real difference; without it, not only Ramon Garcia's freedom, but even his life, may be in jeopardy." I know that this flyer will stay magneted to the refrigerator door for a month, that I will feel a slight niggle of guilt each time I look at it. But that I won't make time to write the letter. After all, if I took the time to write every letter I wouldn't have a life. I know that finally, a month later, when international pressure has either freed Ramon Garcia or not, I will throw it in the wastebasket.

Then there's a cream-colored envelope, my name typed on the outside, "The Dalton Foundation," in the corner. A thick envelope. I tear it open. "Dear Ms. Etters . . . We are pleased to inform you . . ." I've gotten the Dalton Fellowship. I fold the letter back up, put it back in its envelope. Ten thousand dollars. It's too much for me to deal with right now. I don't want to think about it.

Matt comes into the kitchen, showered, dressed. I slip the Dalton envelope under the pile of papers. He's got to leave for work in about an hour. "You want to go up to 24th Street and get a cappuccino?"

"I can't. I have too much to do."

"Say that again. Three times. Slowly."

"I can't, I have too much to do. I can't. I have to do much to do. Okay, okay."

We sit on the patio of the café on 24th Street. The sky is pure California blue. I like being in places—Wyoming, the Greek islands—where the sky overwhelms the earth. I miss the light on Santorini. That pure, holy sun. The unbearable blue. I could go back to the Greek islands, I've never liked working with water colors, but maybe there—

Stop thinking about what use you could make of things, I order myself.

The cold of the marble-top table beneath my arms, the warmth of the white cup I clasp. Decaf caffe mocha. Yes, please, with whipped cream. The silence between us.

"You look sad," Matt says.

"No." I take a sip of my caffe mocha, leaving myself with the hint of a white moustache. "Clara was crying. About my father. And it just seemed so—odd."

Matt rests his hand on mine. The index finger with its slight stain of yellow. The few tufts of dark hair on his knuckles.

The callouses of his palms. I became an artist to try to turn off that flow of words, words, words: those voices that are occupying armies in my head.

Sunday, we go to brunch at Matt's father's.

"Are you taking me home to meet the folks?" I ask.

"No. I'm taking you home to get a free meal."

Matt tells me that these brunches used to be dozens of bagels piled on a plate, lox and whitefish, scrambled eggs, toast thick with butter, pickled herring in cream, rye bread, salami, cheese, kosher dills, olives, lasagna, ziti.

After the divorce (from Matt's mother) the Italian food disappeared. Now his father's on Pritikin. Matt grumbles that brunch will be torn greens, eight varieties—his father's new wife, number three, grows them in her organic garden—and skinless grilled chicken breasts with black beans and salsa.

"You must be Elizabeth," Matt's father says. His name is Mitch. He's younger than I expected. Then I remember that he was twenty-four when Matt was born. I'm halfway between them. This is his wife, Constance. She's my age, maybe a couple of years older.

"We're so glad to finally get to meet you," Constance says.

Sometimes I think there are only four conversations in San Francisco and they are repeated endlessly with slight variations: my dysfunctional family and the twelve-step program I am working to recover from growing up in it; the toxins in our food and how my sister's best friend's cousin cured herself of cancer by drinking spring water and eating bean sprouts; real estate ("four hundred thousand dollars, one, *one* bedroom"); and the wrong-headedness of u.s. policy in Central America.

I tell Constance the salad is delicious (it is) and we start having conversation number two. She takes me into the kitchen to show me her composting system. I'm impressed. She's really working on cleansing her body of toxins; she and Mitch are trying to get pregnant, she confides. I wonder if she knows I *am*. I wonder if Matt knows she and Mitch are trying.

After Matt and I went out for our first drink together, the next morning I called Ann Marie, left a message on her tape. At ten minutes to eleven she called me back. I met someone; I think he's interested in me.

"Oh shit," she said. "My eleven o'clock is here already. Can you meet me for lunch?"

I never go out for lunch; I don't want to interrupt my work. Usually never.

We met at her office. Ann Marie was sitting behind her desk, her blond hair pulled back, wearing her reading glasses. On the wall behind her was a collection of masks: a rough-carved African mask, a Balinese god of creativity, a golden Mardi Gras face. Her bookshelves were filled with hardbound tomes. I saw Ann Marie as she appeared to her clients: solid and wise. She locked her leg braces into place as she stood. She had polio, too.

A miracle: one of her clients had flu. She had three whole hours off. We were like kids out of school.

She wanted to take me to a restaurant on Union Street. "Union Street?" I said, "my reputation will be shot if anyone I know sees me on Union Street."

"If anyone sees you there, they'll be there, too," she pointed out.

We sat outdoors in the sunshine, eating Caesar salad and drinking white wine. I knew I would be hungry again in a few hours. This was not like eating at La Cumbre, my taquería in the Mission where they serve prole food, where a bean-rich carne asada burrito for lunch lasts me until eight that night.

The sun was warm on my face. I was happy to be alive.

After lunch, Ann Marie said, "I'm going to buy you a present."

"What?"

"You'll see."

So I picked up the check from lunch.

She led me to a trendy Union Street store. No, not a store, a shop. In the back, silk underwear hung in open wardrobes. I liked this air of luxury, and felt guilty, too: it seemed self-indulgent, commodified. Although when you are a disabled woman, the equation *woman equals sex* does not apply to you, and you are breaking the role assigned to you (become a social worker, develop inner strength, be a wonderful aunt) when you dress like you love your body.

"Jesus," I said. The pair of underpants I'd been admiring was $34.

"Don't look at the price tags," Ann Marie ordered.

I took the underwear into the changing room. "Come with me," I said. It was a bit crowded for the two of us, with her crutches and my cane, but we managed.

"You look great," she said.

"Do I?" I was afraid of looking ridiculous, lace next to a shriveled limb.

"Yes," she insisted.

"Did you read that article in the *Rag*? 'Public Stripping?'"

"I *knew* you were thinking," she said. "I knew the wheels in that brain of yours were turning around. I started that article, but I couldn't finish it. It was too painful—Come on. This is it. I'm buying that for you. And turn off your brain, would you please?"

Ann Marie is the first real friend I've had who is disabled. All our lives we've wanted someone who would understand us the way we understand each other. But sometimes we are so close that we bleed into each other.

The article, "Public Stripping," was about a woman's memory of having her "case" presented at grand rounds. You would sit meekly in front of an audience of doctors while your deformities, your disease were described. Atrophy. *Pedes equinovari*. Pronounced lordosis. Scoliosis. Your body would be on display as a living, 3-D visual aid. At some point in the lecture, to show off your scoliosis, your hip misalignment, you would be told to remove the thin cotton gown in which you had been shivering. Sometimes you were allowed a baggy medical version of a G-string, to cover your crotch. The vaccine got invented six months after I had polio, so I was the last of my tribe, a medical curiosity, a living museum piece.

I enjoyed getting dressed that night, putting on the black underpants and the black lacy bra that Ann Marie bought me, black leggings and a teal silk blouse. I liked the way my leggings hugged my flesh, showing my legs, one strong like a tree trunk, the other a thin stalk. I unbuttoned the top two buttons of my blouse. I looked at myself in the full-length mirror. I felt crippled *and* sexy. Finally.

We saw *Notorious* at the Castro. Matt asked me if I was hungry. I said yes, and he said that he had some cold pizza at his place; we could go there and heat it up.

I climbed back on his motorcycle. I spread my legs around him, balanced my cane between us. I was afraid he could feel the beating of my heart, the pulse of my crotch. I didn't know where we were going. I liked this feeling.

We ended up at his studio. I hadn't realized he lived there. He kissed me in the elevator, pressing the weight of his body against mine.

"Beer or scotch?" he asked when we got inside.

"Do you have any fruit juice? Bubbly water?"

He squeezed orange juice for me by hand.

"Go ahead," I said, "have a drink."

He poured himself a scotch. Good, I thought, the smell of it on his breath will put me off him, a bit. Keep me from doing anything foolish.

He played a record. It was punk and raucous. I admit it, I listen to oldies stations now, or KPFA, the political station. He wasn't trying to seduce me—he didn't play something smoky that would put me in the mood, or music that would try to bridge the gap of years between us (Tracy Chapman, maybe).

I looked around his studio. It was functional. Not "functional" as in Whole Earth Access: matching $4.95 black coffee mugs, a streamlined espresso maker. Functional as in yard sales and Mort's House of Discounts. I liked his nontrendiness, his dedication.

"What are you smiling about?"

"This picture," I lied, touching a photograph on the wall.

"That's my mother. Me," he said. He's three years old, sitting astride her shoulders, canvases in the background; she's smiling seductively at someone off camera.

"Is that her work?" I asked.

"Some boyfriend's." He showed me the pure black brushtroke on rice paper. "That's her work."

"I thought you were older when your parents got divorced."

"I was."

I sat down on the couch facing him, my legs drawn up toward my chest, the tails of my shirt flopped between my legs. I looked slightly provocative, slightly. I was taking a risk: his couch was old, filled with dust. I might have started to cough, and then to wheeze. I sipped my orange juice, he sipped his scotch. We ate our pizza. We chatted about openings we had been to and movies we had seen. The tension of the evening drained away. I felt sad. We lapsed into silence.

"What are you thinking?" I asked.

"How much I like you," he said. He wasn't at all coy. He looked straght at me. I believed him. "What are you thinking?"

"I don't know," I said.

"That's cheating," he said. "I told you."

"I guess I'm thinking of a lot of things. How much I like you. How scary all of this feels."

"Yeah?"

"You know, the last time I was out there, on the market, I was young—"

"My age?" he asked, smiling.

"Oh, not that young," I said.

"Stop worrying," he said. "This is easy."

"Nothing's ever easy," I said.

We kissed. I'd forgotten that anything could feel this good. He touched my breasts. I reached up and unhooked my bra so the silk of my shirt rubbed against my breasts as he rolled my nipples in his fingers.

A couple of times before it had been this easy with a man. When I was with Danny, and seeing other men, a few times, knowing we wouldn't ever see each other again, there were men with whom my body could be as honest as it was being then, times when with a stranger in the dark, histories fell away, and I was unashamed, pure.

We stayed entwined after we made love.

"I have to move," I whispered. "My legs are getting stiff." A sucking sound as we pulled ourselves apart: my wet cunt letting go of the condom. We lay together in easy silence. Then he asked me, "What happened to your leg?" Flat out, no hemming and hawing, and do you mind if I ask you a personal question? No politically correct, "What's your disability?"

"It's more than just my leg. I had polio."

"No, really."

"Really," I said. He thinks polio's like scurvy or diphtheria, some strange disease from the distant past.

He propped himself up on his elbow. "Polio? How come?"

"In '53. The vaccine wasn't invented until '54."

"So how does that affect you?" he asked.

I wished I had on my glasses; I would have peered at him over the frames.

"How does it affect me?"

"Am I being too personal?"

"No," I said. "It's just such a big question."

"I meant more physically," he said. "You know, I saw your piece, the one where you stood up on the chair and said 'stature' in that deep voice."

I laughed. It's always strange to hear your work being described by someone else. He was talking about a performance piece I had done a few years ago, about creating art as a disabled woman. In it, I read a list of words, culled from reviews, that criticized work by saying that *it limps along, is blind to, falters*; words of praise could have passed as a decription of Arnold Schwarzenegger: *robust, strong, stature.*

I wake up in the morning feeling nauseous, wanting to turn off my alarm, roll over, go back to sleep. But I wake up happy, too. I like earthquakes, I like it when the ground starts to roll and the dishes start to rattle. I like to get shaken up. I like what's happening in my body, now. New sensations that distract me from old pains. I climb out of bed and, for my first dozen steps, my ankles feel as if shards of glass are embedded in them. The hormones of pregnancy are loosening my joints so that my pelvis will expand; but because I don't have adequate musculature, my bones clank and jar at the joints.

I hate my pain. I love my pain. I love it for its urgency, its harshness, the way it refuses to be ignored, the way it makes me know myself in a new way.

I get out of bed and get going. I'm so good at going on. Give me a crisis and watch me cope. I'm downing a cup of coffee that's two-thirds decaf, getting ready to teach my three classes today.

I'm nervous about my exhibit that opens the week after next. I wish there was something left to do about it, something to do besides get nervous.

It was one of those ideas that came to me in a flash, and before I had time to think it through I had called up my friend Marlene, who I had known would say yes. She did say yes, sure I could take her picture, and we set up a time.

Two days later we rode the freight elevator up to my studio.

I locked the door behind us and she started unbuttoning her blouse.

"Gee," I said, a word I'd never heard myself use before, "don't you want to have a cup of coffee or some wine? Anything?"

"It's not like we're going to sleep together."

She took off her blouse; she took off her black knit pants. I was repulsed by her body. Her legs were short and stunted. She had had surgery as a child, and her legs, like mine, are covered with thick scars. But worse than mine. A politically incorrect habit, this ranking of other disabled women's bodies against my own. I put my eye behind the camera and started to shoot. It's easier when I'm watching through the viewfinder.

"I'm cold," she said, and I turned on the electric heater.

"Did you ever have pictures taken of you when you were a kid?" she asked. She didn't say any more than that, but I knew instantly what she meant: in a bare room, in a hospital, by a medical photographer. "You're going to have your picture taken!" a nurse announced, and a savvy kid like you knew that meant that you were going down to the x-ray department. But instead of going down to the basement to be laid under those battleship-green x-ray machines, you were taken to the ground floor. A knock on the door, the photographer came in, you were stood against a blank wall, the hospital johnny was removed, you stood there naked. He hid behind his camera (maybe he was embarrassed by the whole procedure, too) and took pictures of you through a camera that used old-fashioned plates.

"What did they do with those pictures?"

"Medical textbooks?" I said, and shrugged my shoulders. "They have them in there. With those black bands across the eyes, like they used to have in porn magazines."

For the next six months, I took pictures of disabled women naked. Most people I asked said no, but I was amazed at the number who said yes. I took pictures of friends and of friends of friends, of women who leaned seductively towards the camera and women who shook the whole time I was taking their photographs, a nineteen-year-old who had lost her leg in an automobile accident at sixteen, and an eighty-year-old woman who had been disabled with polio at the age of eighteen months, whose body had grown into its disability like a gnarled tree.

I met a one-armed woman who wore a miniskirt and black fishnet stockings. I met a woman who had never shown herself naked to anyone before.

I told everyone, honestly, that I wasn't sure what I was going to do with the photographs. I just needed to take them. I might do an exhibit; if I did, I'd let them know and get their permission.

Then Ann Marie told a friend of hers who owned a gallery about my photographs, and then everyone was telling me how wonderful they were, and I was getting ready for a show. I only had to leave out two photographs because the women didn't want their pictures shown.

In my class for disabled women at the Independent Living Center, we have a new student. Corinne has fuchsia hair and angry eyes behind Coke-bottle lenses. "Is this class going to be stupid?"

"Why do you say that?"

"This is going to be some picture-taking for cripples and retards, isn't it?"

"Corinne," I say, "I'm a serious artist. This is a serious class."

When it's time for her to introduce herself to the group, she says, "My name's Corinne. What am I supposed to tell you? My diagnosis?"

"If you want to."

"I'm 'low vision.' I want to go to art school, but fucking Voc Rehab won't pay for it. They want me to be a goddamn medical transcriber." She wants to show the world that she

sees. "I told my rehab counselor, maybe the way I see is right.
Maybe the edges of things really are fuzzy. Maybe they really
do bleed into each other. Maybe things are clear only when
they're right under your nose. Now he thinks I'm insane."

I say, "You all remember," speaking clearly and loudly,
enunciating each word so that Rachel, whose brain damage
affects her hearing, can hear, "that we have the month of August off."

Corinne wants to know why. "Because the Arts Council
only funds projects for eleven months."

"Can we meet on our own?" Rachel wants to know.

"You can ask Kathy if you could use this room. I bet she'd
let you."

"But you wouldn't be here?"

"No," I say, "I need a break. I love teaching this class. But I
need a break."

We are critiquing Cecilia's work today. She holds up her
first photograph.

"Ahhh toookkk dis phphpphotocrafff iz of mah muudder
indd hhhherr ketchen."

"Did everybody get that?" I say as loudly as I can without
shouting.

Theresa nods, drool escaping from her mouth. She swipes
at it with the back of her hand. Rachel calls, "No, what did she
say?" and Sherry shakes her head.

"Cecilia, can you repeat what you said?"

"Ahhh zed, disss photograbbbb iz uf mah mmmuuudder.
Innnddd hherr kkkkittshun."

Sherry turns to Rachel and says, "It's of her mother, in her
kitchen."

"Oh," Rachel says, "of her mother, in her kitchen."

"Maahhh muddderrr, zzzheeee lufffffs hhhurrr ki-ki-
kitsshun."

"Can you pass it down to Corinne?"

Corinne holds the photograph an inch from her eyes,
moves it back and forth to take it all in.

"I'm starving," she says.

"Corinne, let's keep our focus on Cecilia's photograph," I reprimand. Then soften, and add, "There's some plums in the plastic bag."

Corinne examines the plums as if they were oddities, some food she'd never seen before. I suppose that she doesn't eat fruit, on principle. I like her. I like her rage.

During the break, Corinne walks around and examines the pictures on the wall. I've hung portraits from a poster project I did the year before, "Disabled Women: Hidden from History." Our foremothers, Helen Keller and Frida Kahlo, Harriet Tubman and Carrie Buck, Dorothea Lange, glare down at us. Corrine points to Harriet Tubman and says, "Who was this babe?"

"She was a leader of the Underground Railroad."

"What was her problem?"

"She had a seizure disorder."

"Oh," says Corinne.

I'm drained. My head aches from concentrating on Cecilia's voice. Sometimes I hate being here; sometimes it's just too much for me. No one's polite and glib here, no one has big shiny white teeth and fire-engine-red lipstick. No one wears silk clothes. We are naked with each other from the word go. More than naked, we wear our insides on the outside.

I am like air to these women. They love me. If I do it, if I go through with the pregnancy, I'll have to give up my grant. I wouldn't be able to keep working—Ann Marie keeps telling me that I'll be too exhausted. I have no reserves of energy. I'll have to say goodbye to these women. I'll never get Corinne to uncross her arms and smile.

Plus, I couldn't afford to keep working. Health insurance, a matter I've conveniently managed to push to the back of my mind. I'll have to go on ssi, so I can get Medi-Cal.

I escape to the bathroom, where I sit on the toilet and meditate. My five-minute break. I allow the tension to drain from my body. I allow my thoughts to become bubbles that rise to the surface and then dissolve.

I get to Diamond Sutra, where I am meeting with Phyllis and Cathy, a quarter of an hour early. Another reflex we share, we adult daughters—the shorthand term we use in the Bay Area to talk about adult daughters of alcoholics—we arrive too early, afraid of being late, afraid of letting others down.

I'm as hungry as I've ever been, hungrier even than when I've been on steroids for my asthma. How rude would it be to order an appetizer before they get here? Instead, I make my lists in my planner. The intro for this forum, one hour to write. Go to the post office. Shopping—buy oatmeal, eggplant, yeast, flour (white and whole wheat). All these things I have put off doing. Pregnancy makes me so tired. I'm only drinking one cup of coffee a day now.

I sit here, in Diamond Sutra restaurant, the menu open in front of me. I could order Jamaican black bean soup or Chinese chicken salad, Mexican chili. Expropriation not just of raw materials but raw culture. What do I want instead? To be authentically American, eat hot dogs and potato chips?

I finger the sleeve of the white cotton blouse I am wearing. If it could talk, what would it say? Would it tell me of the defoliants sprayed on crops before harvest time, of the women bending in the hot sun to pick cotton, in Egypt or Haiti or the Sudan? Of the men growing dizzy from the smell of chlorine in the plant where the cotton is bleached pure white? Of the women at the mechanical looms, in a factory in South Carolina, maybe—the air alive, almost glowing, with millions of filaments of fiber that will lodge in their lungs and cause brown-lung disease? Finally, I pull a blouse off a rack in a shop on 24th Street that sells only only natural fibers, and say to Anne Marie, "I love this." A white North American woman, pulling a plastic charge card out of her leather wallet.

Phyllis and Cathy arrive. Phyllis and I embrace. She's a midwife, a midwife who wears a leather jacket and rides a motorcycle, but a midwife just the same. Her hand lingers on my back. How am I doing? I wobble my hand in the air. A gesture that is getting old.

I've met Cathy once before. She is nearly ten years younger than me, from Women for the Nicaraguan Revolution. She's a lesbian, works at The Copy Shop on Market Street. (I suppose a hundred years from now some women's historian will write her PhD dissertation on the concentration of lesbian employees in photocopying stores in the late twentieth century.)

Cathy looks at the menu, lets out a sound that's somewhere between a whistle and a sigh.

"Is this too expensive for you?" I ask. "I can chip in—"

"Sure," Phyllis says. "We can—"

"I'll just get some soup," she says. It's this odd Bay Area self-righteousness, where one proves one's political worth by how little one has.

"Get whatever you want," I say.

We look over our menus. "I'm in the mood for meat," I announce, and laugh. "Is that going to gross anybody out?"

I order lamb chops. Phyllis and Cathy order salad.

"Shall we . . ." I ask, taking out my paper and pen. We rough-out times: my intro will start at 8:15, Phyllis and Cathy will each talk for twenty minutes. Twenty minutes, does that give them enough time? We want to leave plenty of time for discussion.

I say "Have we gotten any . . ."

"Flak?" Phyllis says.

"I was going to say 'negative feedback.' I guess 'flak' is more apt."

"Not yet," Phyllis says. "I mean, we worded things pretty carefully. There's something," she adds, "I wanted to talk about. I'm not sure of how emotional to get. You know . . . to talk about the impact Patricia's death had on me—I don't know how—I don't want to get up there on the platform and burst into tears. I don't want to be too—"

I think of a scene in *The Golden Notebook*, when Doris Lessing describes a meeting held after Khrushchev's revelations about the fate of the Jews under Stalin. A member of the British Communist Party, who had gone to the Soviet Union to investigate, spoke coolly and rationally to a mixed group of sympathizers and Party members about the trials, official and unofficial anti-Semitism; and then, privately, after the "sympathizers" had gone home, told the inner circle of beatings, murders, medieval torture instruments being brought out of museums to be used against Jews. The two truths.

"My feeling is," I say, "you should tell the truth. The whole truth, the emotional truth."

Cathy glares at me. "I think there are people out there who are just waiting to seize on this."

"It's true. There are. But I still think—"

Her eyes fixed on mine, she says, "The revolution has made tremendous accomplishments." She sounds like a leaflet, parroting statistics about infant mortality, vaccination. "Don't you think it's arrogant for us to endanger that in any way?"

"I think the alternative is to turn the Nicaraguan revolution into some kind of an idol."

This table swells to the size of a continent. I am here, Cathy is there; we shout across to be heard. I hang a label on her (Politically Immature) as surely as she, squared-off across this table, must hang a label on me . . . Petty Bourgeois? Liberal? I hate her, however momentarily, for her youth, her easy sureness, her ability to look good in second-hand clothes, her capacity for awakening guilt in me.

I want to grab Cathy's hand and ask, Whose daughter are you? Where did you come from? Did you come from a six-bedroom house in the suburbs, with white carpets and white drapes? Did you get fed on privilege until you choked on it? Or does your self-righteousness grow out of a walk up three flights of stairs every night, coming home to the phone ringing, your mother saying she was working overtime—sorry, sweetheart—there's some chicken in the freezer and no TV until you've done your homework?

I wish I could say to Cathy, I am the daughter of a man who fought for freedom in a country far from home, who made me a vessel for his hatred, of all that was weak and female, who sentimentalized the stalwart Spanish peasants who could do no wrong—a man who talked about freedom and then slammed my head against the wall. I'd like to tell her that I only trust politics when it happens close to home, when it happens within us, when it feels like it will split us open.

Cathy, tell me what set you going. Was it a bus ride through Guatemala? Not the sight of another passenger on the bus, a mother, balancing a scrawny, gray-faced baby in her arms, not the sight of the mother's bared breast, thin and milkless, but her combing the child's malnutrition-whitened hair with her fingers: a gesture of hope against a world of impossibility. Was it *that* that set you going?

Accidents of history, which send Cathy in one direction, me in another, and the woman who has just walked in, with a perfect haircut and a perfect suede jacket, laughing on the arm of some man, in yet another.

Cathy is there, implacable, demanding, What about the Third World? What about the children who starve to death, every day, day after day?

And I am here: What about those revolutions that don't free us, that ask us to tell lies in their name?

Political differences. A short-hand term.

# 6

A truth that's deeper than the truth of dreams: the truth of the body.

Bone truth.

Home truth: a truth that is searching, poignant, close. The Anglo-Saxons called the body the *banhaus*, the bone-house.

The shift from embryo to fetus is marked by the development of the first long bones, on the seventieth day of fetal life. A physiological process, which will or will not occur within me, as it once happened to me, inside my mother, and to my mother inside of her mother. Each of us unfolding out of the one who came before; and, in our turn, unfolding others out of us. If it's a girl-child, a girl-fetus, swimming around inside of me, then soon her ovaries will be formed, with all her ova, too. My future grandchildren warm within me.

Daddy, I read an article in the paper the other day that said there were certain physical reactions common in those suffering from post-traumatic stress disorder: those who had been physically or sexually abused as children, combat veterans, rape victims. We startle easily, for instance. It's a joke among my friends, how I jump when someone comes up behind me unexpectedly. The memories that are stored in my nerves.

Daddy, I want to remember the thing itself. Not words like *abuse, physical violence, dysfunctional*. I want to see it as it was.

I have been called into the living room of the house on River Street, the dark living room with its magnificent, aging furniture that my grandmother bought in the twenties and thirties: Chippendale chairs covered in worn red damask, from her Colonial period; the divan modeled on a pharaoh's throne from her Egyptian period; the heavy dark beams overhead. The air in that room is thin; I have to work hard to breathe. You have both the doors closed, the one that leads to the kitchen, the one that leads to the front hallway. You breathe in, and the air goes into your bad lungs, where the asthma you have passed on to me, the asthma that lurks in my cells waiting to explode, festers. You breathe out, and the air is infected with your hate.

What led up to it? Did you say: *You're in big trouble, young lady.* Or was it: *You fucking little bitch.* I can hear your voice saying both of those phrases. But I can't remember. There are flashes of the violence itself, of you, crouched on top of me, your hands around my throat, desperately choking, choking off my air. I am dirty, a cesspool, I stink. Yet I fight back, fight to live.

Later, with other men, men I loved, I experienced a sensation of melding: the pleasure of union, of two bodies becoming one. But earlier, with him, I was shit, dead like him, without arms and legs—they melted and swelled, into my filthy belly, my gut. When I went down under his hands, it was like going down under the anesthesia.

But what led up to it? What came after? Of that, I have no memory. Was I defiant? Did I talk back? Did I make my hands into fists, plant them on my hips, say, "I wasn't doing anything wrong." Did I plead? Say, "I'll be good, I'll be good, I promise I'll be good"?

Nothing.

A black hole: an area of gravity so dense that light, and the history light carries, cannot escape from it.

Loss of memory: common experience of trauma victims. The automobile accident, the gun firing, the time around it, are all erased. Except that I can remember the thing itself, his body crouched over mine, his hands around my neck, his face above me distorted with rage, the sensation of drowning as my air is choked off. Perhaps it's that the silence afterwards was more painful.

My mother rescued me. She came and stood in the doorway, while my father hollered, "What did you call her for? What the fuck did you call her for? This has nothing to do with her!"

There. It's over. I left the room. Was I ordered out? Or did I slink away? No one walked up the stairs with me, tucked me between clean sheets, pressed a warm cloth against the red marks that in a day or two will be bruises. The next morning, I woke up, and came downstairs. My mother set a glass of orange juice in front of me. She said, "Good morning." And afterward? I must have ached for days. Last year, when the Democratic Convention met in San Francisco, two friends were beaten by the cops at a demonstration. The next day, one of them came over. She was stiff-legged, had to walk up the stairs almost sideways, set herself down gently on the couch. She wanted to take a bath in my tub; she only had a shower at her place. "I hurt so much," she kept saying. "God, I hurt so much." She had been leaving the demonstration: there had been a full moon that night, she and her lover, Lupe, were going to drive across the Golden Gate Bridge to eat a picnic supper in the Marin headlands, watch the moon rise over that bulk of rock that juts out into the Pacific. She kept talking, about what they had been planning to have for dinner, about how they hadn't meant to do anything, they'd been leaving the demo, cutting kitty-corner across Mission, when she'd looked up and seen the cops glaring at her, furious. Alice had said she raised her hands, like in a cowboy movie, *I give up, don't shoot.* But one of them ran towards her, swinging his billy club. Lupe tried to grab the cop's arm. Another cop put Lupe in a choke hold; she wet her pants. Alice repeated "God, I just hurt so much."

I filled the tub with hot, hot water and brought her cups of raspberry tea; played a Miriam Makeba tape for her while she soaked her aching muscles. I perched on the toilet; she lay in the bathtub, telling her story over and over again. The full moon, suddenly looking up and seeing the cop coming at her.

And what do I remember, of the other times he beat me? Nothing. How did I feel those next days—guilty? Angry? Disgusted? Ashamed? Did I ache? Were there bruises?

But there's nothing. No memory. I do all my tricks. I sit and meditate. As I fall off to sleep, I repeat, It is safe to remember now—when you wake up, you will remember your self, afterward. You will remember how you felt, physically. You will remember how your eyes met afterward, yours and his, the next time you passed each other in the hallway, sat opposite each other at the breakfast table.

But I don't. It's gone.

At school they called me "Smiley."

Battery. Later a battery of psychological tests determined that I was hostile to authority, lacked ego-strength, had a distorted notion of the male body, and of my own body. (When asked to draw a female, I drew a stick figure with a skirt, the sort of image that appears on the doors of women's restrooms; when asked to draw myself, I drew more or less the same picture, but gave the figure two crooked legs. The next assignment was to draw a male. This was a fairly realistic picture, but something was missing. I kept adding things: shoelaces, a belt, a belt buckle, cuffs on the pants and shirt. Handing it to the psychologist, I realized with a shock what it is I had forgotten: the man had no face.)

Daddy, when I was seven, eight years old, you used to help me put on my leg braces in the morning. I would sit on your bed in my white cotton underpants and T-shirt; you wore thin blue pajamas from Sears. Sometimes the fly would gape open and I could see the dark tangle of your pubic hair and pale curve of your penis.

Daddy, you would take my dead white leg and lay it within that man-made leg of steel and leather straps, pulling tight

across my flesh the leather straps that had turned yellow with
my sweat.

(Daddy, there's a hole in my life. I remember being an
eight-year-old kid, flat, hairless; and then being ten, with
breasts and periods, pubic hair. I don't remember anything in
between: not my breasts swelling up out of my chest, not hair
beginning to come in under my arms, between my legs.)

I always wonder if something happened then. Daddy, one
day did you let your hand linger between my legs? Did you
ease a finger inside between the elastic of my underpants and
my leg, calmly, as if this were your right? Or did I only
breathe in the tension in the air, did it only seep in through
my pores? Did I only sense through the length of time you
held your eyes on me, through the things you turned away
from, what you wanted? Did you feel disgust at your attraction to me, who was not only female but crippled, lesser on
two counts?

Daddy, did I only dream it? Did you? Can I put your dreams
on trial? Can I find you guilty for the charge in the air, for the
things that were so well-known they were beyond words?

Daddy, was Stalin right to see betrayal in the hearts of
those who did not yet suspect their own treason?

Maybe it wasn't you at all. Ann Marie says that the world of
the hospitals is the world of our fathers. I sit across the
kitchen table from her: she is sipping her coffee, I am sipping
my herbal tea. She says, "I can't tell you, how I often I hear it
in therapy, from disabled women. That eroticization of
pain. . . ."

Polio was my first lover. Pain let me know my body from
the inside out, filled the blank space of muscles and joints
with her sharp knowledge.

Strangers came into my room and touched my body. They
said, "Raise your arm like this. Raise your leg. Push back
against my hand." They pulled my hospital johnny up above
my waist.

Later, when I had surgery, I was laid on a cold metal table and strapped down. Men and women, faces hidden behind masks, came in. A man put a black triangle over my face, and the whole world spun dizzily away.

I did not see the woman who handed a knife to the man. He cut me open. He peeled back the thin outer layer of skin. A woman put clips on my flesh, to keep it out of the way. The man cut through the quivering yellow layer of fat, pushed the red muscle aside. The women sponged up the blood.

He went down to the bone. He cut away a piece, pried it loose. These tools have different names, but they are hacksaws and chisels. A woman sponged splattered blood and bone dust from the forehead of the man.

When he was finished, he stitched me up with clumsy stitches, so that the scar will be fat and thick. He wrote his hatred of my body on my flesh.

Afterwards, the fever. The body's protest, its white-hot reclaiming. White blood cells gather in colonies of pus at the site of infection; the bones recalcify.

There is no place they have not touched me. They have gone to the bone, down to its marrow. They have been inside me. They have remade me. If he had gone into me with his cock, it would have been called rape. If he had done it with a knife, it would have been called assault. But he's done it with a scalpel, and I'm supposed to be grateful.

Later on, I will tell myself that I am not this lumpy sack, this thing I use to lug my real self around. I am this mind, this pure, pure mind, which someday will burn blue and astonish.

But there's more. Forbidden truth: the physical pleasure of those times. The fear of what "they" will say: it proves that you are whining, dependent, spoiled, masochistic. The fear that naming the pleasure is denying the pain.

❀

Another truth, that sits side by side with the others:

A whole world in which I only lay, day after day, in a hospital bed; a world in which there first seems to be absence of change. But what would pass unnoticed in an ordinary life—the smoothness of clean sheets, the texture of warm toast that has been brushed with melted butter—there become pleasure that filled up a day.

The nurses wore caps and uniforms that showed their rank, what nursing school they had attended; like nuns' habits, from which their uniforms had descended. The garb that made of them a world apart.

After my hospital breakfast, a nurse would come in with hot water in a stainless steel basin. She rubbed white soap against a washcloth, which she rubbed across my body. One day she said to me, "That feels good now, doesn't it?" And I was glad, although I could not have formed the thought into words at the time, to have the physical pleasure of touch, of her hands against my flesh, acknowledged. Then she added, "Getting nice and clean." It was a thought that had never occurred to me before, that I could get dirty while lying there in a hospital bed. But there was a difference in the way my flesh felt. My unwashed flesh was damp and gritty, while the parts of my body that had been washed were taut and dry.

The nurse worked lotion onto her hands. Sweet-smelling yellow lotion from a blue glass bottle with a square red cross on it. She rolled me over onto my stomach, her gentle hands shifted the weight of my body. She lifted my nightgown, laying the sheet across what she called my "rump."

But as soon as I hear that word, I remember that there was only one nurse who called my ass "rump." She was tall, old—although she could have been anywhere from forty-five to seventy; anyone with gray or white hair was old to me—and had an accent. Swedish, I think now. I thought she spoke in that funny way because she was old. Her fingers were strong, massaged my flesh firmly and efficiently. There was another nurse who was young, wore pink lipstick, would sing snatches from rock 'n' roll songs under her breath—"The movie wasn't so hot, it didn't have much of a plot . . ." or "It was a one-eyed, one-horned flying purple people-eater . . ." —while she gently stroked my flesh with her slender fingers.

Then the sheets were changed. The hospital sheets weren't like the sheets my mother had bought second-hand and then patched and restitched when they gave way. In the hospital, the sheets were fresh every day, thick, and the blankets' clean white wool didn't smell of the past.

I would be shifted to one side while the bed was made one half at a time. They had a precise way of doing it, making "hospital corners," shaping the soft fabric into right angles, tucking those under the mattress with military precision. And then the pleasure of an unwrinkled sheet under me.

On some days, a strong arm went around my shoulders, another scooted under my thigh, and I was lifted to a wheelchair, taken downstairs. On the trip down, I passed, out of the antiseptic smell of the ward, to the elevator, that didn't have a hospital smell, that smelled like the outside world. Then down again, out past the gift shop, to a smell so heady it almost made me dizzy, a smell of chocolate and sugar candies, of tobacco, of daisies and mums and carnations arranged in ceramic vases, perhaps with paper hearts on them that say, "Get well soon." The male orderly, a Negro (this was before I had gone to visit my grandparents, and I believed that all Negro men were ministers—Reverend King, Reverend Abernathy—and that they were always on civil rights marches; I couldn't understand what this man was doing there in the hospital), pushed me, slowly and steadily on, past the smell that was my favorite, better even than the kitchen: the room that is marked Laundry. I knew how to sound out letters, but I didn't know this word. It became La-Un-Dry. I did not know what happened behind this door, only that the warm smell of starch and steam reminded me of my mother. Sometimes I heard the lilt of Southern voices coming through the door.

One day the orderly stopped, opened the door, and called in, "Hello, Mabel! I know that laugh! I know that laugh!" I saw a room filled with Negro women. They didn't wear white, they wore green. Against one wall, a line of stout square washing machines, each with a glass circle showing the back-forth, slip-slop of suds and sheets. Closer to me were the mangles, where the sheets were pressed. The women leaned over to pull crumpled sheets out of wheeled canvas laundry hampers; they lifted wads of damp sheets out of the washers, spread dry sheets flat to be pressed. Each downward movement of their arms on the great flat hand of the mangle was answered by an upward rush of steam.

"That Mabel," he said to me, after the door had swung shut on its mechanical arm. I had been allowed, momentarily, into a secret world. (And yet, later that night, why did I feel a sense of shame when I realized the word I had mispronounced la-un-dry is *laundry*, a word I knew perfectly well?)

I came to the last of the smells: chlorine, faint but sharp, from the therapy pool in a separate room off to one side of P.T. In the P.T. room another pair of arms, sometimes a woman's, but here sometimes a man's, lowered me into the whirlpool, where I lay caressed by the swirling water, watching the blue water against the turquoise sides and bottom, the dappled shadows. (Later on, I will love David Hockney's paintings of swimming pools, even though everyone else I know sneers at him, says he's a bourgeois lapdog. I love them because they will bring back that world of warm water, that flux.)

When I became stronger, I went to the therapy pool. There, a physical therapist, wearing the flowered bathing suits with the fluted skirts that women of that time wore, her hair pulled back in a white bathing cap with fake rubber daisies on it, held out her arms to receive me as I slipped into the warm water. Every word that she said to me, or that I said to her, echoed off the turquoise walls, the distant tiled ceiling.

The pool room was so warm that even if I didn't put my head under water, my face was soon damp from condensation, drops of water mixed with sweat clung to my eyelashes. The lights that hung down from the ceiling were surrounded with halos.

At home, in order to get to the office at nine looking crisp and efficient, looking, that is, as if she didn't have children, my mother had to get up at five, wake us up at six to breakfast already set out on the table. Our lunches, in brown paper bags with our names written on them in magic marker, waited on the kitchen counter, with four pennies stacked in front of each—our milk money. There was a schedule for the bathroom. She'd call out, "Clara's turn!" at ten past the hour, "Rose's turn," at twenty past. In the world of the hospital, time was something that swirled and eddied and slowly unfurled, the opposite of my mother's world.

Later, when I was nine years old, my mother left for work each morning by seven-thirty. My father lined us all up at quarter-to-eight before we left the house to catch the bus. This was 1960. Clara was twelve. She always rolled over the waistbands of her skirts to make them shorter.

Every morning she did this; and every morning my father yelled, "Show off your goddamn twat, why don't you?" or, "What the hell are people going to think of me? Huh? You going out dressed like that?"

Every morning Clara cried, "But, Daddy, no one wears their skirts long anymore."

"Jesus Christ. I thought we had brought you up differently than that. Everyone does it. Everyone does it! What the fucking hell. Then by all means, go ahead, you fucking do it, too. Go out the door looking like a goddamn streetwalker. It's all right. Everyone does it."

Clara never waited till we got out the door to roll her waistband over and hike up her skirt. And every morning my father yelled, "You goddamn slut!" Sometimes he said, "You're

not too old to go across my knee," and once even grabbed her
and pulled her underpants down, holding her across his lap,
while his hand came down again and again against her bare
skin.

Another time, when we were living in Cambridge, a sanitary napkin had been left, folded in half and wrapped in toilet
paper, on the top of the toilet tank in the third floor bathroom. For some reason, he was up there, saw it. I remember
being called into his study, remember that for a weekend the
household was in a state of crisis over the fact that a sanitary
napkin hadn't been thrown away. What did he say when he
called me into the study? Another black hole.

No, that's not enough, to call it a black hole. If I can't remember, I must imagine it. But don't give up on memory.
Begin with his desk, the wood polished so it glowed. The
desk, of course, inherited from my grandparents. My grandmother had died only a year or two before, so it hadn't yet
lost the gleam that had been worked into it by those Negro
maids in my grandparents' house, polishing the grain until it
shone like gold—except that gold has never been alive, and
the wood of this desk had not just richness but variation, a
pattern showing the wood's history of growth. I see the magnificent desk, piled with old newspapers, yellow check stubs,
mail, those piles of papers that were always in danger of tip-
ping over, through which he used to paw and mutter, "Now
what the hell did I do with that . . ." Although mutter doesn't
convey his rage, our fear. There's the battered desk chair,
bought at the Salvation Army or some fund-raising rummage
sale. Next to the desk, there's the lamp with the yellowed
shade, the lamp he's always pulling closer to the desk, fiddling
with, tilting the shade: it has a 60-watt bulb. (Once my
mother bought 100-watt bulbs by mistake, and Jesus Christ,
100-watt bulbs? It's killing him now, paying the electric
bill. . . .)

Even though I can't remember what he said when he called
me into his study, I can hear his tone of voice. Stripped of its

power, this voice would be called whining or hysterical; but full of its power, of its life-and-death power over me, it is something else. What else? I flip through the thesaurus, trying to find a word to name his voice—*bombastic* comes closest, but it's still wide of the mark. Maybe there is no word, because it's a state that men get into only with women, this whining/threatening, self-pitying/terrifying state.

I can see the room, hear his voice. Now it should be a simple step to make out what he says. *You're disgusting, filthy.* Yes, he would have said that, but he couldn't have said it over and over again, it wouldn't have been enough to fill up the weekend.

Pretend to be him, imagine it from the inside. In order to make the leap, I have to imagine that he hated my body as I hated his. I hated his smells, I hated the bristle on his face when he rubbed his face against mine and said, "Come and give your old man a kiss." I hated when he caught cold, and then had asthma: he filled the whole house with the sounds of his hacking coughs, his coughing up of phlegm, his moans.

Suppose my rage wasn't held in check by my powerlessness? I see an image: a B-movie female Nazi, striding back and forth in front of him—in that dark study with the magnificent desk—wearing leather boots, cracking a whip.

But my disgust in his maleness arises out of those beatings, out of his hatred of me. Where did that hatred come from? I think of his own mother, that matron in black who smelled of lilacs, and try to imagine her flesh exciting hatred in him. Perhaps.

Still, I'm no closer to learning what words came out of his mouth. Did he play detective? Yes, that's what he would have done. It would have been a way of prolonging the confrontation, drawing it out. An interrogation. All three of you, you three girls who have your bedrooms on the third floor, were menstruating at the same time. Three girls, three guilty possibilities. Clara would have been called in first, then Rose, me last. They both said they didn't do it, so it must be you. It must have been you who left the sanitary napkin there. No? Well then which of your sisters did it? Someone did it.

I would deny it, though I'm not at all sure. The third-floor bathrooms had been made over from two tiny closets. In one was a toilet, in the other a sink, shower, and wastebasket. There was no wastebasket in the one with the toilet, so I always set the used sanitary napkin there, picking it up when I left. But maybe the phone rang, or maybe I just forgot. I didn't dare confess: I didn't know what the punishment would be. My sisters would be furious at me for not confessing sooner, sparing them.

After a while, I was dismissed; Clara was called back in again. The round of interrogations began again.

(Mama, you always said, A victory for one is a victory for all. In unity there is strength. But that lesson didn't sink in very far.)

Daddy, I love detective movies, film noir. When I watch them, I feel a thrill that is a cousin to the terror I felt as a child. But it's transmuted: in the interrogation scenes the woman is always sleek and contained. She lights a cigarette, blows a cool jet of smoke between pursed lips. She doesn't tremble or quail. She remains beautiful: no one will ever see her with a bruise, a split lip, a black eye. The camera cuts back and forth: the male interrogator is glowering, the woman's head is down and tilted to one side. I am both the watcher and the watched. And then there's the parting long shot, and the credits roll, the lights come up. I turn to the friend or lover sitting next to me, suggest a bar or a café. We get up and walk out into the cool night air. It's over.

What tied my mother to my father, made her stay loyal to him when he was gone, when he beat her children, when he drowned her and himself in gin? Was it a physical passion that held her to him? Was it some need she'd inherited from her family? But how could there have been any passion in that dry, dry house in Mechanic Falls?

Once in a feminist reading group, we read Joanna Russ's "Autobiography of My Mother." In the story, the narrator imagines herself and her mother as contemporaries, going out together to pick up men. The woman whose turn it was to lead the group had us write for half an hour about our mothers, imagining them not as our mothers, not as mothers at all.

So I sat there, on the floor of the flat on Dolores Street, with my back propped against an overstuffed chair, and filled up sheets of blue-lined paper.

When my mother was five years old, she told her two-year-old sister Katie to jump out the window. Katie, who idolized her, did. There was a bush underneath the window; Katie walked away with scratches. The story is an anecdote that gets trotted out every now and again at family gatherings.

In this new version, this version in which you don't become my mother, you tell Katie to jump out the window, and she looks up at you with that cherubic two-year-old's face, clambers up onto the window ledge and jumps. But this time there's no bush. Katie falls to her death. Eleanor never confesses; her mother never accuses her. But her mourning, her suspicion, her anger, fill the air. Eleanor doesn't become a good girl; she becomes a bad one. She doesn't become the Eleanor McKenzie who sits on the hard pew of the Episcopal Church, furrows her brow and stares at the minister when he reads, "It is easier for a camel to pass through the eye of a needle than for a rich man to enter the kingdom of heaven." She doesn't take meals to the poor at Christmastime. She doesn't become valedictorian of her high school class.

Instead, Mama, Eleanor, you leave Mechanic Falls at seventeen. You've had it up to here with your family, with the Depression, with this jerkwater town. You will never become brave Eleanor Etters raising her five daughters in the fourth-floor walk-up in Springfield, taking in typing and ironing. You will never kneel down between the rows of the vegetable garden in Jefferson, tying the rangy Kentucky Wonders to the bean poles. Instead you stand by the side of the highway, your skirt hiked up above your knee. A truck driver hauling a load of apples to Boston pulls over; you clamber into the cab. I see your face, the face I saw in the tiny Brownie Instamatic black-and-white photographs taken when you were in college. Standing posed in front of a fountain somewhere, you were wearing gloves and had dark red lips. (As a kid, I wondered how you could have been so beautiful, like a movie star, and now be so haggard and worn and ugly.) I see that face, and I meld it to images from the movies: you're Claudette Colbert in *It Happened One Night*, Lana Turner in *The Postman Always Rings Twice*. It was easy. As a bad girl you're not my mother anymore, just some woman with her flesh, her genes.

No, I have to make myself see you, the woman I know, the woman who was as beautiful as a movie star at twenty and became haggard and ugly fifteen years later. Imagine you feeling for him the longing I feel for Matt. I see you with your arms open to him, see a flash of him naked, coming towards you. But then you both turn into skeletons. I shut down. I refuse. Refuse to imagine it.

# 7

The early morning ring. The alarm? No, the phone. Glance at the clock. 3:23. It's not a wrong number, I know it, but still I hope it might be.

Matt has stumbled to the phone before me, he's holding the receiver, saying, "Hello." And then holding the phone out to me, "It's Clara."

"Go back to sleep," I say. I stagger from the bed, my body still mostly asleep, steadying myself on the bedpost. I touch his shoulder. "I'll wake you up if I need you."

Holding the phone, dragging the long cord behind me, I go in the kitchen and shut the door.

"Here I am," I say.

"He's dying," she says.

What else is new? Something must be, or she wouldn't have called.

"I mean, he's really going fast. He had a stroke."

I wait for more, but nothing comes. I stretch the long cord of the telephone behind me as I fill the kettle with water.

"I'm making coffee," I say, to explain the sound in the background.

American Airlines tells me not to hang up and re-dial, as this will only further delay my call. I keep expecting Matt to walk in the door, put his arm on my shoulder, rub my back, ask me if I want anything. He really has gone back to sleep. I have to pee. I clutch my crotch and jiggle up and down like a child while I hold the line.

A human being comes on the line. Times and flight numbers. I give her my frequent flyer number. When this is all over, I'll get a free trip. I'll go to Europe, to Greece, maybe I'll even go to Hawaii. I actually have a moment's pleasure thinking about the possibilities.

When I open the kitchen door, I see Matt standing there, naked and shivering in the hallway.

"What are you doing?" I ask.

"Waiting for you," he says. "You went in the kitchen and shut the door. I figured you wanted to be alone while you were on the phone."

"I was making flight reservations."

I lean against him. He holds me. We're both naked, but there's nothing sexual about our nakedness. We're stripped and alone, two animals without fur or feathers, pathetic as Chihuahuas.

I pack. Socks, underpants, bras, two pairs of jeans, a pair of slacks, five shirts, a dress. Matt pulls on the closest thing he has to pajamas: a pair of green scrubs that a friend of ours lifted from SF General. He makes me toast and jam, more coffee. Then I'm all ready to go. Only twenty minutes since Clara called. More than three hours before my flight leaves. Odd, how when you want time filled up, everything gets done so quickly.

I get out the ironing board, the tall stool, the basket of ironing, and turn on the television. I watch a *Star Trek* rerun. Matt sits on the couch.

I always thought there'd be a thunderclap of pure love or pure hate when he died. I just don't care.

"Do you want to talk?" Matt asks.

"No." I am ironing a white blouse, starching it. The smell reminds me of nights in Springfield when my mother stayed up late, starching and ironing white cotton shirts for strangers.

After a few minutes he says "Okay. I'm going back to bed. Wake me up. I'll drive you to the airport."

At the gate, Matt and I hold each other, and I feel myself letting go, letting go physically at least, sinking against him.

I flip through the flight magazine. I could buy tapes to help me lose weight, become successful, stop smoking, achieve inner peace—if I had only $2999 I could take a three-week vacation to Bora-Bora. "Paying too Much for Data Entry? . . . We'll Do It in the Caribbean." I read an article about the evacuation of the U.S. embassy in Viet Nam at the end of the war, a first-person account. As the last Americans dash for the last helicopters, they are throwing tear gas behind them, fending off the Vietnamese who thought the Americans were their friends.

I get a cab at Logan. The cabdriver starts to tell me jokes.

"I don't feel like talking. My father's in the hospital."

"Hey, lady," he says, "you want to know how to tell if a problem's psychosomatic? Stand on your head. If your feet start to hurt, it was all in your head."

"My father's dying," I say, angrily.

When I get to the hospital, one of the nurses says, "Your mother left just a little while ago. She went home to get some sleep. Karen, can you take her down—"

Karen holds out her hand and I shake it. She asks me, "Have you been in an intensive care unit before?" as she leads me to my father's room. She explains about the heart monitor, the respiration monitor, the i.v. tube.

She tells me he is conscious, but that a lot of brain damage has occurred, is occurring. He doesn't have control of his bladder or bowels. He's been catheterized. "I know how hard this must be for you," she says.

The words: *No, you don't understand. I want him to suffer,* flash on in my mind like a neon sign.

"Thank you," I say. What am I thanking her for? For buying my dutiful daughter act?

"Down, down," my father is saying. "The white. What? Wha'dya? Wha'dya? Hey, hey. How. Call, call. Call it!" He is shouting now, "Wha'dya say, huh? Wha'dya say to a drink? Carrots. No. The. Shit. Shit. Gamble. Fuck. I want a carrot. I want a fucking carrot. Get me the blue plaster. The blue plaster. Get me the. Out. Dog. Dog. Dog."

I sit next to him for a few minutes. Then I go down to the lobby and buy a *New York Times*. This takes me half an hour. The hospital corridors are so long, now that I'm pregnant. My ankles hurt, I get short of breath. I have to stop, like the post-op middle-aged men walking down the hallway, hunched slightly forward, dragging their i.v. poles behind them. I sit down, like them, winded, not struggling for breath, but working for it.

It seems like I read everything in the *Times*, even a few of the sports stories, but still scarcely an hour has passed.

My father is shouting in the background. "Lucky Louis! Lucky Louis! Lucky Louis!"

A doctor comes in. I'm still shocked when doctors are younger than me. He introduces himself and keeps talking, explaining things to me. I see his lips moving, hear the words coming out of his mouth.

"Lucky Louis! Lucky Louis! Lucky Louis!" my father is shouting.

"What is that?" I ask. "That shouting?"

Some areas of the brain are destroyed, others left isolated.

I nod my head.

He hands me his card. Any questions, we can call.

"How are you doing?"

"I'm tired," I say. That's not a lie. I'm sick of lies.

The nurses come in and out. Checking his drip, checking his heart monitor, checking his urine bag. One of them lifts up his nightshirt to check the catheter. I turn away, but not before I catch a glimpse of the plastic tubing running from his soft penis, the sparse old-man's pubic hair.

My purse is on the floor next to me. It has my planner in it—a cheap knock-off of the yuppie version that I got at

Pay'n'Save for $4.99. It has long lists of Things to Do. Write Louise, Francisco, Hallen Foundation (! — deadline the 15th); call Jay, Arla, Celeste. I don't write the letters and proposals I need to write; I don't make my phone calls. I stare out the window. I go down to the waiting area and pick up *Redbook* and *Ladies Home Journal, Time* and *Newsweek.*

I wish dying were something weightless and New-Age, spirit moving into another dimension. I wish it weren't so gross. I wish my father's belly wasn't filling up with trapped bile; I wish he weren't catheterized; I wish his breath didn't have this musty smell. Everything smells more, now that I'm pregnant. It's like when I first quit smoking; but then the world felt fresh to me, without the haze of tobacco smoke. Now, everything makes me queasy, the smell of his body, the smell of gin that oozes out of my mother's pores.

A nurse comes in to check my father's i.v. line. She is wearing blue scrubs with Property of Massachusetts Linen Supply stenciled on them. Twenty-five years ago, when I was in the hospital, the nurses always wore white dresses, white stockings—even in the heat of summer—white shoes; they bobby-pinned their caps stiffly to their heads. Now they're allowed to wear these scrubs, running shoes. Things can change, I tell myself, they really can get better.

Clara comes by. She has called Rose and Jenny. She has sent a telegram to Helen, who is in Zimbabwe doing her field work. She's taken care of everything. I want something useful to do.

My father is quiet. He's curled his legs up towards his chest, a baby asleep.

My mother is spending the night at the hospital. "I don't think he should be alone now," she says.

I take a cab to the house. I let myself in, turn on the heat, turn on the television for company. I sort the mail: *The Nation, The New York Times* go in one pile, the junk mail in a second, a third pile of the few things (bills, one letter) that will need someone's attention. I read the past few days' *New York Times* and *Boston Globes* that I find lying around the house. I go to bed at two in the morning (it's eleven on the West Coast) but I can't sleep. I get up and take a hot bath. I didn't bring a nightgown. I don't own one. At home I'm either naked or I'm dressed. But it doesn't feel right to wander downstairs naked in my parents' house, so I put on a white nightgown that is hanging in my mother's closet. It's cheap polyester, scratchy. I open the refrigerator door. The shelves inside the door are filled with Vitamin E and L-tryptophan, bee pollen. The labels on the plastic caps say $15.98, $18.98, $4.95, $27.95. Bags of wheat germ and tofu from the food co-op sit next to spotted and misshapen vegetables and fruit. These aren't the big glossy tasteless objects you get in the supermarket; they're organic.

What did they do? Fix tofu stir-fry and wash it down with a double martini? Have whole-grain cereal with wheat germ and organic bananas for breakfast, along with a screwdriver made with fresh-squeezed organic orange juice?

He was trying to save himself. He wanted to live. Not as much as he wanted to die, but he did want to live. Were these things here on my earlier visits and I just didn't notice them? I stand there, in the triangle of light from the refrigerator, in the dark kitchen, wearing my mother's polyester nightgown, sobbing.

When I was in New Mexico with Matt, we stopped at a tourist shop, Hecho en Mexico, and Matt told me he'd buy anything I wanted. I got a Mexican Dia de las Muertes figurine: a skeleton prostitute, lying in a bed with a mirror hanging next to her, two pointy breasts her only flesh, holding out her arms to a skeleton john.

Later that day we hiked out to see some petroglyphs.

We walked alongside the deep green Rio Grande. My open-toed sandals sank into mud, which oozed up between

my toes. Wild mint and wild sage released their pungent
smells as we crushed them beneath our feet. I was breathing
hard but I wasn't panting, or wheezing. Then we had to
scramble up rocks. Matt kept his hand on my back. "Move my
right leg for me, will you? Can you set it up on that rock?"
Once or twice I fell, scraping shins and elbow, raising red
marks that would be bruises the next day. A cactus caught in
my jeans; I knocked it free with my cane. I thought the petro-
glyph would be giant. Instead, it was only a foot or so tall. It
looked like a child's drawing, etched deeply into the rock, a
figure with a square box for a body. Its lack of grandeur surprised me. Underneath, Rodney '76 was scratched into the
rock.

We sat, winded from our climb, passing the water bottle
back and forth.

"You don't think of guys named Rodney as defacers of ancient religious sites, do you?" Matt said.

Twelve hundred years ago, sixty generations ago, someone, man, woman, child, made this same trek up these rocks,
scraping shins and avoiding poison ivy, back when bison anti-
qua roamed across what were once the grasslands, now covered with sagebrush, to the west. They made this trek up
these same rocks, to carve this picture. Perhaps they did it as a
holy act. Or maybe in the same spirit that Rodney '76 left his
mark.

*I was here. I lived. I had two arms, two legs, hands, feet. I was
here.*

These things have stayed in the place where they were
made. No one owns them.

Matt and I were dizzy from the altitude, exhausted from
the climb. We didn't fall asleep but we half-dozed there on
the rocks, in front of that stick man.

I suppose it was the deep sound of thunder in the distance
that woke us. The river below rolled and pounded against the
rocks. Again, thunder. Next to us, on a bed of pine needles, a

dried turd—coyote or deer or maybe even human. Out there, its smell blended into the hundred other smells of decay and growth. Iridescent bluebottles grazed on it. The sun went behind a cloud and I pulled on my sweater; the sun came out and I took it off. Birds called and answered, called and answered.

We slept that night under the open sky, in sleeping bags we'd bought especially for this trip. We bought polyester sleeping bags I wouldn't be allergic to; I schlepped them to the laundromat and washed them in hot water to get rid of whatever dust mites might have taken up residence. The goose-down bags Matt already had he'd inherited from his father, who'd bought them for a camping trip in Nepal. ("Camping in *Nepal?*" "My father was into it. When I was seven, we spent our summer vacation in Timbuktu. It was hell . . . the heat, the flies. He just did it so he could say, 'When I was in Timbuktu . . .'")

I saw why people who lived, night after night, under that blanket of stars made constellations: to find an anchor in that infinite formlessness.

It was only eight-thirty when we stretched out our sleeping bags. We were tired from traveling and from that thin air at the top of the world. In the east, the sky was almost gray; it bled to turquoise in the west. We lay there in silence, watching the night move across the sky. The shrill call of the cicada gave way to the evening *chirrup, chirrup* of crickets. A raven's caw. Wind thrumming through the wild sage. The mountains, so distant that their pale color was impossible to name as gray or green or purple, melted into the clouds.

And then it was dark, a moonless night. Far from the lights of the city. Pitch dark. Pitch dark: I suppose that comes from the blackness of pine pitch. But I thought of the verb *to pitch*, of how night this deep unmoors you, makes you feel as if you were hurtling through space. I reached out for his hand, at the moment when he was reaching for mine.

We turned toward each other. There was nothing slow and seductive between us that night. We pulled off our clothes. On that vast, treeless, unsettled plateau, nothing held the heat of the day. Our skin broke out in goose bumps. We clung to each other. Night was full, enveloping; impossible to imagine that, an hour ago, we were slowed by the heat.

I always make love with a candle lit on the nightstand or with the hall light seeping beneath the door. I want to be able to open my eyes and see the man I am with—to reassure myself with a glance to his face, his chest, the curve of his forearm, that he is who he is. Not my father. Not that my father ever fucked me; but he was the first man. When he crouched above me with his hands around my neck, throttling me, the air was charged with sexual tension. My first lesson was that to be a woman is to be beaten, to be a man is to beat.

Men say: "In the dark, all cats are black." It's a joke they make to each other, when they've fucked an ugly woman. A cunt is a cunt. In the dark, a man is a man. In that dark New Mexico night, I saw through Matt to my father.

For a while, in the early seventies, I lived as a lesbian. Making love with women was easy. Too easy. It wasn't with women, with women's bodies, that I needed to make my peace.

Did I think of any of this, as I lay there? No. It's a knowing that suffuses my cells, my joints, my flesh. Always present, never conscious.

I moved my mouth down, kissed Matt's chin, neck. He tasted faintly of the day, a slight saltiness in his unwashed, grainy skin.

He stroked my right leg. I moved his hand away.

"Why do you always do that?"

"Because it hurts," I said. "Abnormal nerve growth." There are only dense medical words to describe this physical sensation.

"If I'm more gentle."

"No. Then it hurts more."

"I want to make love to all of you."

"Well, you can't." I smiled, and rolled on top of him. "You can't," I whispered into his left ear and then again in his right. I flicked my tongue across his earlobe, then ran it along the whorls of his ear. I traced a path of kisses down his body, kissing his belly, his thighs, his balls. I took his cock in my mouth. I'm good at this.

At a meeting of my women artists group, someone asked, "Are there times when we feel that we have to pretend to be men?" The answer that popped into my mind was, "No, I'm too busy pretending to be a woman." In relation to other women, I don't feel that I pretend to be female: that feminine world of nurturance and easy talk goes down to the bone. It's with men that femaleness feels like a costume I've pulled over myself. Not that the need isn't there, a hole at my center that pulses *I want, I want, I want.*

To be disabled is to be neutered. You are not feminine because disability is limping, gallumping, crooked, scarred, broken, bent, lesser. It isn't not masculine, either; it is weak, wasted, limpid, limp, pale, wan, wilted, withered, foundering, incompetent, lesser.

The next morning in New Mexico, I woke up under the blue vault of sky. Nothing makes me happier than open space.

In all those houses we lived in—the farmhouse with sloping floors in western Mass; the apartment up four flights of stairs in Springfield; the big house on River Street in Cambridge—in all of those houses, my father ruled. Even in the apartment in Springfield, we lived there because he did not. Everything was poor and small because he was gone.

The front door shut and we were home, enclosed. Prisoners' slang for prison: *inside.* Those dark ceilings, solid walls, those houses in which the kitchen, the women's room, was always at the back; those houses in which there was always a master bedroom; in which the bedrooms were always upstairs, out of sight, as if it were a shameful secret that we slept, that the efficient, masculine day gave way to a watery night when we lay naked underneath flimsy nightgowns and dreamed.

I remember a night I spent on the Lower East Side of New York in 1968. The answer to my question, "Where should I sleep?" had been a shrug and, *"You know. Wherever."* I dragged a mattress into the kitchen. The next morning I woke up with a three-year-old in a soggy diaper sucking on a bottle sitting stoically on the bed next to me. I woke up happy: how wonderful it was to sleep like a nomad, to be in a house in which the rooms were not rigidly defined, to wake up with a child you had never seen before staring thoughtfully at you. Freedom was the word I used to describe this happiness to myself.

Later, when I was twenty-two, twenty-three, in a disciplined revolutionary party, I would feel ashamed of myself for having used this word, freedom, a word that describes what the Black people of South Africa struggle for, a word that describes the yearnings of the people of Viet Nam. To think that I used that same word to describe the sensation of waking up on a filthy mattress in the kitchen of a roach-infested apartment in New York!

Now I understand. I understand my thrill at waking up that morning in the flat with rooms that were not labeled Kitchen, Study, Master Bedroom. The idea of rooms that could change according to our needs was an early vision, unconscious, of the possibility for a feminist future. My involvement with the party that labelled my desires as petty bourgeois, my pain as self-indulgent, was a drug that got me through the rough first years of that new decade.

I understand why, in 1968, it made me so happy to chant, "The streets belong to the people." I could not have articulated then the pain of privacy, home, family; the hope for a fluid world in which boundaries were not set in wood, concrete, and brick.

Daddy, there is no place where you are not. Even there, under the pure blue New Mexico sky, the joy I felt was only the flip-side of my hatred for you, of those rooms in which you shut me up.

Now, in my old bedroom in the house on River Street, pain wakes me: a spasm shooting through my back. I draw my knees up to my chest, fold myself up like a fetus. It's this mattress, it's too soft. This pain is just a visitor, it's not here to stay.

Galway Kinnell said, "The body makes love possible." Yes, I think, and it makes hate possible, too. I fall back to sleep.

I am holding the old black telephone in my hand. It is heavy and familiar. I realize that whenever I pick up a modern plastic telephone, it doesn't feel right, because it doesn't feel like this one.

Helen hasn't called. Now I have something useful to do, tracking her down. Maybe I could even direct-dial Zimbabwe. I look in the front of the phone book. There is a country code for Zaire but not for Zimbabwe. I call the operator, who puts me through to the international operator, who says, "This might not be easy."

"My father's sick," I say. "We sent her a telegram—my sister—but I don't think she got it. She hasn't called."

After a while the operator comes back on to say that she can't get through right away. She'll keep trying. She takes my number and tells me she is Operator 42.

"Can I give you two numbers? My home number and the hospital's?"

"Certainly," she says. She is so kind. Why does it have to be death that breaks down walls between strangers?

A few hours later, the phone rings in my father's room at the hospital. "Miss Etters?" the operator says. She hasn't been able to reach my sister: the phone seems to be out of order.

She suggests that I contact the State Department. So I do. I get connected right away with the appropriate person. This is everyday stuff to them.

Four hours later, when I am back on River Street, the phone rings and I cry when I hear Helen's "Hello."

"Now everyone is convinced I'm CIA. You should have seen the car they sent to deliver your message—"

"Daddy's dying. We sent you a telegram."

"I didn't get it."

"There's something wrong with your phone . . . the phone at the center."

"It needs a new part. It has to come through Cairo."

My sister takes a deep breath, then breathes out. I can feel it, six thousand miles away.

"I don't think I can get back."

"There really isn't any point. Only that we'd love to see you." We are silent.

"Where are you? You sound like you're next door," I say, laughing and crying at the same time.

"I'm at the Embassy," she says. "There's a color photograph of Ronald Reagan right above my head. Everything here works. The lights, the fan, the telephone," she is starting to cry. "While I was waiting for the call to go through, one of the secretaries asked me if I wanted something to drink. She took me into the kitchen. She opened up the refrigerator door and there was juice and mineral water and Coca-Cola and Diet Pepsi and—and then I went in the bathroom and the toilet works and the faucet works, the water's hot, and there's toilet paper.

"One of the babies—I've been interviewing her mother— one of the babies just died of measles . . . I've got to go," Helen says. "I can't stand to be here. In this place. I've got to get out of here. I'll find a phone that works someplace else. I'll call you later."

❀

They say that your vision is probably gone, that you can see only shapes and colors now. Daddy, that world you lived in where things were always so precise, where one thing stood at neat angles to certain other things, that world is gone. Daddy, you have exploded into my world of color, my world where the edges of things bleed into each other.

But you are surrounded by numbers flashing on machines. They've put a padded clip on your finger with a shining light on it that somehow (the nurses have explained it to me) measures the level of oxygen in your blood; this machine flashes it in a constantly changing read-out. The respiratory therapist arrives to treat your asthma, our old shared bane. She holds the nebulizer, you breathe in and out, in and out. The bitter taste of the medication starts to collect in your mouth, and you fight to get away from the plastic mask.

I want this to be over. I want him to die.

Time runs backwards. Every day he is more childlike than the day before.

Daddy, you are sinking down, down through all the lies and hatred, down through whatever it was that made you the dead man who haunted my life, down past all the lessons that taught you hate; Daddy, I watch you and I see the child you once were.

The nurses and the social workers are so empathetic. They say, it must be so hard to see your father like this. But it isn't. The man I had hated is at last dead. A child who could be my own child has taken his place.

I lift your head up with my arm and I sponge away the dried saliva that has gathered at the edges of your mouth, caught in the dark stubble of your two-day growth of beard. For the first time in my life, I touch you without being forced, physically or through social compulsion. For the first time in my life, I touch you without revulsion or fear.

I lay your head back down against the pillow.

My father will never build his city of the future, his city that began in his bedroom as a child, the toy city built from the Erector sets his father gave him for Christmas; his city that became a dream of what could be when the forces of production were harnessed for the good of the people. Daddy, you dreamed of a city where, as Lenin said, the public urinals might as well be lined with gold as with lead, a city where the wealth of ages would be put in public repositories, where you could go and borrow a Rolls-Royce or a diamond tiara for a day or two, as books are borrowed from the library—the wealth that the labor of the working class had created.

My father will never see the shining city he died for.

Spin, spin, Jacques is spinning. Jacques who will become Jake, who will become my father.

Spin, spin, Jacques is spinning. The cells that will become me locked within him, my asthma, my blue irises, my good eyesight and bad lungs. It is January 17, 1918. Jacques is only a year and a half old and knows nothing of dates, although to his mother's delight he says over and over again, "one-two-three, one-two-three, one-two-three."

*I like Marie. I don't like Marie. Dust under the divan. Dust is a puppy. I want a puppy.* Dizzy Jacques tumbles down onto the floor. He lies on his back and stares up at the ceiling. He is not supposed to be in this room. This is his mother's reception room, now done in art nouveau neo-Egyptian. Black marble columns with gold fluting on top; her divan is designed to look like one found in the tomb of an Egyptian pharaoh. She gets angry at her husband when he calls it a sofa. She has cards printed with her name rendered in hieroglyphics: a sphinx, a peasant with his arms outstretched, a papyrus. Later on she will get bored with this room and redecorate it in Tudor (and plant a Shakespeare garden, with every plant mentioned in his plays, rosemary and thyme, verbena). She fills her house with pretty objects and her soul with dust.

Jacques is not yet Jake, he does not yet know the phrase *conspicuous consumption*. He does not know that labor creates all wealth, that he is the child of parasites.

"Jacques, Jacques," Marie calls. "Little master. Naughty. Naughty."

He clambers to his feet.

Marie only pretends to be mad. Her hand on his bottom, then her arms around him. Naughty, Mr. Jacques. What are we going to do with you, Mr. Naughty? Marie smells of hair pomade and roses and sweet sweat from the place where her two breasts meet.

The women who love him, the women who wipe his messy bum and wipe his tears and rock him to sleep and feed him from their breasts, those women are not allowed to walk in the front door of the house (unless the little master is with them). They come to the back door, their feet crunching against the gravel walk, and in through the kitchen. The women who love Jacques smell differently every day, coming back from their Sundays off rich with the smells of sex and their own children, the smells of the trams they took across town and their kitchens where ham hocks and collards stew on the stove for hours. Tuesdays they smell of starch from their newly washed uniforms; by Friday, they give off an acrid smell of exhaustion and bitterness.

Jacques' mother always smells the same. She wears a lilac scent especially imported from France.

Then Marie is gone. There is someone new, with olive skin. "Hock," she calls him, and then, when Jacques corrects her, "Hawk." She has a moustache above her lip, and since he isn't quite sure he asks, "Are you a man or a lady?" He hates the paleness of her skin, the hair above her lip, the way she says his name. He hates her; she isn't Marie.

He wails, "I want my Mammy, I want my Mammy." Mammy, he really called her Mammy. Shame, shame, Jake. Your parents bought you the love of a Negro woman. You had a cool mother who wore a silk dressing gown and smelled of lilacs and a black Mammy who smelled of sweat and left her own children on the other side of town.

He cries so hard Marie comes back. He overhears his mother calling her a "Negress". Why does that word sound dirty?

Where are you, Mister Naughty? I make a big poo. Dirty bum, sweet bum. She sang him a song. *Sweet briar*, those were the only words he remembered. She sang to him, smelling of earth, sang to her little boy who was made of nonsense. "My naughty darling, you're mine, aren't you?" she whispered into his ear.

"Why are you giving Marie money?" he asks his mother.

Laughter all around. You don't think she works for free, do you? Laughter, laughter.

Jakie, Jakie, naughty Mr. Jakie. Dirty bum, sweet bum, give me a kiss. Do you love your Marie? She was paid to say that.

(The Communist Party was the place where men of all colors could meet and shake hands as equals. It was the place where the color of a man's skin didn't matter.

But it mattered so much. How could he ever name the longing aroused in him by their touch, by the color of their dark hands grasping his white hand? By the memories stirred by their smells, the timbre of their voices, the way their hair curled against the napes of their necks?)

Spin, spin, Jacques is spinning, the cells that will become me locked within him, my blue eyes and weak lungs; little Jacques is spinning down.

The phone rings in my parents' house on River Street on Tuesday morning at 4:30 A.M. One, two, three, four rings and the answering machine clicks on, my father's voice saying, "This is 891-4237. Please leave your message . . ." I picture my mother turning in her bed, as I turned, left side to right, or right side to stomach, deciding not to hear the four clear rings.

❈

It was a hemorrhage from esophageal varices that killed him. A fairly common complication of cirrhosis. The textbooks say that this is one of the most formidable emergencies in medicine.

The obituary in *People's World* reads:

> Jake Etters, a veteran of the Abraham Lincoln Brigade and long-time fighter in the struggle for social justice, died on August 7th at Massachusetts General Hospital. He was 72.
>
> Etters was the son of a wealthy Detroit lawyer and his socialite wife. Although he appeared to be set to become a loyal member of the upper class, his life was changed when he witnessed the death of twelve workmen who fell from a faulty scaffolding while building the Golden Gate Bridge. Seeking to understand what sort of system would allow cost-cutting to put the lives of men at risk, Etters read everything he could get his hands on about working conditions, unions, capitalism, and socialism. His readings led him to become active in the militant struggles of the '30s.
>
> At the age of twenty, within weeks of his summa cum laude graduation from the Massachusetts Institute of Technology, he traveled to Spain and enlisted in the Abraham Lincoln Brigade, to fight against the German and Italian invaders of Republican Spain. One of the longest-serving members of that Brigade, he rose through the ranks to become an officer. Those who fought with him described Etters as a man admired and loved by all. The strength of his dedication to democracy was so great that when the International Brigades were about to be repatriated, he attempted unsuccessfully to slip into a

Spanish battalion in order to continue the anti-fascist struggle.

Returning to the States, he pursued his graduate studies in engineering at MIT. He married his wife, the former Eleanor McKenzie, in 1940. He served in the U.S. Army from 1942 to 1945, fighting in the European theater and receiving several citations for valor.

At the end of the war, he accepted a position as an assistant professor at Jefferson College in western Massachusetts. There, he lived quietly with his wife and five daughters.

In 1955, he was fired when he refused to sign a loyalty oath. During the difficult years that followed, both he and his wife were forced to work as sales clerks, door-to-door sales-people, and as office clerks, frequently losing their jobs when their employers learned of their "subversive" links. For several years, they managed to survive by working odd jobs and raising their own food in their country home in Jefferson.

In 1965, with the chill brought on by the Red Hunts of the fifties finally thawing, Etters was able to return to work in his chosen field when MIT offered him a teaching position. He remained there for nearly twenty years.

After his retirement in 1982, he fulfilled a life-long dream by traveling to the Soviet Union with his wife.

He is survived by his wife and five daughters: Clara Tagliaferro, 39, a physician; Rose Etters, 37, a professor of history at Florida State University; Elizabeth Etters, 33, an artist; Helen Etters, 32, an anthropologist; and Jenny Etters, 30, a social worker.

A memorial service will be held in the parish house of the First Unitarian Church, Arlington Street, at 2:00 P.M. on Saturday, August 15. The family requests that donations in lieu of flowers be sent to the Friends of the Abraham Lincoln Brigade.

# 8

When I was nineteen, I tried to strip myself bare of the past. I tried to make myself new. When I was nineteen, I lived in London, went to art college, was married to a man named Danny. How did I end up there? I went to London when I was eighteen because I wanted to be someplace different. I suppose. I don't really remember.

Blanks.

I remember so clearly being seven years old, riding in the front seat of the green station wagon, the red shotgun shell with its black lettering rolling out from under the seat and then rolling back, Helen's damp thigh against mine. I remember his threadbare Orlon socks in the cedar-scented drawer.

But so much else, that came later, is gone.

They tell me that it's all there, stored away in my brain: each day of my last year in high school, the day I left the States, the day I arrived in London. The smell of chalk dust and old bricks in that yellow-brick high school building. The medley of English voices that must have so amazed me as I rode (the train? the bus?) from Heathrow into town: Jamaican and Kenyan and Cockney singing in and out of the expected BBC.

I go to the library; peer again at the microfilm reader. I turn the knob to the left and time reels backwards, to the right and it rushes ahead.

*The New York Times*, May 4, 1968. I must have read these same words almost twenty years ago, although they were firm then, black letters on grayish newsprint. Now what I see is only light, or rather the absence of light.

The things that leap out at me now: the headlines reading COLUMBIA GIRLS BOOKED QUICKLY, ALLIES MAUL FOE; the photo of Robert Kennedy with the caption: "Campaign Scars" (he'd cut his lip and chipped a tooth when pressed by a crowd); the ads for girdles, the ads for suits that trumpet "55% Dacron Polyester."

When I was a seventeen-year-old high school junior reading these words for the first time, the newspaper spread open on the kitchen table, a coffee mug cupped in my hands holding coffee that had been kept warm in the percolator all day, coffee that would be undrinkable to me now, none of these things would have caught my attention: the word *girls* applied to adult women, the ghoulishness of "Allies Maul Foe." I didn't know that in a month Robert Kennedy would be dead; I didn't know that girdles—those awful contraptions of lycra and spandex into which we squeezed ourselves each morning—would shortly be thrown onto the dustheap of history, that polyester content would disappear down into the fine print.

I'm seventeen years old; I drink coffee that is fetid and thick; my friends and I sit in the third-floor rooms at the top of those big old houses that no one then thought of as "Victorian," those rambling old houses that weren't charming then, just funky and hard to heat. We sit cross-legged on the floor in those rooms that had once been the servants' quarters, passing a joint from hand to hand and talking, endlessly talking. Those books we read: Hermann Hesse's *Demian* and Marx's Paris manuscripts, *The Egyptian Book of the Dead*. The things we said in those third-floor bedrooms, with the anxious mothers downstairs, the sweet weedy scent of marijuana drifting out the window and down the streets, *Sgt. Pepper's Lonely Hearts Club Band* (*Now we know how many holes it takes to fill the Albert Hall)* drifting with the marijuana smoke down Prospect Street and down Broadway, down.

Every time Michael Owens got stoned, he would say, "You want to hear something really far out? Do you know that the longest any cell in your body lasts is seven years? So, dig it, every seven years you're a completely new person." I would always think, Then why do my scars stay, my memories? But I would never say that out loud.

And then I'm in London. I'm on my own; there aren't any anxious mothers downstairs anymore. I'm standing in the Leicester Square tube station. I'm eighteen. I've just come from an anti-apartheid demo, where a red-haired man had rallied the crowd against the cops.

"Hullo," the red-haired man is saying to me, having tapped my shoulder. He's ruddy-faced, with a torn shirt, a sweat-streaked face, a wispy red beard. (His nose had been broken twice—once by the cops, he would tell me later; he never did tell me how it had been broken the other time.)

"Hullo," he repeats. "From the demo. Can you give me sixpence for the tube?"

He looks into my wallet as I fish for the coin.

"Buy me a cup of tea?"

"Sure." Immediately, I regret the word, though not the sentiment. Sure sounds overblown, colonial. *Gosh, golly, gee, sure.*

We cross the street to a restaurant with greasy lace curtains, where Danny says, "I'm starving."

"Go ahead. Order whatever you want."

He orders a bowl of tomato soup, three rounds of cheese and chutney sandwiches, a cup of tea, a Coke; and later a cream pastry and a slice of chocolate layered gateau.

"It's been days," he finally says, between mouthfuls. "Since I've eaten."

"Really? Days?"

He goes back. Wednesday, he'd run out of food. He had a pound note, but he was holding on to it for tube fares so he could get to meetings and out fly-posting for the demo. Thursday, he'd seen someone throw a half-eaten fish-and-chips dinner in a dustbin, and pulled it out. That was it. Today is Saturday.

"How do you do that? Go so long without eating?"

"I've no choice, have I? It's bad at first, but then you get used to it. I get a bit light-headed. That I don't like."

He turns his attention back to his plate.

We go back to his place together. He hands me a jar, a jar that had once held marmalade or salad dressing, into which he pours red wine. He doesn't offer it, doesn't ask me if I want wine or tea or water, just thrusts it at me. He stares at me. I gulp it down, even though red wine always makes my head ache and my tongue feel thick.

His room is a room. A single bare bulb hangs from the ceiling. He has no bookcases. His books are simply stacked in piles. Neat piles, though. Volume One of the *Complete Works of Lenin* sits on Volume Two, which sits on Volume Three, etc. The rest of the room is strewn with rubble: clothes, pencils, cups, papers, a Yankees baseball cap, orange peels, dirty socks, leaflets, an overturned lamp, newspapers, cigarette butts. (Later, I would ask him; "Don't you ever clean?" "No, I move.")

He offers nothing. I ask him where he is from, how long he has been in London, how long he has been politically active. He answers me in monosyllables and half-sentences: "Ipswich," "Two years," a grunt that turns into a laugh. Then: "My you're curious."

"I'm trying to make conversation."

"Is that something that your mother taught you to do? Make polite conversation?"

I want to defend her, to say, She wasn't a mother like that, she had her own life, she didn't raise me to be "nice." But I don't.

We finish our wine.

His breath is hot when he kisses me. No romance, no tenderness: he is needy and honest. He unfastens my jeans, tugs them down together with my underpants, enters me almost immediately. I am wet and ready.

I never go back to my room, at least not to sleep. I just go back to pick up clothes, books, my art supplies.

I think Danny is wonderful. I like his cool contempt for every article he read in every leftist paper, for every demonstration he took part in; his cool contempt for me.

Later on, a shrink will say to me, "My, you were self-destructive."

But that is just what we want to be. Danny and I set out together to destroy the selves that were a product of our bourgeois upbringing, the selves that had been forged under capitalism. We want to remake ourselves. We want to let go of everything we had held on to; we want to fall free.

Danny doesn't work, not at a straight job. He goes to demonstrations and reads and passes out leaflets and once gave our last ten shillings to a spare-changer. We live on the air, on the dole, on what we can cadge from friends and acquaintances, on my savings.

We are always finding ways to live without money. Empty jars become glasses. We cull through dustbins finding aluminum trays from frozen food dinners that we wash out and use as plates, old clothes, the two neat halves of a broken bowl (I shoplifted the glue to put it back together).

We are going to throw off the shackles of consumption, Danny and I. Danny says, Look at the Vietnamese, they live on rice. We could do it too. So we buy a fifty-pound sack of rice from the food co-op and eat almost nothing else for weeks—sometimes we get a few vegetables, or find some fruit in a dustbin behind the market.

Of course, we are miserable. Of course, we dream every night about hamburgers dripping juice, about the sharp crack a sausage makes when you bite into it, about the comforting slide down the throat of a glass of milk. Of course. This is our ego, our Western ego that has been fattened on the poisoned fruits of capitalism, that has grown used to the taste of bananas picked by workers in Central America for slave wages, savors the bloody taste of flesh, our ego that always holds onto what it has known.

I'm not just miserable. I am learning so much. Now I cannot walk into a Tesco's without feeling dizzy. The packets in gold and red with their seductive lettering, crying out Buy me! No, me! The vegetables, grown in chemical soil, bred to uniformity so they can be picked by machines.

Of course we are tired, always tired, of course. Capitalism has sunk into our cells. Our bodies have grown used to that protein buzz. Yes, we miss our slap of caffeine in the morning, that will get us up, get us going, so we can go out and work our dreadful jobs at their frantic, inhuman pace. It's hell, eating the same thing day in, day out. We are addicted to the jolt to our tastebuds, the need for the different that capitalism had bred in us. We are remaking ourselves, remaking our spoiled, greedy, white Western selves who always want more, different, more.

The sight of meat! The slices of what were once the muscles of cows, whole legs of lamb, the hearts, the livers, the kidneys. It's true what Danny says, that we numb ourselves to the casual slaughter of humans by numbing ourselves to the casual slaughter of animals. Danny loves to talk about this, how eating must, like everything else, be political. Even eggs, innocent eggs—they were meant to grow into chickens. Milk was meant to feed calves. And we have guzzled it all down, thoughtless, while it clogs our arteries and gives us cancer, killing us, too. Murder is suicide, suicide murder, Danny says. (But still, he drinks milk in his tea. "I don't like tea without milk," he says, and laughs.)

❀

Before all this, I must have sent away for and received an application to Hornsey Art College, filled it out, perhaps wrote an essay in which I clearly defined goals and discussed my strengths and weaknesses, picked out slides of my work, bought an airline ticket. I must have had that passport picture taken in which I grin at the camera, my cheeks chubby and rosy, my long hair tucked behind my ears. I must have stood in the passport office, 3-by-4-inch photographs in hand, and sworn not to attempt to overthrow the u.s. government by force. (Would I have put my hand behind my back, crossed my fingers? I think probably, yes.)

That passport is in my desk drawer, it's evidence, along with the birth certificate that states that I was born on December 21, 1950 at 7:23 in the morning, that my father's name is Jake Etters (although his legal name was never changed, it was always the name his mother gave him, Jacques) and that my mother's name is Eleanor Etters, maiden name, McKenzie. The desk drawer holds birth certificate, passport, résumés laser-printed on cream-colored bond paper (holder of BFA from the Museum School and MFA from Cal Arts, recipient of Hallwood Fellowship and Jenkins Award, one-woman shows at . . .): evidence that even at the times I don't remember, there was a woman with my face, my past, living my life.

What is in these blank spaces? I must have lived through these times, because to get from point A to point B, you must go through whatever lies in between: slowly traverse the distance between the sixteen-year-old girl called Lizzie—who wore bell-bottom blue jeans (from the Army-Navy Surplus store on Canal Street) and a blue cotton workshirt, chainsmoked Marlboros; the girl whose nails were ringed with black from mimeograph ink but who slept every night on sheets changed weekly by her mother; the girl who ate meals that were balanced, according to the notions of that time: steaks, lamb chops or chicken; corn, peas, broccoli emptied out of plastic freezer-bags, boiled white rice or instant mashed potatoes—and the girl-woman who, at nineteen, slept on a bare mattress, wore clothes pulled out of dustbins, and ate rice, rice, rice.

One night Danny said to me, "I've got to go out for a while," fingered sixpences out of the pile of silver on top of the bureau, and left.

I understood. I was proud of myself for knowing that I was not to ask questions. I understood that perhaps he was taking the tube across town to a meeting held in a safe house in Wembley or Islington, or perhaps picking up a package of wires and plastic explosives, or a folder of papers. Perhaps he went to a call box to ring a "contact," perhaps to wait in an alley beside a call box for the telephone to ring.

Danny, it thrilled me. That night, as I moved about the flat alone, or sat on the sofa with my legs curled under me, my fat art history textbook spread open on my lap, wrote notes with my fountain pen in the notebook with the speckled black-and-white cover, got up to plug the kettle in, make another cup of tea, I was me, Elizabeth Etters. But I was also a figure being watched by an imaginary camera, The Woman Who Waits. When I glanced at the telephone the camera held the shot; when I heard a noise that could have been Danny's footsteps on the stairs and glanced up, I watched myself from the outside.

Danny, did I love violence? Did I feed on it? Did I yearn for an act of hate, the embodiment of my rage, as consuming and as sharply defined as an act of love? Daddy, I loved the rhetoric of guns and violence. When I was in high school I hung a poster on my bedroom wall of Huey Newton, sitting like an African prince on a reed throne, with a gun clasped in both hands before him. I used to mutter under my breath, "After the revolution," and make my thumb and forefinger into a cock and barrel.

I loved violence. True. But I remember, Daddy, the day in

the early sixties when the Freedom Riders rode into Mississippi; the whole family went to Debbie's parents', our "sympathetic" friends, to watch the news on television. I remember the gray-and-white images: the bloodied heads, the night-
sticks, the few seconds when the camera kept filming after it
was knocked to the ground, catching glimpses of random
pant legs and shoes before a dark shape—a nightstick? a
foot?—smashed the lens.

I remember too, Daddy, some unnamed thrill— No, thrill
isn't the right word, it's too easy, but it captures the way it
touched me physically, the way the knowledge came into my
body. Suddenly there was no more middle ground, there was
nothing muddy left anymore. There was only the one who
clubbed and the one who was clubbed, the oppressor and the
oppressed, the father and the child.

I had a friend who was carried off into the whirlwind, Sarah
Huntington, a former Radcliffe student, with honey-blond
hair and honey-brown eyes. She and I spent the summer of
1967 together, working on an anti-war organizing project.
Once we spent the day passing out leaflets at the beaches. At
the end of the day the guy who was our leader, although we
never would have called him that, thought we should head
back into Boston. We'd all come in the same car. Sarah
wanted us to stay and put on our bathing suits, swim and lie
in the sun. The two of them got in an argument, and Sarah
planted her hands on her hips and said, "Che said, 'The revolutionary has a duty to preserve his sense of joy and wonder at
life.'"

We stayed. She turned to me as I lay next to her under the
hot sun, doing my revolutionary duty, and said, "You know,
Che really didn't say that," and we both laughed till we held
our sides in pain.

She chopped off all her hair about halfway through the
summer, but she was still beautiful. She once went four days
without eating—because, she said, she needed to know she
could do it.

And then, I was reading a manifesto, a polemic, a tract, with her name at the bottom, in *New Left Notes*. From the tangle of rhetoric (*revolutionary, manifest, overthrow, self-determination, colonized, imperialism*), there emerged two words: the gun. "Having made the decision to take up the gun . . ." The article was always in front, *the*. Not a gun, guns, weaponry. A single sacred object: *the gun*. When you picked it up, you had crossed the line, the only line there was to cross. Bullets never equivocate. They answer yes or no; dead or alive. Daddy, I wanted to believe that it was that simple. Danny, I wanted to believe that hatred, like love, could be made flesh.

Sometimes, Sarah, I imagined headlines: from the *News*, EX-DEB IN FATAL SHOOTOUT, or the *Times*, FBI SEEKS THREE IN WESTCHESTER BANK ROBBERY.

When I am twenty-three years old, I will be standing in a post office with my Republican aunt in northern New Hampshire, and I will see Sarah's face staring back at me from the Wanted posters on the walls. My aunt will chat with the postmistress ("The blackflies are terrible this year"; "It's all the rain we had in June") while I stare at her. Sarah hadn't ever been arrested, so they won't have a mug shot. Instead they will have a picture from a high school yearbook or society page: Sarah, in pearls and black velvet, hair pulled back in a tasteful chignon. Sarah Huntington, b. June 12, 1948, wanted as an accessory to murder.

I went back to the States to find refuge in the movement that had been my home, and found that it had splintered into a thousand pieces. All that was left was a notion of being oppositional, of going against the grain, of being part of the despised, the forbidden. I had a lover who was a drug dealer. Gary kept a gun on the top of the antique escritoire, which he had bought because his mother had always loved "that old stuff" and it cost five thousand dollars. The dull black gun rested on top of the polished mahogany—the loaded gun waiting there. I couldn't stand to be in the same room: the gun made me too nervous.

Now I sometimes wonder if it wasn't all part of some fantasy of Danny's. Perhaps on those nights when the phone rang and he looked at me and said, "I have to go out," swept the pile of silver into his pockets, and left, he was really going to a pub to wait for an imaginary contact; walking the London night streets fantasizing that he would jostle a passerby and slip him a folder; or riding the tube and dreaming that he was worthy of the life of a fugitive? Was it all play-acting, Danny? Was it all to entangle me?

Our bathroom smelled of piss and shit (our own and Nazquel's, the cat) and the nook that was our kitchen trapped the odors of coffee and grease from our pre-rice-diet days, and the main room smelled of sex and cigarettes. We weren't going to fall prey to that relentless propaganda that taught you to hate your smells and then buy deodorants, anti-per-spirants, scented soaps, cleansers, air fresheners to rid your-self of them.

Our hair grew as it grew. When it got in our eyes, we cut it ourselves. Our bodies smelled like bodies. Our house smelled like a cave. We schlepped our laundry home from the laun-dromat without drying it; we saved 50p. that way, lugging the heavy wet wash home in an industrial-strength green plastic bag we had found on the street. We strung our clothesline throughout the bathroom and hung our clothes to dry, the wet sweet smell of laundry seeping through the flat for the days and days it took it to dry in those damp rooms.

Our home away from home was The Electric Cinema in Notting Hill Gate. It was painted day-glo green. Day-glo pink bubbles floated up the walls. Inside each bubble was a quote from that fount of all wisdom, Bob Dylan. "He not busy being born is busy dying," "Don't follow leaders. Watch the parking meters."

The Electric Cinema had a festival of new films from Latin America. We saw *Blood of the Condor*, *Macunaima*, *Antônio das Mortes*. In *Antônio das Mortes* the dead rise, beautiful women turn into hags, men die while the camera lovingly records each detail, the blood jetting from the wounds, the mouth, death's stagger and rattle. I thought I would faint. I closed my eyes. I couldn't stay there anymore.

Danny couldn't stop talking about it all the way home on the tube. It was the most political film he'd ever seen. It's overthrowing the bourgeois aesthetic. It's a whole new language.

"But, Danny," I said, "I almost fainted."

Did he ever say what I thought he said next? He might have. Or else I might only have inferred it, understood it from the sideways look he gave me: That was what revolutionary art was, *something that made girls faint*.

It's true, he said, the Third World is more advanced than we'll ever be. Lin Pao is right: the peasants of China encircled the cities, choking them off, and the Third World is going to strangle the developed enclaves of Europe and North America. But dig it, it's not going to be military, or at least not just, it's going to be cultural. Danny was shouting, the other people on the tube were staring at us.

For the next month, we went nightly, almost, to see those films—some were surreal, some were ponderous stories of strikes. A couple of times, when we didn't have the money even for the Electric, we stood on the street and begged. Danny loved them all. Sometimes I got so freaked out that I began to sob; once I climbed out of my seat and crouched on the floor, shaking.

I go to the artsy video store where they have more copies of *For Joshua Who Will Be Twenty-Five in the Year Two Thousand* than they do of *Rocky*, to see if they have *Antônio das Mortes*; I want to see how that movie would look to me now. But they don't have it. The woman behind the counter tells me it's not on videotape.

They do have *Satyricon*, though. That was another movie that we saw in those days, another one that made me shake and quail. I rent it, play it on a friend's VCR. But it's not the same as sitting in a dark theater, with strangers. I'm sitting in a sunlit living room; I hear the mailman coming up the walk, the ice cream man ringing his bell and calling out, "Helado, Helado." The characters aren't larger than life anymore; they're smaller than my hand. The video screen turns them into impressionistic points of light.

Now I watch the way the camera flies from gentle eroticism to grossness to walls collapsing in an earthquake. I note that I have no time to catch my breath, am aware of the juxtaposition of violence and sensuality. I note my own disorientation.

When I sat with Danny at the Electric Cinema in Notting Hill Gate and watched this film, I entered into it. I didn't watch my disorientation, I *was* disoriented, directionless, swirling within the vortex Fellini created.

Danny and I lived on rice in our filthy flat and went every night to the movies, to those movies that were making me crazy. And still I took the tube faithfully across town every day to go to my classes. I always turned in my assignments. I always gave the teachers what they wanted. What a good girl. We had gotten married. It is something that we did like that , in the middle of a paragraph. It was so I wouldn't get deported, Danny argued, if I were ever arrested.

Danny's old friend, Rob, came into London from the commune where he lived in Wales. He was older—in his early thirties—and Danny idolized him. Rob talked incessantly about possession. He didn't want to own anything, not even a pair of socks. He said possession is poison. He said that desire to own, to accumulate, is what drove the U.S. into Viet Nam, is what drives capitalism. And doesn't it have its roots in the desire to possess another human being?

They kept talking, drinking cup after cup of tea and talking. I left for school.

"Rob wants to fuck you," Danny said. Just like that; we never used euphemisms then. I remember that I was shocked, relieved, repulsed. Relieved? Yes, I wanted to get out from the weight of Danny's love.

I remember how Rob smelled of brown rice and beans from his macrobiotic dinner, how his tongue, pressing into my mouth, felt too thick and urgent, clumsy. I tell myself to stop marking the differences between the two of them—the scratchiness of his beard, the awkwardness of his fingers as they unbuttoned my blouse.

Then what is elemental took over. It felt good to have a tongue carressing my nipple—any tongue. I let myself sink back through the years, till I became a baby who soaked up touch. I transformed my repulsion into an act of giving to Danny.

The three of us slept in one bed together: Danny on one side, Rob on the other, me in the middle. All that long night I kept waking, a confusion of limbs pressing against me, my body prickly with sweat, Rob's cum drying between my legs.

I got up at six the next morning and turned on the hot water heater. I couldn't stand being naked so I got dressed and sat down on the toilet and waited for the water to heat up. I waited an hour. I wanted the water good and hot. I soaked in that hot, hot bath until the water turned gray, and cold.

We dove into it. We dove into it with a fervor, trying to break through those bonds of our training, our "needs," our jealousies. We read Wilhelm Reich, we read Engels' *On the Origin of the Family, Private Property and the State*; we went to see *WR: Mysteries of the Orgasm*. If we were frightened of something, repulsed, we knew that meant that we needed to go there, to do the thing we were frightened of, to see what it was we were afraid of.

We cracked ourselves open like eggs, heart and guts spilling out.

To my mother I write (always in that neat, neat hand) reports of demonstrations and meetings and books and articles read.

I could remember that time we spent together as a drug-induced hitting bottom. But we never took anything that brought us down, nothing that blunted the world, that made it more fuzzy. When we got high, we wanted to go to the edge, to go further, to blow our brain cells into the future, to roil our truths to the surface. We dropped acid, we ate peyote that my friend Michael brought from the States, we took speed if we needed to get an article written, fly-posting done. It wasn't to make ourselves "happy," not that boozy false-cheer that passed for happiness in our world.

Mama, I just didn't want to be dead like you.

Danny would have bad trips sometimes. Once he thought the cup of tea I was handing him was a cup of blood. That same night he saw a blouse flung over the bathroom railing, and he thought I'd killed Nazquel, skinned it, and hung its hide there as a warning to him.

The morning after was hard (mornings-after were always hard). I would feel detached from the world—as if I had just dropped down to planet Earth from a distant galaxy. How odd that people lived in things called flats and houses, arranged themselves into families of one variety or another; how strange that my art mattered so much to me, that I cared one way or another about this or that painting I had made.

So, at twenty, I succeeded in the thing I had been trying to do for so long: I destroyed myself. I destroyed that outer shell of glue and wire and flimsy cord.

No, this is all wrong. I can't speak in the first person. The "I" had dissolved.

She was still alive; she still breathed air into and out of her lungs in a steady rhythm, her heart still beat its steady thumps. Only now she understood that the beating of her heart counted for no more than the beating of any other heart.

She tried to explain to Danny how sometimes she is aware that her body is made up of atoms and those atoms are made up of sub-atomic particles, points of hurtling energy; how she is aware that she is mostly emptiness; and how that frightens her. She uses the word *alienation* to describe this, but Danny corrects her. No, this sense of estrangement from herself that she feels is only her ego holding fast to what it knows, fighting its own death. She is almost free, he tells her.

She wakes up alone in the morning in the cold London flat and thinks about Frosted Flakes. She thinks about toast, not whole wheat toast, but white toast—white toast dripping with butter. She remembers going out for breakfast on Saturday mornings with her friends when she was in high school: the yellow of the egg running onto the bacon, the toast, the home fries, drinking cup after cup of coffee until she was jangling and almost high.

And then she thinks about the brown rice in its brown sack in the cupboard under the sink.

Her husband didn't come home last night. That's all right. They've agreed on it. He is with some other woman, or perhaps with a man.

She takes pills that are supposed to stop her from being depressed. In fact, they make her sleep. The more time she is asleep, the less time she is depressed, or at least awake to her depression, so she supposes that they are working.

She does not get up. She is so tired. She could go to college today but the thought of the crowded tube, the comrades who will ask her why she wasn't at the meeting last night, the thin air in the classroom are more than she can bear.

When the drugs her G.P. prescribed didn't stop her from crying, she got an appointment with a psychiatrist. She had to wait six weeks to see him. The office does not look anything like her image of a psychiatrist's office: book-lined shelves, art. Just a wooden desk, four wooden chairs, a few manila folders stacked on a desk. The doctor sits center stage. He is clean-shaven, or at least beardless, with a bad haircut, a cheap suit, and the omnipresent English pallor. He asks her how old she is; he asks her how many siblings she has; he asks her what her father does. Does her mother work? What does the expression "A rolling stone gathers no moss" mean? Can she repeat the following sentence back to him: "Mr. Jones, the butcher, lives at 734 North Crescent Road in Highgate. His telephone number is 237-8621."

At the end of the session, he gives her another prescription for anti-depressants and tells her to come back in a month.

She fills it. The pills are small and yellow. She takes them home and swallows all of them. She is surprised at how easily they go down.

# 9

My mother has it all so well arranged. On a tablet of yellow legal paper, she has written our names, the tasks assigned to us for the day of his funeral. She drinks neat gin out of a water tumbler while she makes these thorough lists. After so many decades, she's adapted to life underwater.

I am sent early to the Unitarian Church. Bob Carmichael is there, setting up folding chairs. He likes to be called Reverend Bob. I call him Bob.

He has been the minister here since I was in high school. He's over six feet tall; he must weigh at least 250 pounds. He's a mountain of a man, craggy. An odd body for a Unitarian minister. They tend more towards the Ichabod Crane type: marathon runners, knowledgeable about their cholesterol levels. He looks more like a high school football coach, a machine politician.

"Elizabeth Etters," I say, to sort myself out from the four other blue-eyed girls with big grins, my sisters.

"Of course, Elizabeth," he says, laying a hand on my shoulder. "How are you doing?"

"All right. I guess I'm still numb."

"Uh-uh," he says, sympathetically.

He must be used to this comforting of the grieving; it's part of his job.

We aren't Unitarians, but the Unitarian church is the place where we get married and hold memorial services. (We never say "funerals," there is something too religious about that word.) I know the Unitarian Church best from meetings in the parish house of the Boston Committee for Peace in Viet Nam, the Fair Housing Campaign, the High School Students Rights Project.

The parish auditorium is paneled in pale beech. It could be the rec room of a fancy community center or a hotel meeting room, except a butcher-paper mural runs around it: the history of South Africa, as seen through the eyes of the fifth- and sixth-graders in the Unitarian Church Sunday School. Albertina Sisulu and Winnie Mandela look like fashion models; bullets leave a dotted trajectory as they fly out of the guns of South African policemen and into the hearts of Sharpeville strikers.

"We can have the podium at the front or the chairs in a circle . . ."

"Oh, a circle," I say. I am sure of that. I am glad to be sure of something.

A woman dressed all in white—white shoes, white stockings, a white skirt and a white blouse—comes and sits down in one of the empty seats.

"I'm Elizabeth Etters," I say to her, and she shakes my hand and looks at me quizzically.

"Are you here for meditation?" Bob asks. "I'm sorry. The meditation group is meeting in Room B today—" He writes a note in black magic marker directing the meditators to Room B.

Have I heard that the new assistant minister is a Buddhist?

"Someone told me that," I say.

"It's been interesting, getting exposed to that whole philosophy . . ." He keeps talking. I don't really listen to him, but the timbre of his voice, the ebb and flow of his words, are comforting.

"One thing I've found with the survivors of cancer deaths," he is saying.

"What?"

"One thing I've found when a parent dies of cancer . . ."

I can't believe it. My mother must have told him cancer. I should tell him the truth. But I don't.

I am worried, the way I always am before a party, that not enough people will show up. But the room is full ten minutes before the service is scheduled to start, full of gray-haired and white-haired women and men, and my red-eyed sister Clara goes to fetch some more chairs.

Some of these old women and old men have driven hours to stand in this room. My "aunts" and "uncles."

When we lived in Jefferson, we'd all pile in the car on a Sunday and drive to Springfield, to Boston to visit them. My mother kept track of whose turn it was to sit in front. A car radio was a luxury then. We sang with my mother: "The Wheels on the Bus," "We're Building a City," "Last Night I Had the Strangest Dream," "Down by the Riverside." We played games endlessly. Homonyms: b-o-u-g-h and b-o-w; r-e-d and r-e-a-d; b-r-e-a-d and b-r-e-d. I spy with my little eye, something beginning with C. A cow? No, not a cow. A Chevrolet? No, not a Chevrolet. Give up? A cupola. A cupola? Jenny starts crying. It's no fair! She doesn't know what a cupola is.

One day in Springfield, everyone else went out sledding, but it was too icy for me. (Where had my mother gone?) Sol and Ruth said "She can stay here with us. We'll give her a special surprise." I hardly knew them. Ruth squeezed my arm and said, "We'll have a good time, won't we, dearie?"

I was scared of them; their house smelled funny.

"Do you have a TV?"

"No," Ruth said.

"We don't have one either."

"Hey," Sol said, "I have something that's better than a TV." He shuffled over—he was wearing leather bedroom slippers—and took a scrapbook out of the sideboard. He opened it, pulled a lock of blond baby hair, fine as silk, tied with a ribbon.

"Do you know who this belonged to?"

I look at him for a long time, finally shake my head and shrug my shoulders.

"Me," he crowed. "It belonged to me!" He held it next to his bald head, and laughed and laughed and laughed.

He showed me a photograph of Ruth, the day they got married. He showed me pressed violets, gathered sixty years ago; he remembered everything about the day they were picked, the streetcar ride, how his mother held his little brother out the window of the streetcar to piss.

"Why didn't you go in your car?" I asked.

"She wants to know why we didn't go in our car," Sol said. "Our car? Who had a car? A car, we didn't even want to have a car, we were happy to take the streetcar, the bus, with everyone else."

Ruth leaned forward, "And when the workers at the shipyard went out on strike, and I didn't have money for the fare, I'd walk out there every morning to walk the picket line—"

"Listen," Sol said, grabbing my arm. "I want to tell the girl something."

But Ruth hadn't finished, ". . . So I thought, well, here, I've got a bundle of Daily Workers, I could fold one of these up and put it in my shoe. But—"

"I want you to listen to this," Sol said to me. "You, you can't imagine what it was like. In the thirties. Before. Not so much the poverty, the things it does to people. I saw my own brother and my father come to blows over a chicken wing. Over a chicken wing! People so skinny their eyes took up half their face. For days, we'd have nothing to eat but potatoes. Potatoes, potatoes, potatoes, potatoes."

Ruth had given up on her story of the walk out to the shipyard. She lit a cigarette and tapped the ashes against the edge of a yellow ashtray.

"My buddy Mark, his father was a tool and die maker, and he hadn't lost his job. Mark's father was bringing in maybe twenty dollars a week, and to us, this was wealth. Mark invites me over to his house for dinner. The coming Friday. This is wonderful, I can't tell you how happy I am. All week long, it's what I'm thinking about. His mother made meat loaf. Now, at our house, when we had meat loaf it was this much meat," Sol holds his fingers apart a fraction of an inch, "and the rest was loaf. But at the Kaplan's, it was meat, meat, meat, maybe a little bit of crumbs. I finish eating, and his mother, she says to me, 'Sol, would you like a little more to eat?' 'Well, Mrs. Kaplan, I wouldn't mind a bit more meat loaf.' 'Sorry, Sol,' she says, 'the meat loaf's all gone. Let me get you some more potatoes.' I tell you, I felt like crying. I never wanted to see another potato."

"She doesn't want to hear this, Sol—"

Sol said, "Yes, she does. So, it's 1934, I'm sent abroad. Do you know what that means, *sent abroad?*"

"To go to another country?" I finally said.

"*Sent abroad.* It meant to go to the Soviet Union. I was going to the Soviet Union, I was leaving behind this suffering, this hardship, the sight of man fighting his fellow man for a job, of some people walking around with bellies out to here while other men were starving. I was going to the workers' paradise. I was a kid, I had stars in my eyes."

"I'll get you something to eat," Ruth said, rising.

"Why don't you give her some of that—you know, that Coca-Cola. . . . So, I get to the Soviet Union, I meet my new comrades, we go out to dinner, we get to the restaurant, the waiter doesn't even ask us what we want to order, he just brings us over these plates, sets them in front of us. Do you know what they were? Potatoes. Potatoes! My friend says something to the waiter—I can't understand a word of Russian, but I know he's telling the waiter to bring us something else. A few minutes later the waiter comes back. What has he got? Boiled cabbage. Boiled cabbage! This is what we get to eat, boiled cabbage and potatoes. But, you know, something—"

"Here's your Coca-Cola, dear," Ruth said. "Maybe you should have a little bit more cake—"

"Don't interrupt. Don't interrupt. I'm coming to the point of the story now. We eat boiled cabbage and boiled potatoes, but I don't mind. And do you know why I don't mind? Because it wasn't brother turned against brother, fighting over crumbs. It wasn't one child starving while others were spoiled rotten. This was the finest restaurant in Moscow and we were eating potatoes and cabbage, the same food that they were eating in the poorest hovel. We sacrificed together for the common good. Do you see," Sol said to me, laying his hand on my arm, "do you understand?"

That legacy of endless talk. Those urgent hands that took my arm, settled on my shoulder (sometimes the knuckles were gnarled with arthritis; the hands of the woman my mother called "the Duchess" had shaped fingernails and jewelry so fat it looked make-believe): "Listen, honey," "Listen, Elizabeth," "Let me explain something to you . . ." They told me about strikes and picket lines, about being under house-arrest in South Africa, about witch hunts, about freedom rides, sit-ins, organizing the farm workers in the San Fernando Valley in '32, those urgent voices wrapped themselves around me.

Sunlight pours into this room, reflects off of blond pews. No, they don't call these pews . . . seating, I suppose they say. Only a few people are dressed in black.

There are two kinds of funerals. When relatives die, the services are held in churches filled with calla lilies and the scent of burning candles. There's talk of God and gardens and grandchildren, and later crustless sandwiches are eaten off red-and-white plates with hunting scenes etched on them.

How solid those dead are, leaving behind wills that have been duly executed, estates that will be passed on to their children.

Then there are the ragged funerals of the old warhorses who have devoted their lives to the struggle. The memorial services are always held in the basements of community centers or the parishes houses of Unitarian churches; someone always shows up in T-shirt and jeans.

Daddy, now someone is talking about you. They are talking about your five wonderful daughters, about how you fought for democracy in Spain, against fascism, against nuclear weapons, for civil rights, against apartheid.

I'm not mourning you, Daddy, I'm mourning the father I never had, the baby who lived in your body for your last few days.

Daddy, I remember getting called into the low-ceilinged living room of the house in Jefferson or the somber study of the house on River Street so you could have a talk with us. The rooms were always dark: the dim light of a single lamp, the heavy mahogany furniture that had been passed down to you by your parents, the opulent couches that your mother had consigned when she was redecorating, first to the basement and then to you.

One night you called the five of us into the living room of the house in Jefferson. Some crime had been committed. Maybe Clara had been listening to rock 'n' roll; maybe we had been watching television. The five of us were lined up on the couch, shoulder to shoulder. We were wasting our lives. (How old was I? Ten? Eleven?) Did we know that half the children in the world didn't have enough to eat? Did we know how lucky we were?

You read out loud a poem about the International Brigades.

*They tramped across the earth—*
*they sailed the intervening sea*
*When the call went out like a fierce shout*
*from the throat of Liberty.*
*From plough and bench to battle trench*
*the steady march was made:*

*To save the land came a fighting band*
*of men who were unafraid.*

You start to cry. You pull up your pant leg to show us the scar that winds around your left leg.

Daddy, Stalin does not live any more in the red citadel of the Kremlin. Even when he was still alive, even when a solitary light burned in a window all night, so that passersby could look up and see its glow and imagine the towering figure with the thick dark moustache bending over his desk, even when the phrases heard on the radio ("He lives, works, and thinks for us") or learned by children at school ("I want to be like Stalin"), even when those phrases echoed, consciously or unconsciously, in the minds of those who stood on the cold Moscow streets and saw that single light burning, even then he was not there. He lived in a suburban villa.

The photographs always showed a towering figure with a bushy black moustache and black head of hair; but his moustache was gray, his hair thin and white. He was slight, old, pot-bellied. A frail wizard behind the smoke of doctored photos and the amplifed, thundering voice.

In March of 1953, Stalin's body lay in state. The streets were jammed with millions of mourners, pressing endlessly forward, forward in the still deep Moscow winter. Some slipped on the ice and were trampled to death by the crowd. Finally, after waiting for twelve, fourteen hours in the bitter wind and cold, the mourners filed quickly past the coffin, with only time to glance at the corpse. When, after several days, the flow of people was brought to a halt, the line of people still waiting stretched for seven miles. They did not go away; they simply stood there, stood silently in the cold, cold night.

It will take months for the embalming of his body to be completed. All that will be left will be the frame of bones, the fragile casing of skin and hair, and teeth. The blood, the liver, the intestines, the crumbly gray brain of the man who was once a boy beaten by his drunken father, his drunken shoemaker father of whom he was ashamed, all that will be sucked away. The outer shell of flesh will be preserved in an atmosphere of perfect balance and control: humidity, acidity, air itself held at bay.

We are standing up and singing now, a song that you sang in Spain. The tune is "Red River Valley." We have the words on a Xeroxed sheet. "There's a valley in Spain called Jarama . . ." The voice of the old man standing now at the podium, leading us in song, wavers.

Daddy, on September 11, 1973, I am home for a visit. We are watching television; it's ten, ten-thirty. We are waiting to hear the news of the coup against the government of Salvador Allende. "The beleaguered Marxist government," the news announcers say between commercials, "Coup. Stay tuned."

My father says to my mother, "Give me your glass." But when he comes back, he has a bottle of gin and a bottle of vermouth tucked under his arm. I am afraid he is going to drop them, and I watch his wobbling path around the coffee table to his chair. There. He made it.

The news comes on. A bomb falls into the Presidential Palace. A still photograph is shown of Allende, wearing a too-small white helmet, with a machine gun slung across his shoulder. He looks almost comical, a pudgy country doctor playing soldier, until you look at his face, the face of a man going out to die in a battle that has been lost.

"Bastards," my father says, and turns the channel of the television set. On the next station the news announcer is saying the same thing, the safe conduct offered and refused, the presumed death of the . . .

My father changes the channel again and again, but the news is always the same.

He keeps turning the knob, looking for the place where time runs backwards, where the bomb will be shown rising up from La Moneda, the rubble imploding on itself and becoming whole again, where the bullets will fly backwards out of the heart of Dr. y Presidente Salvador Allende.

"Bastards," my father says again, and punches the on-off button. The television goes dead. He drains his glass in a single gulp.

Then it's over. I've gotten through it. Jenny and I stay behind to help fold up the chairs. In the background, we can hear a rumbling chant coming from the Buddhists in Room B.

"I'll meet you outside in a minute," I say to Jenny.

" 'Kay."

I walk down the hall, and stand in the doorway and listen to the rising and falling of the voices moving in unison. The woman in white is there, along with a couple of teenagers, others my age.

They stop chanting. Someone stands up and tolls a bell, once. I listen to the pure sound against the silence.

The day after his funeral, at the Neptune Society, they hand us a can that holds his ashes. The ashes and dust that were his soul are now his body.

My mother has taken the Basic Plan ($150). In a few weeks, I know, one of us will make a joke to one of the others (me to Jenny? Jenny to Clara?) about the Shoebox Plan.

My mother has sold the house. Already.

She asked twenty thousand dollars less than the realtor suggested ("It's just not right to make that kind of profit," she said) and it sold a few hours after it went on the market.

Now, two days after the memorial service, the four of us are helping her clean out the house.

What will we find behind the old Kenmore refrigerator when we move it? Bobby pins, safety pins, Bic pens, shopping

lists written in my mother's always-neat hand? Flyers an-
nouncing demonstrations and boycotts that have slipped
loose from their magnets and drifted underneath years before, now yellowed and covered with a thin blanket of dust?

My mother has bought five black magic markers, so that
we each have one. She has stacks of boxes from the liquor
store. She has contacted a thrift store run by members of the
Hmong community. They will be by tomorrow to pick up
the stove and refrigerator, the boxes we have packed. Alcohol
doesn't make her high and happy, it doesn't even make her
drunk. Somehow her body is able to filter out the anesthesia
that it needs, discard the rest.

I am sorting my father's black and maroon socks, threadbare at heels and toes, into a cardboard box. I throw out his
undershorts, add his droopy undershirts to the pile in the box.
There are places where the fabric has come apart from age,
and my mother has mended them. Why did he keep wearing
these? I wonder if the thrift store will find them worth selling.

There, Daddy, I am done with you. I have packed away
those socks and undershirts and boxer shorts. Daddy, once I
was a child and the things you had were so mysterious. Now
I am an adult. Now I know the roots of your power.

My mother says to let her know if there's anything that we
want. I could take this old bureau, with its cedar-lined mahogany drawers, the dresser that his father passed on to my father, take this bureau with its inlaid squares of pale veneer.
But of course it wouldn't be practical to schlepp it back to California with me. I'd have to hire a van; it would be crazy. And
anyhow, it would overwhelm my tiny California apartment.
Engels saw the motor of class society as the desire to pass on
one's possessions after death, a physical afterlife. Not *one's*
possessions, *men's* possessions. Father to son to a rejecting
daughter. Father to son to some stranger.

I go to the linen closet. That shouldn't be too hard. I open
the door; in the far left corner is a big Tampax box, piles of

white sheets and worn wool blankets, the old enamel bedpan that my mother carried the summer of 1963, when I had surgery for the last time, back and forth from the bathroom to my makeshift bedroom on the first floor. Later I shoved it to the back of the closet; it seemed obscene.

Nothing's easy. Those mended sheets. When I was a kid, I'd get woken up by the sound of a worn sheet ripping, caught by a toenail or tugged during sleep. I tried to sleep carefully to keep that from happening. The towels: why couldn't they give themselves the smallest bit of luxury, of comfort? Good towels instead of these scratchy, twenty-year-old ones, frayed and torn. And those sheets, stacks and stacks of threadbare white sheets. What were they saving them for? What disaster were they hoarding them against? Why couldn't they trust the future?

I load the mended sheets into one box, I load the threadbare towels into the other.

I take down the box of Tampax. It's an old, old box. Under the brand name, instead of, "Junior" or "Super Plus," it says "For Waning Days." I shake the box, which feels almost empty. There are three tampons left. I save it, along with a single torn, threadbare sheet.

Another closet opposite, where they stored winter clothes in summer, summer clothes in winter. My mother says she's already taken everything she wants. No, she didn't say want, she said need, everything I need. The boxes fill up so quickly with thick coats, my mother's imitation Chanel suits, my father's thick wool suits. I fold up the flaps on the cardboard boxes and write "Men's Clothes" and "Women's Clothes."

A black metal file cabinet is stuck in the back of the closet. I call to Jenny, and she comes and helps me drag it out. Old insurance papers, bank statements, Jesus, this is tedious, sorting through this stuff, things my mother saved, our grade school report cards, five smart girls, straight As, all of us, always. Pictures we drew in kindergarten. I save my pictures; I save my report cards. I put the other things in a pile for my sisters to sort through.

I open one of the bank books. There are steadily mounting figures, beginning in 1965: $100 one month, $186.23 another month. By the end, they had almost a hundred thousand dollars in a passbook account. Still, they didn't have enough money for new towels.

I open a brown accordion file. It holds paper, photographs, the passport my father got when he was twenty years old. There's a sheaf of typed pages, the paper yellowed, typed with a manual typewriter,

> Heroes of Spain, by Jake Etters . . . This book pays tribute to the brave men of the Abraham Lincoln Brigade. Coming from all across America, they were the sons of the "best" families and sons of sharecroppers and factory workers; some were idealists in the first bloom of youth, and some were veterans of earlier wars and battles for justice at home. They were united by a common ideal: defense of democracy in Spain . . .

Underneath there's an old-fashioned photo album, with a leather cover with ornate gold scroll-work, black pages with gilt edges.

"Jenny," I call. She comes and sits next to me on the floor in the hallway. We spread the album open on our laps.

My grandmother—she couldn't be more than twenty—stands in a grove of poplars on the banks of Lake St. Clair. She is wearing a loose-fitting garment, an imitation of a Greek tunic. It is early morning, the focus is soft; her arms are curved above her head. She is Beauty. In the next photograph she holds a scale and looks fierce: Justice. My grandmother poses as Truth and Charity and Melancholy.

"Isadora Duncan in Detroit," I say.

"That's not Isadora Duncan," Jenny says.

"I know, Stupid. It's Grandma."

"No."

"Sure, look at the mouth." I point.

"Grandma was a hippie," Jenny says in amazement.

My grandmother's gauzy costumes flutter about her. She is a bird in flight, a heron. But when a heron lands, imperious on one leg, its rump sticking preposterously out, it becomes a fussy dowager.

At twenty-three, she married my grandfather. In the wedding photographs she is slender and beautiful, swathed in lace and pearls; he is portly, settling into middle age, a top hat and tails. The soft focus is gone. My grandfather looks proud of his new possession and my grandmother looks resigned. I look at those two faces and a thousand questions arise. Did they maybe love each other, she finding in his alkalinity a remedy for her own high-pitched nervousness? Did she think of the things she would be able to buy with his money, the strings of pearls, the cameos, the art?

I turn the page, and there you are, her precious Jacques. Daddy, you are dressed in a long gown of white Brittany lace. Your mother holds you in the crook of her left arm, rests her right hand against your chest. The pose is conventional, but the love is real.

My grandmother, a woman of her class and time, must have given birth to my father in a haze. Twilight sleep, it was called: at the very end of her pregnancy, she was admitted to a nursing home, given a narcotic potion that kept her sleeping or wavering on the edge of sleep for days or weeks, vaguely aware of, yet unable to remember, a thrust of pain, a fumble of hands between her legs, a slimy child being pulled from her body.

How did you come from these two, Daddy? Later, when I went to their house, they always seemed flat, as if a dimension were missing. Or was that just youth looking at age? Life is chance, dice in a cup. One sperm is admitted, the other not.

Shake my mother and father together, and I spilled out. Shake me and Matt together, and what will happen?

Daddy, did you learn your hatred from your father? Something he learned from his father before him, and his father before him? Look again at those photographs, taken back before there were Instamatic cameras and cheap and easy developing, those stiff black-and-white photos that could hang above a mantelpiece. There were no snapshots taken then of Mom sprawled exhausted in a chair, Dad mugging for the camera. Can I imagine my grandfather's cold, formal face distorted with rage, his hand raised above his head? Or Grandma, her hair here pulled so neatly into a chignon, imagine instead her hair wild around her face, imagine the tears coursing down her face as she pleads with him, "No. For the love of God, stop. Please!"

I stash the manuscript and the photographs in the box I am taking back to San Francisco.

We eat tonight at The China Palace. It's where we used to go for an occasional night out, back before Chinese food became authentic. It serves sweet-and-sour pork and egg rolls; you cannot order eels, bok choy or seven mushrooms stir-fried.

The waiter asks if I'd like a drink. What a wonderful idea. I'd forgotten about alcohol, forgotten about it as an ordinary substance, not a destroyer of lives. I glance at the back of the menu and order a Polynesian Paradise. It's the most expensive drink on the menu. "Elizabeth," my mother reprimands automatically: I'm being childish, silly, wasting money. It arrives, just as I had hoped it would, festooned with maraschino cherries and orange slices and a pink paper parasol, and tastes of grapefruit juice and grenadine syrup and rum, of sweetness and a touch of oblivion.

My mother's eyes seep tears. She lifts a tissue to her eyes and wipes them. Clara sits next to her, patting her hand. I look around at my three competent, childless, loveless sisters. We are not scared of trekking off to Zimbabwe, of defending our doctoral dissertations, of making lives for ourselves as artists, of getting arrested protesting apartheid, the u.s. embargo of Nicaragua. It's only love that scares us, only love. Five daughters, verging on middle age, still haunted by the past.

Mama, I remember the day when you were late coming home, and we watched television. When you finally came home, after dark, you told us about the Sharpeville Massacre.

Mama, that day stands out for me because afterward things went back to the way they were.

Every morning, Mama, you got up at 6:15 and took a shower; then dressed, putting on first your white nylon underpants and white cotton bra that you still, even after we had moved to Boston, ordered from the Sears and Roebuck catalog, in which the underwear was illustrated in black and white, like the sickroom supplies and the Snap-On tools. Then you wiggled into a girdle and fastened your stockings with garters. Your stockings you bought always in the same color ("Cinnamon") so you never ended up with a single unmatched one. You put on a white nylon slip, one of your imitation Chanel suits that you had bought at Filene's or Loehmann's, a pair of pumps.

You fixed us breakfast and our lunches to take to school while you drank your coffee, ate your breakfast standing up. We weren't allowed in the kitchen. It would have been too crazy, all of us crowded in there.

You went off to your job. You raised money for Beth Israel Hospital. I think you were good at it. You didn't have any qualms about manipulating people away from their money, for a good cause. I don't think you particularly liked it, but it was the kind of decent job a woman could get in the sixties. You worked so that we could go to private colleges. That was important to the two of you.

You never talked about your work.

You came home every evening and took down two glasses, beautiful Finnish glasses with pebbled bottoms. You took the ice-cube tray out of the freezer. It was aluminum, with a lever on top that you yanked up to free the cubes. There was a scrunching sound. You stood at the sink and pulled the metal lever which moved the dangling dividers, then fished out three cubes for his glass, three for yours, left the tray, with its remaining six cubes, sitting there in the sink.

Then you went to the liquor closet and carried out two bottles. The vermouth bottle was always the same, Martini and Rossi, a green bottle with a green-and-white label, a pattern of vines. Sometimes the gin was Beefeaters or London Dry; sometimes it was Liquorama. You stood at the counter and poured both glasses full of gin, then tipped a bit of vermouth into the green screw-top cap, shook half of it into my father's glass, half of it into yours, and added an olive to each drink.

Each evening you fixed dinner as you and my father drank. You broiled steak or pork chops or chicken. You pulled a package of frozen vegetables from the freezer (always the house brands, with names like Scotch Buy and Fresh-Freeze); you mixed instant mashed potatoes or boiled white rice. Sometimes you'd make us hearts-of-lettuce salad. You'd take a head of iceberg lettuce and slice it in half and then divide one half into three sections, the other into four. You made salad dressing in a special carafe that came with the Good Seasons powdered mix. The carafe had lines marked for vinegar, oil, water. After you added those, you poured in the mix and shook it up. There were three flavors, French, Italian, and Blue Cheese, but they all tasted the same.

While you were fixing dinner, my father would say, "How about another drink, Ellie?" and you would tilt your head to the side and say, "Oh, I suppose I will." You always tilted your head to the side and thought it over, but the answer was always the same.

Before you went into the dining room, you gulped down the last of your martini. There was a bottle of wine with dinner; and then at eight o'clock it was time for highballs—bourbon and branch water. You really only had one, you just kept freshening it all evening. By the end of the evening your words dragged, like a record played at too slow a speed, and you stumbled when you got out of your chair and finally toddled off to bed.

And then, the next morning, you got up and dressed, your Sears-and-Roebuck underwear next to your skin and your decent imitations of high fashion on the outside, and went off to work, and came home and drank your martinis and your wine and your highballs, and went to bed.

It wasn't that you never spoke to me. You said, "Good morning"; you said, "Here's your lunch"; you said, "Pick up your coat"; you said, "Good night."

There wasn't really anything wrong, was there, Mama? Didn't you do the things you were supposed to do? Didn't you get up every morning and make us breakfast, go off to work, come home, fix dinner?

I almost fall asleep in the car on the way back from dinner. It's an effort to get up the stairs. I go into my old room. I don't turn on the light. This room is ugly. It depresses me. I undress in the dark, dropping my clothes onto the floor.

Someone's turned on the television downstairs. I can hear the muffled sound of laughter coming up through the floorboards.

I am wide awake. My apartment at home in San Francisco always feels too small. This house feels too big.

When Grandpa Etters was an old, old man and I was fifteen, I sat next to him on the back porch swing. Sometimes he called me Eleanor and sometimes Estelle, his wife's name. The present had disappeared, leaving the past in plain view. He told me of his father's body lying upstairs, because there was no money to pay the undertaker, in the cold, cold house with no coal. At twelve, he became the man of the family. He worked fourteen hours a day, standing at a chest-high desk, wearing a green eyeshade, adding long columns of figures, having no prospects but the prospect of standing forever at that same desk, leaving for work in the cold darkness of morning and coming home in the cold darkness of night.

Later, the rest of us would laugh, sitting around the dining room table, as I repeated those stories, which we have all heard time and time again: the walking five miles through the snow, fourteen hours a day at work.

His story had an Horatio Alger ending: the eye of a benefactor lighted on him, upon the resolute lad who worked so diligently to support his family, and he was lifted out of poverty, lifted into the airy world above him.

Grandpa gave his son the things he had longed for. At twelve, Jacques was still a child, building the future in his room, that city made from thin steel girders, a skyline grander than the New York skyline, those fanciful bridges and underground tunnels. What else can I buy you, Jacques? Another cardboard carton filled with miniature steel girders? A childhood that goes on and on?

Grandpa gave to his son the thing he had wanted most in life. And did my father think he was giving us the things he had always needed—political principles, a life that was more than an accumulation of things? And will I give my child the thing I wanted most in my life—a childhood without violence, without rage—and ruin her life in some other way? I think I'm different, I think it won't happen to me. After all, I've got feminism; I understand the power dynamics of families; I've got insight coming out of my pores; I'm an artist; I live with my pain; I've had eighty-six skijillion therapy sessions; I go to my meetings for adult children of alcoholics— even though I refuse to work the twelve steps, I go.

But maybe all of that won't be enough.

# 10

Night.

Where am I?

Not in the first house I knew, that old farmhouse with sloping floors in western Mass, not the apartment in Springfield where Helen and Jenny breathed in the bed next to me, not on the bare mattress in our flat in London. Suspended in time, alone in the dark, I could be anywhere, any of those old houses or funky apartments where I have lived.

Those rooms, those arrangements of contained space, don't swim back to me in order; they meld into each other. In my mind's eye, I'm walking up the stairs of the house in Jefferson, but when I get to the top and turn into the hallway, it isn't bare floorboards; instead, it's carpeted with a runner in shades of brown and yellow. The number three is on the door. It's my apartment in Jamaica Plain.

The elevated train ran half a block away. The gray formica-topped kitchen table I hated that now would sell in a Melrose Avenue antique store for hundreds of dollars. (I remember walking along Melrose with Matt, when we were in L.A., reading a sign, Antiques from the Fifties and Sixties. I laughed. He said, "What's so funny?" and so I repeated it: "Antiques from the fifties and sixties." "I still don't get it," he said. "Someday you will.") The wooden desk in the study off the kitchen, the box spring and mattress on the floor of the bedroom, the brick-and-board bookcases. The apartment where I lived "when I was crazy."

The other histories depend on each other, the official history that we spoke of proudly is cut away to reveal the sinews and bones of the histories of which we didn't speak, the histories of dreams, the histories of what we've forgotten. These years are different. I've packed them away in a box, sealed it shut. This time of my life is so close. It isn't covered with that hazy wash, like those childhood memories; it didn't happen in another country; there are no acts of imagination necessary. It's almost here. Not quite in the present tense, but not in that distant past: "We used to . . ." "In 1956 . . ."

I don't want to admit that she was me, that I am her. But she had my name. I have the scars she burned into me.

I can't even use that word *I*: it's too proud, too upright, assertive. I was *you* then, the object of berating voices in- and outside of my head.

Two years (minus a few days) after you come out of the coma you went into following your suicide attempt, a year and a half after you leave the mental hospital, a year after you leave Danny, you wake up in a rumpled bed, on dirty sheets, alone in the apartment on the third floor of a brick row house in Jamaica Plain. Even now, when J.P. has been gentrified, houses a few blocks away getting stripped of old paint, floors sanded, architectural details uncovered, this place will never be done over. The Red Line runs four houses away, on elevated tracks, straight down the middle of Washington. When you first lived here, the sound of the train would wake you up from a deep sleep. Now you don't even hear it.

You wake up on a rumpled bed. You wake up with an image: a dead, still planet hanging in the middle of a blank universe. You wake up thinking: *I want to die.*

Mornings are always the hardest. You know this mood will lift—will lift a little—during the course of the day.

You look at the clock. It's nine-thirty. You overslept again. You worked last night, at your job as a desk clerk at a seedy hotel in Somerville. You work from seven at night until three-thirty in the morning. By the time you get home, it's four. You always go straight to bed, but you're so wound up that sleep takes awhile. You should be able to get by on four and a half hours of sleep a night. You have read a book about yoga that says this is all you really need. Every day, you sit in the lotus position and meditate, and at the end of the meditation, you tell yourself, "Tonight you will sleep four and a half hours. You will wake up feeling rested and happy and wide awake." But you never do. You wake up feeling tired and guilty for having overslept, with that voice in your head that seems to have its own existence repeating *I want to die*.

Last night was a bad night. You fucked up at work. You forgot to check the expiration date on a credit card. The night supervisor said, "I just pray to God we can collect on this," and rolled her eyes. When you got home, you held a lit cigarette a fraction of an inch above your arm. The fine hairs of your forearm sizzled and melted. You almost always stop there. You are satisfied by the smell, by the thrill of coming so close. But sometimes that's not enough. Sometimes you need to go all the way, to burn the flesh you hate. Last night, you did it. You added one more scar, on the inside of your thigh. You hate your scars. But at least these are your scars, not the ones the doctors have carved into you.

You speak the language he has taught you.

You don't bathe. You don't brush your teeth. It doesn't matter what you do: you always feel filthy. When you actually are filthy, it's easier. When you're scrubbed and clean and you can still feel the grit collected in every pore, then you know you will never be free.

You get dressed. You wear either your black pants with one of your four T-shirts or the flowery Marimekko dress that was handed down to you by your cousin—these are the only clothes you own. You do your laundry every four or five days. In winter, you wear a coat over your underwear when you go to the laundromat. You throw every piece of clothing you own into one machine and wash it on cold.

You have two saucepans, one frying pan, two coffee mugs, three plates. One chair, a table, one sheet. Danny would approve.

You were going to get some reading done this morning. You have a paper due in a few weeks for your art history class. Your paper is about Frida Kahlo. The professor is young and hip and a leftist and sardonic; he's always saying that he's more of a feminist than most of the women he knows. When you go to talk with him in his office, about your paper, he steeples his fingers and sneers and nods his head and says, "Interesting." You know he is laughing at you, even though he gave you an *A* in a class you took with him last term. Maybe he gives *A*s to everyone. More likely, the *A* was part of the joke he is playing on you.

You wait in the hallway outside your Voc Rehab counselor's office. You are always waiting in those days: waiting at the food-stamp office, waiting at the welfare office, waiting at mental health clinics, waiting not to be crazy anymore. Now you are sitting in a gray metal chair upholstered in green plastic. The people who walk by make a point of not looking at you, walking past with their heels clicking; when they make phone calls, they get put through to whomever it is they want to talk to.

You don't. Last week, when you had been waiting for three weeks for your voucher so that you could buy your textbooks for school—three weeks after the semester had started—you called your Rehab counselor and were told that she had moved to Colorado and her cases split up between three other counselors, and the woman who answered the phone would have to check who it was, but someone else would get back to you "in just a few minutes." You waited by the phone.

After two hours you finally called back and said, "Someone was supposed to call me back, and didn't."

"Who do you talk to?"

You said, "I was a client of Shelly Mandelbaum's," and the voice said, "She's no longer working at this office." "I know," you said, "I called two hours ago, and you told me you were going to get back to me in a few minutes . . ."

"It wasn't me."

"Well, whoever. Someone was supposed to get back to me. I need to talk with my counselor."

"Well, who is your counselor?" she said.

"I don't know," you said. "That's what I'm trying to find out."

She took your name and social security number again, and said she'd have to check the files, and she would get back to you in a week or two.

"A week or two?" you said, "Let me talk to your supervisor, please."

She said, "My supervisor is in a meeting."

"Can you have her call me back?"

"I'll give her the message. She's very busy today," she said. "I can't promise she'll get back to you."

"Look," you said, "the semester started three weeks ago. I don't have my books yet, because I haven't gotten my purchase order."

"You'll have to talk with your counselor about that."

"I don't know who my counselor is. Look, please, can't I talk with someone who can help me?"

"I'll give my supervisor your message—"

"School started three weeks ago, I don't have my goddamn *books* yet—" you shouted. She hung up on you.

The day after, for the first time in your year of dealing with Rehab, they return a phone call. Your case has been assigned to the supervisor. You know it is because you have been deemed difficult.

Now, you are sitting in the supervisor's office. She's telling you that you are too emotionally disturbed to be working,

and probably too emotionally disturbed to be attending
school.

You start crying.

She thinks that since you have such a problem with manag-
ing your hostility that you should work in a sheltered environment. A sheltered environment, how lovely that sounds.
Except that you know what it means: less than the minimum
wage, a social worker breathing down your neck, most of
your fellow workers are retarded.

No, you tell her, you don't want to drop out of school. You
want your vouchers for your books. It is four weeks into the
semester now. You need your books.

It's a problem with the state house, she tells you. It's not
just your book vouchers: she had a student who had to drop
out of school, because he couldn't get his tuition money in
time. It will be at least another month before you'll have the
vouchers for your books. Your counselor reminds you of
how tenuous your situation is; the office pulled some strings
for you, they don't usually fund people to go to art college.

You get in your green vw bug and drive to school. The ashtray is overflowing. There's candy-bar wrappers in the back,
overdue library books, old newspapers. You have dreams,
night after night, about cars. You dream that you are driving
two cars at once, you dream that you are driving across a
bridge when the steering wheel comes off in your hand.

You can't find a place to park. You always have to leave for
school an hour or so before class, even though it's only a ten-
minute drive, because you have to drive around and around
looking for a parking place that's close enough to school for
you to walk from the parking space to class. You wish you
had a watch, but you don't. You know it's getting late. You
turn on the radio, hoping to hear the time. Shit, it's ten minutes of eleven already. There's a space, finally. Two blocks,
not too bad. You slog to class, listing to one side, lugging your

art supplies, your arms aching, your legs aching, out of breath, sweating. You are "up" in Judith's class today: your work is going to be discussed.

You love Judith, your painting teacher. First off, there is her name, Judith. She doesn't shorten it to Judy or worse, Judi. It's Biblical, but Old Testament, not New. Justice, not miracles.

Judith wears sleeveless shirts and doesn't shave her armpits. You don't shave your armpits either, and you like your armpit hair, but are embarrassed to wear sleeveless blouses. Judith wears red-red lipstick on her thick lips at a time when none of you wears any make-up. The women's movement has galvanized one of your mother's friends to finally leave a miserable marriage; she starts a business to support herself called Eve, which sells unadulterated bath oils and soaps and pure cosmetics, but you see even that as a co-optation, a way for the patriarchy to resell us what we are revolting against in a slightly new and much more expensive box. But when Judith wears her red-red lipstick, it is different.

Judith is striding into the room, Judith with her wonderful Aztec profile and sheaf of long dark hair and full skirts and Earth shoes.

"Oh, God," she says, "peanut butter," wiping the edges of her mouth. "I'm so sick of peanut butter." She tells the class that a friend of hers was getting government-surplus food. When he couldn't stand any more peanut butter and powdered milk, he gave her the big aluminum cans, with their black-and-white labels. Manna from heaven, she had thought, but now she feels like she can't face one more peanut butter sandwich. She tells you how hard her life is: she teaches here part-time, she has a studio in her basement. "I buy my clothes at thrift stores," she says. "I know you all buy your clothes at thrift stores, but it's different when you've been doing it for twenty years. Believe me, the thrill wears off.

"I'm not just up here bitching and moaning," she says. "I want you to know what you're getting into."

Judith can't get hired full-time because the men on the fac-
ulty think her vaginal imagery is reductivist. Hugh Lamberg,
the darling of the painting department, isn't reductivist: his
canvases, on which a single square block of a single color appear, parody the stripped-down grammar of modern art, they
take us to the limits of formalism, they make us confront the
question of what art is.

You know all this. You know that Louise Nevelson said,
"For forty years, I wanted to kill myself . . . I have been so
lonely for long periods of my life that if a rat walked in, I
would have welcomed it. I don't think I realized the price that
would be demanded of me for what I wanted."

"Elizabeth Etters," Judith says. People walk up and look at
your three paintings: *Woman with a Gun, The Braided Rug, The
Things He Left Behind.* The class is almost all women, a few gay
men, and one straight man who is openly combative.

In *The Braided Rug,* you show your mother at the center,
making a braided rug. It was what she worked on every night
for years, in your house in Jefferson, after you came back
from Springfield. She took your old wool clothes, things that
finally, after years of wearing, had worn out. She cut the fabric into strips, folded the strips into thirds, tucking the raw
ends inside, sewing them up into cords. Three cords were
braided together, and then the braids sewn into an oval, using
a thick black thread called carpet thread and a frightening
hooked needle. Your mother sits at the center, and you and
your four sisters are tiny figures on the periphery, tied to her
by the cords of the rug.

Judith says, "I'm very interested in the technique you use,
the center and the periphery. Have you read Lucy Lippard's
*From the Center?*" You shake your head. "You should." You
make a point of writing it down. Another book that the library won't have in, because everyone wants to read it; and,
of course, you can't afford to buy it.

"You know," Judith says, turning towards the class, "When

you have something you do well—this isn't particularly directed at you, Elizabeth, it's for everyone—your central
figures and the figures on the periphery, for instance, don't
allow it to be a crutch. . . ."

They all say that the blank, set face of the mother makes
her look malevolent. (But that was how she looked, you want
to protest.) And the way the other figures are tied to her. And
the thing she is making, whatever it is, is so ugly.

At the end of the discussion, Judith lets you speak, and you
say what it was you were working toward. How you wanted
to show your mother's resourcefulness, her ability to gather
the threads of your lives together; how you wanted to show a
women's art form.

"But it's so dark," Laura, who has long straight blond hair
and grew up in Connecticut, blurts out.

(I still have that painting in the alcove off my studio. When
I look at it now, I see what everyone else saw: a woman filled
with repressed anger, who is stripping her children. A woman
who spent night after night making an ugly rug that a few
years later, when my grandfather died and my father inherited his big oriental rug, would be consigned to the attic.)

*The Things He Left Behind* is a painted collage of your father's
bureau and newspapers with the headlines FUGITIVE REDS
HUNTED and MR. K. SAYS: STALIN A MURDERER. You paint your
mother's ironing board and her old Remington typewriter.
You're at the center, alone. It's you and it isn't you. You're
not wearing leg braces, using crutches. When you first started
here at the Museum School, you did self-portraits. Your first
painting teacher always dismissed you as sentimental, because a picture of a cripple is, by definition, mawkish—
*Christina's World*, the *Christmas Carol* etchings of Tiny Tim.
You knew that if you painted the crutches and braces they
would become the focal point of the picture. So you have left
them out.

The painting that people really want to talk about is called
*Woman with a Gun*. A woman is sitting with an expression on

her face that could be summed up as quizzical and happy at the same time, looking at a black gun in the foreground. The gun is almost photo-realist. It's not a self-portrait, the woman you've drawn is lanky, tall, has a horseface—no, it isn't you. The gun is real though. You don't have money for clothes, scarcely enough for food, but you have managed to buy this gun. You think about killing your father with it.

The feminists in your class are shocked. Women are peaceful and loving. Are you saying that we ought to be like men? The anti-feminist man springs to your defense. This is a piece of art, not a piece of propaganda, he says.

"I don't want to get too far away from Elizabeth's painting," Judith says, "but let's take a few minutes to talk about that. Do we think that those are mutually exclusive terms?"

At the end of the discussion, the anti-feminist man asks Judith if she believes in art for the sake of revolution.

She laughs her rich, throaty laugh and says, "No, I believe in revolution for the sake of art."

Hanging on your refrigerator is a flyer that comes every month from Womanspace. At Womanspace tonight there is a talk on matriarchal religions; tomorrow there will be a performance by a feminist theater group. But their talks are always three dollars; the performances usually five dollars. You can hardly ever afford to go. Never mind the fact that you work five nights a week, and want to paint on your nights off. Yet every month when you get their flyer, you mark events, promising yourself that you will go to them. You tell yourself that this month you are going to set aside some money, you are, and you're going to get there. This time when you go to Womanspace, you're not going to think that people are giving you strange looks, you're not going to think that everyone can tell by the way you dress, by the way your eyes shift, by the way you hold your mouth, by the way you shake, that you're crazy. You're not going to be shy about going up to other women and saying—whatever it is that other people say. You are going to have artistic friendships, like the ones you read about in the biographies of artists. You are going to stay up until four in the morning drinking cheap red wine and talking.

The women at Womanspace talk about how painting is dead, this medium that separates the creator from the creation, the finished, static product which becomes a commodity. Women's art is flux; it is change; it is process. But you could never get up in front of a group of people and perform. You know that. Anyhow, when Sarah Cunningham dons her cap of plastic snakes and becomes Medusa and then picks up a bow and arrow and leaps around the stage as Diana, everyone else thinks she is profound and revolutionary. You think she is ridiculous. You can't make yourself believe in the Great Goddess, no matter how hard you try.

You know you should lose this desire to leave something behind you; that this desire to leave an artifact that reflects glory on you as an individual is male, because it's male arrogance that hates and fears death. Women know that we are parts of cycles, that we live on in a hundred ways, in the flesh of our children, the hearts of those who have loved us; we honor the decay of our cells back into the sweet earth. You don't need this arrogant masculine assertion of the self.

But you do.

You have an appointment at a mental health clinic. You are being evaluated at this clinic, to see whether you are (a) crazy enough and (b) not too crazy to receive therapy. You don't have to worry about meeting criterion (a); it's (b) you are concerned about.

At the mental health clinic, the social worker who comes out to greet you is young, male, with sandy brown hair and a thin moustache. He leads you into an office with a bare brown desk, the sort that teachers have in classrooms. The chairs are molded plastic. His is turquoise; yours is hot-pink.

He has spruced up the office by hanging a poster of a country sunrise and the line, "Today is the first day of the rest of your life." You take one look at him and know that he owns every book by Rod McKuen and every record by Simon and Garfunkel.

He looks at you, smiles, says, "How're you doing?"

"Okay," you say. You don't say anything else. He doesn't say anything else. Five minutes pass.

"You seem pretty depressed."

"No. I'm not depressed." You know what depression is. This is not depression.

"Can you tell me what brought you here today?"

"I want to find a therapist," you say.

He uh-huhs empathetically. You hate this man. You hate his turquoise and pink plastic chairs, you hate his cheerful poster on the wall.

"And what do you want from therapy?" He pushes his glasses back up the bridge of his nose.

You try to answer his question. You know that a normal person, someone with "problems," would have a handy answer to this question. They could say, "I have a problem relating to men," or "I'm nervous all the time." But the more you think about the answer, the more things get tangled up in your brain. You think maybe you should begin by telling him how you used to be. Where should you start? Maybe you should start by telling him about Danny? But now a lot of time has gone by. Whatever you say, it will have to be weighty enough to account for the time that has elapsed.

Finally you say, "I want to be normal."

"Normal?" he prompts.

"Yes."

He keeps trying to make eye contact with you.

A week later, you will get a letter from the clinic telling you (but you knew this was coming) that you have fallen into category (b). "Our limited resources mean that we have to make difficult decisions about who would benefit most from our assistance . . ." One more mental health clinic has told you that you are too crazy, beyond hope.

One night, you wake up; you can't breathe. For a fraction of a second, caught between sleep and consciousness, you think that someone has broken into your apartment and has fixed his hands around your throat. But, no; you hear a whistling from your lungs. You had asthma when you were a kid, you haven't had an attack in almost twenty years. But it's back again. The disease you inherited from him. Proof that his cells are locked within you, that you are his daughter.

You search your face for signs of his features.

You are split in two. Your good cells are female, your bad cells are male. In all your memories of your mother, she is down on her knees in the garden in her big straw hat, or in the kitchen kneading bread. She gave you life; she makes the garden grow; she kneads the yeast into the flour so it can rise.

Daddy is death, and she is life. It's that simple.

You wake up, angry at yourself for oversleeping, get out of bed and make a cup of coffee, pull on your men's white button-down shirt that you bought at the thrift store on Centre Street, and start to paint. You are painting a picture of Danny. Or trying to. This is a picture you have worked on and put away, worked on and put away. First you painted the newspaper clippings that he cut out and pasted onto the wall, MPS WILL NOT RAT ON CATHOLIC GHETTOS, HEATH TURNS ON; then the cigarette butts overflowing out of the ashtrays, the salmon table, the window in the background showing the steel skies and steel rain, mud-red bricks. You painted his face, but when you were done, he looked like Rasputin, with his wispy red-blond hair and his beady eyes. And that's not what you want. You want to show the craziness, but you don't want to caricature it. You want to show that it was a wonderful thing that we did, Danny, you and I, when we tried to live like the Vietnamese, when we let ourselves know the glossy horror of supermarkets, when we smelled the poisons in the air; when we tried to remake ourselves.

You think of painting him Janus-like, two-headed; but that splits him in half, and the saintliness and the mania were one.

You want to paint a picture of how it was at the end, the two of you crouched naked, animal-like in your filthy cave of a flat, but you are too ashamed.

Judith says not to be afraid. Judith says, "Remember, if you don't fight the water, you float." But Judith never ended up huddled on the floor, sobbing, naked, a cornered animal. Judith says, "Don't aim to be mediocre, aim to be great." Judith tells you to paint with your bodies. She looks at you, and says, "If you have a—a defect, a hindrance, a—incorporate that into your work."

You still love her, even though she said this.

You want to make everyone happy. When you are in Judith's class, you want to paint just the way she paints. When you are in the class taught by the sardonic, hip professor who calls himself a Marxist and talks about how personal art reinforces bourgeois notions of the individual, you want to stop doing these sloppy, painful paintings that are merely spilling your guts on the canvas.

You thought of yourself as so determinedly ugly then, yet you had lovers. Lots of them. You fucked and fucked and fucked, thinking you could fuck yourself free of that hatred of the flesh.

Sometimes Danny would slip into the body of the man you were making love with. Sometimes you could drive him away with an incantation: *This is another man. He is in another country. He is far away.* Sometimes you can drive him away, but sometimes you can't.

You are in your last year at the Museum School. You still live in your apartment in Jamaica Plain. You still own two saucepans, one frying pan, two coffee mugs, three plates; one chair, a table, one sheet; the Marimekko dress handed down from your cousin, the four shirts. You have two pairs of pants now because one day, when you were in Cambridge, you saw a wooden box on the sidewalk with Free Box stenciled on it, and found a pair of pants inside.

You have a therapist now, too. You have finally found a clinic that thinks you are salvageable, though they think you're psychotic, and they prescribe Thorazine. You tell them you are taking it. You took it once and slept fourteen hours, then woke up feeling like your brains had been sucked out and replaced with thick wool. If you really took it, you would have to drop out of school. So you lie.

Your therapist is a therapist-in-training. She gets to practice on you. She is always edgy; she chain-smokes. Years later, you realize you must have terrified her.

Sometimes you know what has made you crazy: it is the feeling of suffocation, the suffocation by the ether and the suffocation of your father's hands. The suffocation of asthma, when you can't breathe out the stale air in your lungs. The asthma that you've inherited from him, proof that his cells are your cells, he's trapped within you.

You're not depressed anymore. You are still miserable, but there's nothing low and groaning about it: it's high-pitched and wild, fueled by hate.

Obsessed, like a hysterics' love affair. You rehearse his body: his steel-gray hair, his jutting chin and sharp cleft features that look as if he has stepped out of a socialist-realist painting. Your father's angry face appears before you a hundred times a day; again and again and again, he looms above you, the dead man who fathered you.

The dictionary defines *hatred* as strong dislike or strong aversion, just as it defines *love* as warm affection, attachment, liking or fondness. Those words don't get at the physical charge of either emotion. You are "in hate," a state as strange as being "in love." You think this should free you, but it doesn't. Now when you wake up in the morning you don't see a dead planet in a motionless universe, you see his leering face instead. You don't shake anymore. Now you vomit, two or three times a day. You get skinnier and skinnier. The skinnier you get the happier you are. Half of your cells are his cells—can you purge him from your body?

Your apartment isn't filthy anymore. It's spotless. Sometimes you wake up in the middle of the night and think, maybe, about the black gunk that has collected in the indentations on the stove's knobs. That's it. You can't get back to sleep. You get out of bed, pull the knobs off the stove, and, using a table knife and steel wool, scrape away the hidden dirt.

I thought the past was a tumor. I thought if I could cut it from my memory, that I would be cured, that I would be clean, free. But it is my hatred of him that cut my body free of his, that made me.

The only reason I didn't kill my father was the fear that murder wouldn't be enough; that having committed the ultimate act, I might still not be purged

The light coming in through the windows is different. I must have fallen asleep. I'm awake. I am in my parents' house on River Street in Cambridge. No, my mother's house. My father died four days ago.

I know where I am, but I slip back into the memories of rooms, arrangements of contained space.

My grandmother's house, its hot attic rooms and cool marble fireplace mantel, the high ceiling, the elevator ("It's not an elevator," she used to explain patiently, "it's a lift.") and its two black buttons, Up and Down, each circled with a wreath of golden laurel leaves. That vast kitchen, with its black stove, stout and matronly, and two gleaming identical white refrigerators set side by side.

There was another house like the one my grandparents lived in, the old mansion in Oakland where twelve people lived collectively. The house where I met Jeremy. For the first time since I moved out I can remember those rooms without a sense of guilt.

Tides that sweep across a city: in 1976, we moved into a mansion with rotten front steps, a house that the twelve of us could rent for five hundred dollars a month, in the middle of an all-black neighborhood, surrounded, like Sleeping Beauty's palace, with a thicket that had once been a carefully tended rose garden.

I have never, since I left, driven through that part of town again. It would be easy enough for me to go there. I go to Oakland three or four times a month—to a meeting, a talk at La Pena, for ribs at Flint's. I could leave half an hour early, turn off MacArthur, take a left, then a right.

But I have never driven down that street to see what has no doubt happened to that house: to see that a skylight has been cut into the roof; I have never ventured out of the car on a hot summer's day, wandered to the yard, where they would be, the couple (perhaps younger than me) who own it now, seen the lawn where they play with their two children. I could amble up to them: I used to live in this house. I might tell them the story of the collective. Maybe they had been radicals once, or taken part in one of the big mobilizations at the end of the war. Perhaps not. At any rate, it's a tale they would be able to add to the history of their house. I could hang around for a minute, waiting for one or the other of them to ask if I'd like to come and look around. They'd lead me into that house that once had been dust-filled, dark.

There, above the fireplace, where the National Liberation Front flag had hung, would be a poster, matted and framed. Perhaps a Diego Rivera: the kneeling woman with calla lilies strapped to her back. Once, for a fundraising reception for Casa El Salvador, I went to the wholesale flower market to buy dozens of daisies and zinnias, sweet-smelling phlox. A dozen of those, I said, a dozen of those, and those, spending all of the twenty-five dollars that had been allotted. I made

three trips back to the car, my arms aching; I staggered back
to my car, wheezing and out of breath. Flowers aren't
weightless.

The lamp. What's happened to that fake porcelain lamp, its
base a shepherdess with rosy cheeks and three gamboling
sheep, a memory of a false past, a lamp made to sit next to a
canopy bed? I used to read nights by the light of that lamp
with its frilly pink lampshade, that lamp that must have been
retrieved from the attic of that old mansion on 85th Street in
Oakland. I read Hegel and Engels; on Saturday nights, I lay in
bed and read *The National Enquirer*, eating ribs from Flint's,
having assured the woman behind the counter that I really
did want the hot sauce. (One day she said to me, "You better
take the medium, honey. I was *angry* when I made the hot.")

The twelve of us lived in that house built for one rich man.
The kitchen was in the basement. On the first floor were the
rooms once called reception rooms, and the breakfast and
dining rooms; and on the second floor, the master bedroom,
vast and baronial, and rooms where sons and daughters
might have slept. An uncarpeted, rubber-treaded flight of
stairs ran up the back of the house, a flight of stairs that didn't
have carved banisters and lathed struts. Under the slanted
eaves of the third floor were plain bare rooms: the servants'
quarters.

Before we moved in, we had had a long, long meeting, trying to decide how to allocate that unequal space. The early
suggestion, that those of us who took the large ornate rooms
should pay more rent than others, was rejected. We discussed
a lottery; but we'd only have ended up with an inequality
based on chance, rather than on race, class, gender. Leah suggested that we set up a rota: on the first of each month we
would migrate, so that each of us lived in each room. We
tried that for a few months. I dreaded the end of the month,
having to pack up everything I owned and lug it up or down
the stairs, across the hall. It wasn't just the physical work; it

was the feeling of instability from having no space to call my own. We talked about it, late at night in the kitchen and at meetings. The women felt it more than the men—that longing for stability. Betsy said this was because men's home is the world. Carl said that we must not run away from feelings of disorientation, must not be in too great a hurry to get rid of them. In the end, the master bedroom was shared; those of us who lived in the servants' quarters got two rooms.

I was happy in that house. I was not crazy anymore. The sensation (of becoming sane again) is the same as the first few days after a flu: gratitude for the absence of sore muscles, aching joints, nausea. My chronic misery had run its course.

I remade myself, again. Not with the same drug-induced, love-induced, frenzy I knew with Danny; this was different. Really. We were cautious. We talked and talked and talked, all of us, together.

And I fell in love with Jeremy there because he was good and solid and safe and boring. (And I fell out of love with him for those same reasons.)

I learned word-processing, so that I could get hired at one of the word factories within a huge law firm, where Sheila and I would start a union drive.

We didn't have a grand strategy, just a patient belief in our own spirit, and that the boredom, the meaningless work, the everyday injustice, petty and otherwise, would come together in a volatile mixture and explode.

We worked in the word-processing department, at the back, of course the back, of a law firm that took up two floors of a downtown high-rise. There were carefully tended dwarf palms and stark Japanese flower arrangements outside the offices of the attorneys but not, of course, outside of ours. We didn't get vacation pay, sick pay, health insurance; our shoulders got stiff, our necks ached, one woman developed some strange nerve problem that never was diagnosed, but which must have been repetitive motion syndrome. We had headaches from staring, staring, staring at the fuzzy screens in the rooms with the glaring fluorescent overhead lights. *Name of file to be retrieved?* the computer screen asks, and I type in "Boilerplate A," ENTER, Control C, Control KR, *Name of file to be retrieved?* and I type in "Boilerplate C," ENTER, Control C, Control KR; *Name of file to be retrieved?*

Some people thought the high-pitched whine that computers gave off caused problems, miscarriages, tension headaches; some people thought it wass the electro-magnetic field; some people blamed the pace of work. In South Korea, in Singapore, in Silicon Valley, it's called an economic miracle, these women sitting patiently soldering circuit boards, as fine as lace-making and just as blinding. In the newsletter, which I processed, they said, "Because of our concern with employee health, Crockett, Wilson has installed a health club on the 14th floor. All attorneys and law clerks are welcome to use these facilites." You add, "Lower life forms, including paralegals, proofreaders, messengers and word processors, are not welcome to use these facilities." I was caught, called in before the supervisor. "I want you to think," he says, "about just how embarrassing it would have been to the firm if this had been distributed in this fashion. Just take a minute, right now, to think about it." I never had to work so hard to keep from laughing. But I realized I'd been stupid, too, had jeopardized our organizing work.

In 1977, we thought that history was sleeping, that the people were recovering their strength, that this was a brief trough between waves, and the next wave would be the biggest ever.

We were patient. We met in our study groups and understood the complexities of capitalism, the difficulties of revolutionary change. We studied the objective social conditions, which have never been riper, and yet nothing happened.

Then it was 1978. Years later, you will read a quote from Gramsci: "The old is dying and the new cannot be born; in this interregnum there arises a great diversity of morbid symptoms."

Vincent, we used to call him Mother Vincent, I remember him coming through the doorway, sitting down on the floor in a semi-lotus, the yellow mixing bowl on his lap, as he creamed raw brown sugar into butter, asking, "Chocolate chip or oatmeal?"; and I remember him glaring at me, from across the room, taking notes as I spoke in the meeting.

When Jill left to go to grad school on the East Coast, a young Asian woman, Allison, who worked with Barbara at the health clinic, moved in. We weren't like the rest of the world, we didn't ignore race, pretend that it wasn't to be talked about in polite company.

Allison was newly political. Her anger exploded, exploded after all those years of being asked those "innocent" questions, "What nationality are you?" (She answered, "American," which brought forth a condescending, "No, I mean . . .") and "Are you a math major?" They expected her to be shrewish or demure, a Dragon Lady or Snow Pea, to be intelligent, but in a narrow, clever way—almost-white, enigmatic.

Tom was the oldest of us, in his forties. In the early sixties, he'd spent summers driving donated supplies down South to civil rights projects. He told stories about turning off his headlights late at night on dark Mississippi roads when he realized he was being followed, about getting chased by a southern sheriff and doing a U-turn going sixty by pulling on the hand brake. In 1964, there had been an easy masculine bond between him and the Black men of SNCC, though everyone said Negro then. He had been a good old boy, without the racism. He wasn't guilt-ridden like the white college boys; he was hard-drinking, tough. The following year, when Stokely Carmichael shocked the movement by saying "Black," Tom was one of the few whites for whom the new word felt easy, instinctively right. Black was a word from dreams and nightmares, a word that came from the world of bars and work that made you sweat and smell bad, unlike the careful, educated, distant "Negro." Tom had been a truck driver; he'd been strung out on heroin for a while. He was divorced, had a kid whom he saw for a few weeks in the summer.

We were watching a Woody Allen movie on television, in which Allen raised a rice bowl to his mouth, and gobbled like a cartoon Oriental. Tom laughed, his loud, raucous laugh alone in the vast former ballroom. Allison glared at him. He didn't hang his head; he glared back at her. A few nights later, at our Sunday night meeting, the meeting in which we talked about everything—after we had discussed the toxicity of commercial oven cleaners ("You can make a paste out of baking soda and use that to clean the oven," Vince said. "*You* can make a paste out of baking soda and use it to clean the oven," Sheila said. "I'm not about to spend three hours scrubbing out the goddamn oven." "Okay," Vince said, "I'll do it."), whether we were going to use house funds to buy meat (an ongoing discussion), about noise late at night and early in the morning—Allison said, "I have something I want to raise." Her arms were folded across her chest. Her voice was shaking. "The other night, when we were watching television, Tom laughed at an anti-Asian joke."

"Okay," Tom muttered.

"What do you mean, 'okay'?" Allison asked.

"I'm sorry if your feelings were hurt."

"What does that mean?" Sheila asked. "I mean, is that an apology? An acknowledgement? I have to be critical of myself. I treated it like it was an embarrassing moment. I should have confronted you at the moment, Tom."

"Oh, Christ," Tom said. "This is ridiculous. I laughed, for Christ's sake."

"Do you know how that made me feel?" Allison asked.

"Look, I'm sorry if I hurt your feelings," Tom said, got up and left the room.

Two weeks later, Tom moved out.

When I think about this, my head aches. I try to figure out how it could have been different. Of course, Allison had a right to be angry. Of course, it's easiest to vent our anger on those who will listen to us, take us seriously; in a place where it is safe, or at least safer. It didn't stop there—we devoured ourselves, trying to live better, purer, truer; dancing in ever-decreasing circles. Finally, Jeremy and I fled.

Rosa Luxemburg said that the "collective ego of the working class . . . insists on its right to make its own mistakes and to learn the historical dialectic by itself. . . ."; that "our errors are infinitely more fruitful and more valuable than any edicts handed down from on high." And more painful.

# 11

Another plane. Coming down again through the clouds. Leaning against Matt. Another numb journey through the airport. The glaring fluorescent lights and the miniature models of the Golden Gate Bridge.

When we get out to the car, he holds me against him. The steady thumps of his heart, the smell of him. At the funeral, my "aunts" and "uncles" all smelled so dank and rich. Was it just that they grew up earlier in the century, so that daily showers and anti-perspirants seem indulgent? Or is it that their pasts, their histories, have sunk into them, festered? Matt only smells faintly of the tuna fish sandwich he must have eaten a few hours ago, of darkroom chemicals. Matt smells only of today, yesterday.

We are silent in the car. He holds my hand, lets go of it to shift, takes it again. We don't say anything as we drive 101 into the city, drive past the hills browned by the summer sun, drive past the white rocks arranged on the hillside to read, South San Francisco: The Industrial City.

It's when we are pulling off the Army Street Exit that I finally say, "I didn't know it was going to be so *physical*. Like flu." I work to take a deep breath, work against the weight in my chest, of my chest. And then suddenly, the words are gushing out of me: I'm yammering on about the funeral, telling him the names of the people who came, names that mean nothing to him; the food my mother served at the gathering afterwards; the things we found when we were cleaning out the house. "The Buddhists," I say, as we pull up in front of my building. "I forgot to tell you about the Buddhists."

Matt gets out of the car, hefts my bag out of the back seat. It's an Yves St. Laurent that Jeremy found it in a dumpster off Union Street. It had been thrown out because the zipper didn't unzip all the way. He rests his hand on the small of my back as we walk up the path. The small of my back is one of my favorite places to be touched. My body is demarcated into places where I can't be touched because my nerves blossom in wild, painful profusion; and places my father's hands have poisoned, like those areas toxic chemicals have left dead; and places where I was sliced open. The small of my back is wild territory, unclaimed.

Matt's cleaned up my apartment for me: he knows I hate coming home to a messy house. There's a single lily in an old mayonnaise jar in the center of the dining room table.

"Thank you," I say, sitting down on one of the hard wooden chairs. "Thank you." I am so relieved to be away from the clutter of my parents' lives, to be back to my asthma-induced, Zen simplicity; to be back to the clean and slightly depressing vistas of my apartment. I stop talking about the Buddhists, I don't bother to tell him the story I was going to tell him next, about one of the old women who came to my father's memorial service, and the story she told me of her parents' escape from Czarist Russia.

I stare at the lily. Its ridiculously sexual stamens jut proudly out. A living thing that grew out of the dirt, out of what came before it. A living thing that was not made from hard work, struggle, consciousness. A living thing that simply grew.

"Are you hungry?" Matt asks.

"No. I'm tired. I'm going to go lie down . . . when I get the energy to walk into the other room." I hold out my hand; he comes over and stands next to me. I lean my head against his hip. I feel against my face his cotton T-shirt, his belt buckle, his jeans. His smell is male and good.

"Thank you for cleaning up the house." I take a deep breath. "I got the Dalton."

"I know you did. You got a phone call from them. They need an eight-by-ten glossy of you. For their newsletter."

"Will you take it for me?" I ask.

"Sure," he says.

I tilt my head to one side, paste on a fake grin, and freeze as though he held a camera. I start laughing, laughing until I cry. How can I have a picture taken of me now, now when I'm in this state?

"I'm sorry I didn't tell you. Are you mad at me?"

"Not mad. I'm kind of amazed at how you can shut me out of your life."

"It wasn't . . . it just made the idea of having the baby so much easier. It was too much."

"When did you find out?"

"About ten days ago. The day we went to Noe Valley Café. I'm tired. I'm going to go lie down."

"Do you want me to stay with you?" he asks.

"I'm okay."

"Do you want me to stay?"

I know that if Matt stays, I'll wish he had gone; if he leaves, I'll wish he'd stayed.

"No. I'm just going to sleep."

He tells me that he's going over to his studio to do some work; I should call him when I wake up.

"Okay," I say.

And then I'm alone. I go into the bedroom. Matt's even changed the sheets, pulled them smooth and taut, just the way I like them. I get undressed. I wish I had a white night-gown. It's something I've wanted ever since I was a little kid. A white cotton nightgown with openwork lace insets. I'm going to buy one. I'll start squirreling away my money. I'm good at that, when I want something. I have all these little tricks: putting a dollar a day into a jar, saving all my change. I could, of course, use my Dalton money. But I don't dare touch that; I could fritter it all away on cotton nightgowns and silver earrings and dinners at Indian and Thai restaurants.

I lie down in bed naked.

Waking up, I glance at the clock. 6:02. I hate digital clocks. I got this one at a yard sale for $2.50. I've slept for two hours. They say the grieving process takes a year. I try to figure out how many hours there are in a year—how many down, how many left to go—but I can't do the arithmetic in my head.

I call Matt, tell him I want to go out and have fun. My treat, to thank him for cleaning up the house.

I shave my legs, something I never do. Almost never. Then I'm rummaging through the cabinet, finding the hair dryer, finding some Body Sloughing Lotion that I got as a "free gift" when I bought a tube of lipstick. The finer print on the label says that this will assist my skin in sloughing off dead cells, leaving my whole body fresher and cleaner. I want my whole body to be fresh and clean. I want to be purged and pure.

A friend of mine converted to Orthodox Judaism for a few years. She told me about going to the *mikvah*, the ritual bath, once a month. Before going into the water, one must be absolutely clean: the teeth brushed, the ears cleaned of wax, toenails and fingernails scraped clean of grit. When she first told me about it, I could only think, How oppressive to women, this post-menstrual purification. But now I like the honesty of it, the frank admission that we move through cycles of cleanliness and uncleanliness.

I wash my face with the special soap that Ann Marie gave me as a present on my thirtieth birthday. I've hardly used it. I go through all the steps of the facial cleansing regimen outlined in the pamphlet that came with the soap.

My hair is washed and conditioned; the dead cells of my skin have been sloughed off. I have rubbed myself with lotions. If I wasn't scared of having an allergic reaction, I'd anoint myself with perfumed oils.

I check myself out in the mirror before I leave to pick up Matt. I look great.

Daddy, you're right: I'm a bitch. You're dead and I'm triumphant. I've outlived you. You wanted to kill me: you wanted to pound my brain out of my skull, you wanted to choke off my air. Now I'm alive and you're dead. Life is the only real power, Daddy.

I imagined grieving as a slow wade through a morass of sorrow; I didn't count on this rollercoaster ride. I thought I would be purely and simply sad. I'm everything but sad.

Matt and I go to my favorite restaurant, El Gallego. We've talked about what we're going to order (paella), he's given me the messages he needed to give me, told me that he put my mail in the sideboard, in the far-right top drawer; and then we sit opposite each other, and stare.

"Do you want to talk about anything?"

"No." Can't he tell—by the way I'm dressed, by my shaved legs, the make-up I'm wearing—that tonight I just want to forget? "Just talk to me. You know, about regular things," I say.

So he does. He tells me about the new supervisor at Hutchinson, Rubin who wrote the word-processing department a memo outlining her New Age approach to employee relations. She believes that the department can move from the old paradigm of "win-lose" situations to the new one of "win-win"; she believes that everyone in the word-processing department is a unique and special individual, a gift to the universe. Matt tells me that he is finally printing the pictures he took when we were in New Mexico. This is what I want, ordinary talk, to fill the air.

I gorge myself. I'm not used to the richness of this food. I've slathered butter on the bread. The paella is thick with olive oil and clams, mussels, shrimp.

We walk up to Valencia Street, head for Bajones to listen to jazz.

"I want to talk about the—the pregnancy," he says.

"Matt, I just don't want to think tonight."

"I know it's not a good time, but . . . we're running out of time."

"You want me to have an abortion."

"No. No. That's not it at all. I just don't want to—I just don't want it to be too late and we haven't talked about it."

Earlier, I imagined this evening. I imagined how we would eat dinner at El Gallego and then walk up to Valencia Street, past the Roosevelt Tamale Parlor; I imagined the occasional car filled with young Latino men cruising past with a radio full-bass and booming; and the fundamentalist Christian standing on the corner of 16th and Mission, the words *Jesus, Christo, el Salvador* emerging out of the maze of shouted Spanish, holding the black Bible with the large gold cross on it, which he waves in the air and thumps for emphasis. I imagined everything, just as it is happening; only I imagined that we would be happy, drunk—not on alcohol, but, I suppose, on that state called denial.

"What are you thinking?" he finally asks me.

"Nothing" would be an honest answer. Honest, but unfair. I am exhausted from pregnancy, bloated from dinner—thick, lumbering in this body that already the combined effects of pregnancy and disability have made wobbly and strange. A simple thought would be welcome, a release from the prison of this body. By now he must be reading my silence as a refusal to speak.

"Nothing," I say, to say something. "I'm just feeling how— heavy. I'm sorry. I know you want to talk about the . . . baby. But I can't—all I can think about is how. . . If you want to talk about it, *you* say something."

"The Dalton thing really hurt me," Matt says.

"I didn't tell anybody. I didn't even tell my mother."

"I got that phone call from them, about the picture. I was over at your place. I think this guy thought I was your husband, at first, and he acts like I must know all about it. And then, when he realized I didn't know, he starts treating me like your . . . houseboy, or something."

"I'm sorry," I say. "I know I hold you at a distance. I'm so scared of you—your having power over me."

"It feels good to talk this way."

"Does it?" I ask. "It feels scary to me. I get scared you're going to leave me. When you find out how fucked up I am."

"You're just an ordinary amount of fucked up."

"Really?"

"Really."

At the door to Bajones, I realize it'll be too loud to talk in there. I say, "Do you want to stay outside for a while?"

"No," he says. "Let's go in."

After Bajones, we wander up Valencia Street to Las Flores, where we drink *aqua frescas*. I'm happy until a marimba band, with a transvestite lead singer in a sequined gown, crowds into the tiny bar; then I start feeling crazy, can't get out of there soon enough. I need air, I need silence, I'm leaning against the wall outside, sobbing. Matt's holding me.

My father is gone. It will never happen: he will never go to an AA meeting, see the light, go into recovery, apologize. No, never. He will never have a grandchild, get a second chance. I will never show him my anger. Odd shock to realize that for all my wild hatred of him, for all those nights when his grinning face leered above me, for all those ragings in my head—I even bought that gun, toyed with the idea of killing him—I never once even raised my voice to him. I never looked him in the eye and said, "Daddy, this is what you did to me." Never. Everyone in my life has felt my anger, except him.

I stand outside Las Flores, sobbing so hard that I'm choking. Matt tells me, "Take a deep breath. Come on, Elizabeth, take a deep breath." My face is wet with snot and tears. People passing by on the street are stopping to stare at me. One woman comes up to Matt and asks if there's anything she can do to help.

"Her father just died," Matt says. "We're okay. Thanks."

The woman I have never met before touches my arm, tells me she's sorry, tells me she'll pray for my father. I can't talk. I nod. Matt says, "She'll be okay." The woman moves down the street and I want to call after her, "Don't feel bad for me that way, I'm not a good daughter. Don't pray for the repose of his atheist's soul."

I calm down. Matt takes me to Café Picaro, to wait for him there while he goes back to get the car. I go into the bathroom. My face is streaked with black mascara, caked powder. I lather soap onto my hands and scrub my face with the harsh brown paper towels. I look ten years older than I looked two weeks ago.

In the car, I turn to look at his face. He's as lost and alone as I am, as fragile, as helpless, as new at all this as me. I want him to be a statue, I want him to be a cardboard cut-out of Prince Charming. I don't want to see my own pain reflected in his face.


My friends put gentle hands on my shoulder and ask, "How are you doing?"

If they want to know the truth, I feel free. I'm a hot-air balloon that had been held down with dead weights, suddenly unmoored, rising, rising away from earth. I can do anything. I could toss away this solid life I've built for myself here, take off for Mexico, live in a fishing village on a Greek island, spend hours, days, a lifetime, looking at that line where heaven meets earth. The Dalton is only ten thousand dollars—it's not that much, really—but it would stretch for a year or two in Mexico, in Greece.

I could give birth to my baby in a hospital somewhere where the sheets are worn cotton, where a nurse, murmuring words in a language I only faintly understand, would lay her hand on my forehead.

I could chuck it all, stop going to political meetings three nights a week. I could create sculptures that are about form, that are whimsical. This morning, Daddy, as I was walking to my car, I saw the shattered glass from a car window lying on the sidewalk. The odd jagged squares, hundreds of them, their shapes echoing off each other. Their color different than when the window was one piece. I thought, I could go back to the house and get a pair of gloves and a bag, kneel down, gather these fragments up, use them somehow in a piece. In a piece that wouldn't be "about" disability or "about" being a woman living in a city; a work of art that would only be these shattered fragments of glass.

Is that all it's been all these years, Daddy, wanting to prove that I could be a better leftist than you, that I could hold on, not give up?

I could chuck this life that I've worked so hard to make for myself. Maybe I'd make it: not doing political art in a cold room at the back of the Independent Living Center. Doing work that doesn't challenge people.

Ever since those days in that cramped flat with Danny, I've never been able to get enough light, enough room. I hate the tiny two rooms of my Bernal Heights apartment, the way they get cluttered so quickly. It'll only be worse when I have the baby. If I have the baby. I want a loft the size of a football field. A top floor filled with light. Loft, I like the sound of that word. Loft, lift, light, flight, fly, free. We could live there, little guppy, you and me, and maybe Matt too.

But who am I kidding? Lofts are expensive. Cyndi has a poster on her wall that lists Ten Advantages to Being a Woman Artist. All of which boil down to: you never have to worry about the problems of making it, about having success, acclaim, money. Medical insurance.

It's only that suddenly I'm free to dream, without your dead hand weighing on my shoulder.

❀

The night before I chair the Nicaragua forum, I dream that I was driving two cars at once—an old dream, one that I used to have in the days when I was crazy. But this time, I managed to do it: one hand on each steering wheel. My legs elongated until they weren't my legs anymore, they belonged to a cartoon character named Stretch. I was scared, but I did it.

I get to the Women's Building at seven to help set up. We bring chairs to the room and arrange them; someone takes charge of the cash box. A handwritten sign downstairs directs people to the right room. How many times have I done these same duties, getting ready for a forum, a panel? Fifty, a hundred? And now the room starts filling up with women—some with spiked hair and some who wear their hair loosely about their shoulders—and a few men.

Phyllis puts her hand on my shoulder and asks, "How's your father?"

"He died," I say. My words sound harsh, almost obscene. Maybe I should have said something more gentle, *He passed away, he didn't make it.*

"I'm so sorry," Phyllis says.

"I'm doing okay," I say, and I turn away from her.

"If people could take their seats please . . ."

I introduce myself, lay out ground rules (hold your questions and comments until the end, keep them to under two minutes). "Six weeks ago, a delegation of women, organized by the Berkeley Women's Health Center, made a trip to Nicaragua to report on women's health care there . . . they came back with information which was both encouraging and disheartening . . ." I hear my voice shake. Will I ever lose my fear of antagonizing people? People, too broad a word. It's men who scare me, the men sitting in the front row or close to it, with their dark eyes and dark hair. Men who have fled to this country from El Salvador or Guatemala, men who left Nicaragua twenty years ago. Men who've seen their families or their comrades killed. Are they looking at me and thinking, How dare you? How dare you risk undermining a revolution we've sacrificed so much for? You, a white, North American woman, daughter of privilege.

There, I've done it. I've said my piece. Cathy goes first. She talks about midwifery care, infant mortality, sanitation measures. She still sounds like a leaflet, but this time like a well-written one. Now she's even getting a bit familiar with the audience, telling them a story about an evening in San Juan at a rickety bar out at the end of a pier called The Drive-In Disco. She met a woman there . . .

Then Phyllis speaks. She tells the story of Patricia. Her voice is controlled, but the outline of sorrow and anger is clear beneath the surface of her words.

During the discussion period—discussion being something of an understatement—I am a fair and strong mediator. I'm scared, but I do it.


Tonight Matt and I move into the earnest discussion stage, sitting across from each other at the dining room table, with a piece of blue-lined notebook paper, on which we jot figures. We'll have to buy diapers; how much do they cost? A washing machine and dryer; how much are they and where will we put them? There are compact models, the dryer stacked on top of the washer—we could put them in the corner of the kitchen. We could get diaper service. No, that's forty dollars a month, way too much. Matt says he could take Junior or Juniorette with him to his studio while he works. I say no, you couldn't take her in the darkroom, with all those awful chemicals. And it's hard to work with a baby. In the middle of it all, the phone rings. It's his father. "Can you believe it," Matt says when he gets off the phone. "I was talking with him last week, I told him I'd been playing racquetball. So he calls me to tell me that he played racquetball with a twenty-five-year-old—he actually said that, a twenty-five-year-old—and beat him."

"Your dad doesn't hide it, I'll say that for him. . . . Did your dad ever tell you that he and Constance are trying to get pregnant?"

"No."

"She told me the morning we went over for brunch."

"Really?" Matt stands and shakes his head from side to side, grinning.

"You didn't tell her you were pregnant, did you?"

"No way. . . . Does that make you want to have the baby?"

"Yeah. Isn't that sick?"

I shrug. "My motivations are always pure."

He wants to prove something to his father, that he can be a father and stay an artist, do it better than he did it. Me, I want a balm for my past. I want to have a child so I'll know something whole and perfect can come out of my imperfect body. I want to know my body through pregnancy, and through birth. I want to become rooted to the world through my child.

Years later, I will remember this evening, sitting at the dining table of my home in Bernal Heights—remember that I wanted to feel rooted, connected.

All through the war on Iraq, I will think, *This is what I wanted to know*, with an odd half-laugh. Throughout the years of the Viet Nam War, the "people of Viet Nam" were just that, an abstraction. Heroic, suffering, sentimental pawns. Motherhood made the world new to me.

The night the u.s. attacks Iraq, I will turn on my radio and hear the sound of fighter planes taking off in the background. I don't even need to hear the newscaster's words. The physical sensation of the world, as I have known it, dropping away comes on as quickly, is as acute, as the first shattering contraction of labor. I will burst into tears and then race around in my tiny Bernal Heights apartment, grabbing coats, hats, mittens, gloves. We have to go, I will tell Sam. The war's started.

We have to go down to the Federal Building. Don't worry, I will tell him, as the teachers at his school have advised parents to tell their children, don't worry: you are safe.

But that night—after I leave the demonstration because, after all, tomorrow is a school day and he has to get his sleep—that night, as I lie down in bed, the face of an Iraqi woman will appear to me: she will be wearing a pale green headscarf, have dark eyebrows that meet above the bridge of her nose; she will stare straight ahead. She cannot tell her children that they are safe. I will wish that her face would resolve itself into something else—anger, grief, fear. She only stares straight ahead. I will understand that tonight the world has split in two: on one side are the women who can tell their children honestly that they are safe. On the other side of the divide are the women who must lie to their children as they hustle them into bomb shelters.

A sleepless night.

The second night, at 3 A.M. she will knock softly on my door, a woman I had known from demonstrations, seen at meetings, gone out postering with earlier in the evening. "I hope . . . I'm not—I saw your light on." I will put my finger to my lips, "I can't sleep either," I'll whisper, "but my son, his father . . ." "Do you want to go out spray-painting?" she asks. I grab my jacket, shoes. I watch for cops as she spray-paints on walls and freeway abutments: U.S. OUT OF THE MIDDLE EAST. NO BLOOD FOR OIL. WOMEN AND CHILDREN ARE DYING IN BAG— She will turn to me, "How do you spell it?" BAGHDAD.

The fourth night I will discover a way to make myself sleep: the Brandenburg Concertos. I concentrate on the pure waves of sound and they carry me away to a place without words, without images. I sleep then, for three or four hours, until some dream I can't remember impels me up from sleep, impels me out of bed.

The first week of the war, I will eat and eat. Not the way I usually eat, low on the food chain, oranges and bananas, vegetarian stews. Instead, I run into the gas station where I have stopped (the needle well into red) on my way to the gathering in Palo Alto where I will speak (making broader connections, the voice on the other end of the phone said, and I intoned urgently, yes, yes, to show her that we were on the same political wavelength), a feminist analysis of the language of war. A subject about which I could not have said more than a couple of sentences a week ago. Although now I am listed on the flyer as a "noted Bay Area artist," the flyer which had been run off and distributed in the space of hours. Running into the gas station I grab a bag of barbeque-flavored potato chips, not even stopping to examine the label. If some chemical in it—monosodium glutamate, FDC Yellow #5— kicks off my asthma, I can always go on steroids. I could use the jolt, the extra energy, taking those drugs would give me. But I tell myself that I won't get sick, couldn't possibly, I haven't got the time.

Impossible to imagine that two weeks ago, I was a woman who spent an hour each Saturday morning in Noe Valley Community Foods, selecting organic green peppers, measuring wheat germ and millet out of the bulk bins and into the brown paper bags that I so carefully reuse; that I used to stand in my kitchen, listening to the news on KPFA and slicing onions, green peppers, zucchini, garlic. A lifetime ago. I will not have sat down to eat since that night the radio broadcast the sound of jet fighters taking off. Now I eat desperately, wildly, foods I haven't eaten in years and years, wrapped in plastic. Cheetos, Snickers, impulse items, easy to seize, next to the cash registers in 7-Elevens and A.M.-P.M. Mini-Marts; I eat and eat, seeking to fill that churning hole at the center.

At the end of that first crazy week, I will climb on the bathroom scale, calling out to Matt as I do—"Do you want to make a bet on how much weight I've gained?"—and discover that I've lost five pounds. I look at the needle again, climb off, climb on again. It's true. How could it be? All that high-fat food, the salt. For the first time in my life, loss of weight evokes fear in me. I understand that this restless churning in my stomach could devour me.

I had a child because I wanted to know what mothers know. Now I know. Lucky me. A phrase that my side uses, "civilian casualties," a phrase that I once would have used. As if the deaths of soldiers did not count.

Twice I have to stop at gas stations to pee on my way to my show, even though it's only a fifteen-minute drive. Matt's coming straight from Hutchinson, Rubin, meeting me there. I am sweating so hard that right there in the Chevron bathroom I take the shoulder pads out of my blouse and stick them under my arms to catch the sweat. This won't work. I might be talking to some gallery owner or critic when one of them will start to slip and maybe end up in my champagne. I settle for washing my armpits.

I park the car. I get out and drop the keys, pick them up and then drop them again. My legs are jelly, my cane shakes in my hand. The negative reviews that I will read run through my mind: "One wonders what the photographer hoped to accomplish. If her intention was to shock, she certainly succeeded . . ." Or perhaps, worse, there'd be polite condescension, "Elizabeth Etters, a handicapped artist . . ." My legs may literally crumple under me. What an entrance that would be. I could call out, *This is performance,* before someone grabbed my arm and tried to yank me to my feet. I'm grinning when I walk in.

Ann Marie meets me at the door and hugs me. "This is wonderful." She said no to having her picture shown: if any of her clients came, it might be disruptive to their therapy.

"I've never been this scared before. Not about my work. Do you think people like it?"

"You know, this is tough stuff. But I'm surprised at how well people are responding."

"Yeah? Really? Do you think they really like it?"

Suddenly, Richard, who runs the gallery, is there, steering me towards all the people who want to meet me, and my hand is being shaken and I am saying, "Thank you . . . Thank you so much . . . Yes."

I keep looking for Matt.

A man and woman stop in front of the almost life-size photograph of me. It shows every pore and pock and wrinkle. Every scar and bulge of flesh. The man is explaining something to the woman, pointing his finger at my shoulder and then my thigh. I must remember this is serious. I must remember this is Art.

I look at it from across the room, squint my eyes, and think, *I don't look too bad.* By which I mean, I don't look too disabled. I am supposed to love this body as it is: love the curl of my right foot, love my body's sideways slant. My pastiche, postmodern body, which carries on its own rebellion against the ideal.

A man in a black-and-white Italian silk suit (my sense has been well developed by thrift-store shopping, pawing through racks of polyester looking for gold amongst the dross) is leaning close to my ear, saying that he heard about the Dalton Fellowship, congratulating me. At last I'm getting the recognition I deserve. And I think, Who the hell are you? but smile back politely and say, "Thank you."

Ann Marie, Matt, and I go out for a drink afterwards. White wine, Long Island iced tea, Perrier.

"To Elizabeth's show," Ann Marie says, raising her glass.

"How's it feel?" Matt asks.

"Pretty good. There's this nagging voice in the back of my head that says, You're not a real artist, you just take off your clothes and shock people."

"Stop being neurotic," Ann Marie says.

"Is that what you say to your clients?"

"That's what I wish I could say to my clients."

❁

The phone is ringing. It's nine in the morning.

"You're famous," Ann Marie says.

"You woke me up."

"I'm sorry. I thought you were always up by six."

"I haven't even peed yet. It's okay. I'm taking you to the bathroom with me. I'm on the cordless." I sit down on the toilet. "That was in my previous life. That I got up at six. Now I'm a slug—"

"You got a wonderful review in the *Chronicle*."

"Getting a wonderful review in the *Chronicle* doesn't make you famous."

"You're grumpy because I woke you up."

I walk to my apartment door naked, the cordless tucked under my ear, open it a crack, glance out to be sure that no one's in the hallway, open it, stoop down and pick up my paper.

"What page is it on?" I turn them too quickly. "Oh, shit, I'm making a mess out of this paper." I find it: "'As children, we were told not to stare at handicapped people. But disabled photographer Elizabeth Etters insists that we do stare: her photographs of nude disabled women make us confront . . . Unflinching honesty . . . often surprisingly humorous. . .' God," I say, amazed. "They don't just like it. They get it. And guess what—there's not a trace of self-pity in my work."

"Oh, well," Ann Marie says, laughing. "You can't have everything."

Matt and I celebrate. We go to Hal's and eat scrambled eggs with bacon and hash browns and white toast with butter. When we come home, we take a shower together. He rubs my shoulders, puts his hands on my sides, his lips move against mine. I close my eyes, but I'm scared I'll slip on the wet floor, scared I'll move the wrong way and topple over.

"I can't make love in the shower. I can't do it standing up."

"I'll hold you," he says. "It'll be okay."

"No," I say. "I can't. I've tried it before."

He kisses my breasts. "Not with me you haven't," he says. "Trust me."

I say, "It's not that I don't trust you."

"Oh no," he says, "it's not that you don't trust me," running his fingers along my spine.

"It's not *just* that I don't trust you."

I want to tell him how precarious I am, how everyone always thinks they know our bodies better than we do, and how I don't even know my own body now, now that I'm pregnant.

"I love you," he says to me, "I know you."

"Don't let me fall," I say.

"I won't let you fall."

And he doesn't.

The water heater starts making its odd knock, the one it gives off just before the hot water runs out. Mrs. DeSantini's not about to replace it, not in this rent-controlled apartment. We finish making love, laughing, with cold water pelting our skin.

Little things. The staring out of windows, at the falling rain or the fog pouring down from Twin Peaks. Chopping vegetables, the well-weighted knife slicing through the green peppers or carrots or potatoes, the sound when the blade hits the wood of the cutting board. Standing in front of the dairy case at Noe Valley Foods, deciding whether or not to spend the extra twenty cents for tofu made from organic soy beans. I make those decisions, hundreds a day. To buy or not to buy organic tofu. Choosing between writing the letter about the imprisoned Salvadoran trade unionist, washing your kitchen floor, or going to the movies. Putting off calling an abortion clinic and making an appointment.

Almost. We have almost decided to do it. To go ahead with the pregnancy. Almost.

I ask Matt how he feels. He says, "I'm scared." I want him to say that he'll be big and brave, take care of me, work sixteen hours a day to buy organic baby food and quilts stuffed with dioxin-free cotton. I want him to hold me in his arms and tell me that there's nothing to be scared of.

I call my mother. Her voice is slowed down, a 45 record played at 33 rpms. It's the voice she's always had late at night, after a long evening of drinking. But it's ten in the morning. She says she is doing all right. She says, "That's good," in the same flat monotone when I tell her about my review, my show.

"I think we're going to have the baby," I say.

"Oh," she says. The voice not of a drowning woman, but of a drowned one.

I lie down in bed, exhuasted, but I can't fall asleep. I count slowly backwards, visualizing each number as I do. It's no good. The longer I lie there with my head on the pillow, my body still, the more my mind swirls. I keep telling myself to get up, do something, don't just lie here. Finally, I do. I go to my cardboard box of treasures that I brought back from Boston. I empty out the accordion file. I hold the old photographs in my hand.

Look at our little Jacques! A living doll. Fair locks curling against fairer cheeks, scrubbed and rosy, his sailor suit with white piping. He crows! He insisted on it, insisted on posing with his fire truck that really squirts water and his windmill that he built all by himself (well, almost all by himself). A prize among prizes, our Jacques.

At twenty, he leans against the rail of the ship: angular, dark suit and dark tie fluttering back from the sea wind. He looks just like what he is pretending to be, a rich college boy on his way to Europe. No one would guess what he is going to.

I open the passport. I cannot hate the man who smiles back at me, his face stamped with an embossed seal, an eagle, "The United States of America." He looks proud of himself. Not smug but happy. I flip the page. In purple ink it is stamped, "Not Valid for Travel to Spain." A visa for the landing in Le Havre.

I shake the file and two other photographs fall out. In the first one, my father poses with other soldiers, a blond-haired Michigan lad amidst the dark-haired Jewish boys from Brooklyn and the lower East Side, proudly bearing their guns that will misfire three times out of four. His uniform swims around him, a cigarette hangs from the corner of his mouth. He is trying to look tough, but he just looks foolish.

In the other photograph he is a graduate student, I suppose. He's with my mother, posed in front of one of the buildings at MIT. Something's gone from the core of him; there's nothing in the eyes, the smile looks like a grimace.

I take out my father's manuscript, "Heroes of Spain." It is written in a another language—everyone who believed in this tongue is gone now. I have only these things and fragments of memories to decipher it, to find the truth behind those familiar lies.

Spain. In second grade the music teacher came to our class one day. We were to learn a song from *My Fair Lady*, she said, then blew into the pitch pipe to give us the tone. "The rain in Spain falls mainly on the plain." We were to go around the room and each sing that phrase in turn. I sat in the front row, the first seat. "Elizabeth," she said. She blew into the pitch pipe again. Spain? That's a dangerous word. I must have heard her wrong. I'll get in trouble if I sing it. But what is the right word? I sat there, silent, the lump in my throat so big that even if I could have figured out what to sing, I couldn't have. My eyes filled with tears. Miss Hamlin, the regular teacher, finally took me to the girls' room and put her arm around my shoulder. *What's wrong, Elizabeth?* she asked over and over again. But I couldn't say.

Daddy, I have remade you, remade you out of scraps of memory and imagination, out of the photographs in the old photo album, old newspapers read on microfilm. I have seen you sitting in your dorm room at MIT as the rainy weather moved in from New York, seen you reading an article that I read almost fifty years later, DEAD GIRLS LINKED WITH SUICIDE PAIR.

Daddy, I have seen you a shadowy figure dancing with my mother at a party in an apartment on Prospect Street in Cambridge; seen you, as if in a black-and-white movie from the forties, dancing to a song I used to hear on the radio, "When the deep purple falls, over sleepy garden walls . . . in the mist of a memory, you wander back to me, breathing my name with a si-iii-igh . . ." I have seen a you decade later, walking up the stairs in a dumpy boarding house, my gray father.

I sat next to your bed, when everything you knew and thought, your whole sharp world, dissolved in the ocean of gin you had spent your life drinking. What did I know? Only the rooms you had grown up in, some hints about what life was like for a boy of your class and time, the name your mother had given you. Daddy, I dreamed you a life.

I stood next to your body when you were gone from it. I stood and looked down on your stubbled face, your blue eyes staring straight up at nothing, your arms laid rigidly against your side. Head, trunk, arms, legs, shoulders, feet, hands: you.

Daddy, I know you better than you ever knew yourself.

I have not ceased to hate you; that would be impossible. If I ceased to hate you, I would cease to exist. I was born from your hatred of the womanflesh you fucked, from your disgust, your hatred for the world that had refused to be harnessed to your will. I was the future, the future for which you died somewhere in Spain, the future which betrayed you.

There's only one piece of the puzzle that's missing, Daddy. I must see not just the dead man who fathered me, the shell of bone and sinew and muscle, but see the man who smiles back at me from the passport photo.

At one-thirty in the morning, I pick up the phone and dial an 800 number. I don't even get put on hold, which I take as a sign from the cosmos. I give the voice ("This is Marie, how may I help you?") my frequent flyer number. How many miles do I have? And how many would it take to get to Spain?

"First class or economy?" Marie asks.

The question strikes me as funny: me, travel first class?

"Economy," I say.

Yes, I have enough to go to Spain. Just a minute, she'll check on flight availability. There are no seats available to Madrid on the date I've given her. How much flexibility do I have? Some, I have the month of August off. She's sorry, there's nothing until the first week in September.

Can I get to Paris?

I end up making reservations for a flight to Paris, in ten days. I rent car to drive south from there.

I hang up the phone. I can't believe I did it. I'm going to Spain.

# 12

My father did go to Europe the summer after he graduated from MIT.

Done with college at twenty, yes twenty! Would you like to see the pictures of him, posed in his black mortarboard and gown, with his proud mama on his left and his proud papa on his right? His mother is wearing a hat, drawn jauntily over one eye; her lips are red-red. His father looks remarkably like the fat capitalists in cartoons in *The Daily Worker*. They have resigned themselves to Jacques becoming an engineer.

But look at the unsmiling face of young Jacques. There are voices in the head of this skinny twenty year old. The voice of his father, tamped down, down; the seductive coo of his mother. The voices of the old-time Party members who clapped him on the back when he talked about dropping out of college and going to work full-time as an organizer for the Party. *But, Comrade, We'll need men like you after the revolution. Do you know how they suffered in Russia, from the treachery of the technicians?* (Did they really mean that, Jake? Or did they mean, What would you do as a Party organizer, kid? Your voice cracks when you talk in public. And after you came to the meeting, the guy from the Ford plant wanted to know if there were queers in the party. You, an organizer?)

Poor Jacques: he should be smiling, but instead he is listening to the voice of the volunteer who came back from Spain, who raised his left arm, the one he still had, during the chorus of "The Internationale"; listening to the voices crying out, "*¡Viva la República Española!*" and, "*¡No pasarán!*" He has listened to speeches about the hypocrisy of the "Non-Intervention Committee," organized by the U.S., Britain, and France, which is supposed to stop aid from going to either side, but only stops aid from going to the democratically-elected government. At a fundraising auction, Jake paid ten dollars for a copy of *Mundo Obrero*, November 7, 1936, the front page printed in red, ALL OUT TO THE BARRICADES: THE ENEMY IS ACROSS THE RIVER. (On the second page, there is an advertisement for *Modern Times* playing at the Capitol Theatre on the Gran Via.) His head is filled with the Spanish phrases he has been studying for the past six months—yes, on top of his finals, he has been learning Spanish, out of a phrase book for tourists.

*Uno, dos, tres*, he has said, doing his push-ups in the dorm room, all the way up to *cincuenta*.

He has read the story of Ernst Dorfman of Berlin, who heard of the fascist attack on the Republican government on July 17th, walked straight to the bank where he emptied out his bank account, and bought a train ticket for Madrid, arrived at noon the the 18th, took a tram to the battlefront, and was dead before sunset.

Jake does go to Europe the summer after he graduates from MIT. He goes to Europe carrying a passport stamped, "Not Valid for Travel in Spain," sails on the *Normandie*. He sails to Europe with steamfitters and auto workers and coal miners and Party organizers, men with calloused hands and red necks, all pretending to be tourists.

Jake coaches them on how to act. "You've got to remember, these people have never been hungry in their lives." So don't grab the bread the minute it's set on the table—keep your eyes off the salad while grace is being said. Watch me for which fork to use.

He keeps looking at their faces, trying to find a trace of his own fear.

He never gets drunk, not like the others, he keeps working out, laps around the deck, push-ups in his cabin. If he's not dead tired by the time he gets in bed, his panic keeps him awake all night: *I might die. I might die.*

From Le Havre they travel to Paris, from Paris to Perpignan, where they are smuggled on foot across the border into Spain.

Orly. Passport control. Purpose of visit? I hesitate for a moment and the man behind the counter says, "Business or pleasure?"

"Pleasure," I say.

I can't drive a standard; the cheapest automatic they have is an almost-luxury car, a Renault. I drive south, following the path you went by train. My car is bigger, sleeker than most of the cars I pass. I am driving too fast. I like the fact that the speed is in kilometers, not miles: I am doing a hundred and ten. I like this feeling of power.

I am exhausted, bleary. I keep driving, though I shouldn't really. I should pull off the road, find a hotel. I practice what I will say, remembering my high school French. But I don't stop. I keep driving, driving south.

This landscape is beautiful, ancient towns with leaning walls and moss-covered red tile roofs clinging to the crests of hills, stands of white-barked trees, looming rock formations eaten away by millenia, fortresses from battles lost centuries ago. A hawk glides through the air. For a while, the road runs alongside the train tracks. Daddy, did you look out at the same trees I am looking out at now, only seeing them from the opposite side, from another time?

Finally, I do stop in a little town. The room is ninety francs; the toilet is down the hall. I am hungry and sleepy, but more tired than hungry. I fall asleep in the narrow bed. I have to get up three or four times during the night to pee, padding down the hall in my bare feet. When I wake up, it's three in the morning. I am starving. Of course, there's nothing open.

I take some pictures of my room: a black-and-white photo-graph of the bed, another one of the table and chair, a third of the wardrobe. Then I stand in the doorway and take a picture of the whole room. I want to make some artistic use of this.

I have brought your manuscript with me, a few other books about Spain. I sit in bed and read "Heroes of Spain." Its straightforward accounts of battles and troop movements are broken up by rhetoric about the horrors of fascism, the sim-ple goodness of the Spanish peasants. When I can't stand it anymore, I put it down, pick up Alvah Bessie's *Men in Battle*. I didn't expect to like it; I thought it would be hack stuff, a bet-ter-written version of your "Heroes of Spain." It isn't. It's honest. It's hard. I flip through George Orwell's *Homage to Catalonia*.

These books upset me. I like your version better, Daddy, where there is no doubt, no ambiguity, where the heroes are all stalwart and brave, the people all simple and true. I want to keep you the way I've always kept you, a cartoon figure, the Incredible Anti-Fascist Fighter. My good Daddy. I don't want to know that because they were pure evil, it doesn't fol-low that you were pure good. I don't want to know about the trials within the International Brigades, the executions, the way the Communist Party played up to the petit bourgeoisie, that bullets flew in Barcelona, not against the fascists but against each other. Daddy, I don't even want to know that the men grumbled.

When the *boulangerie* opens at six in the morning, I get a croissant and a loaf of bread. I start driving again, driving south.

I am on a superhighway, crossing the gorges of the Pyrenees. I fiddle with the radio, looking for familiar songs. Here: the Beach Boys are singing about LaJolla and Pacific Palisades. You are beneath me, Daddy, struggling along a rut-ted mountain path. It is night when you cross, the darkness hiding you from the French border guards. You are panting, stumbling; you twist your ankle, you learn the meaning of the phrase second wind, third wind, fourth wind.

You look up, you look through time, at this gleaming highway above you. You see me, pressing my foot against the accelerator, gliding so easily along, listening to the Beach Boys, while your feet blister and swell, sweat soaks your shirt. You look up, you look through time, and you see it all: that you are going to die in a war that will be lost; Generalissimo Francisco Franco, Caudillo de España, President for Life, will govern Spain for nearly forty years; he will die an old man, in a hospital bed, surrounded by beeping machines and the bones of saints, after crying out, "What a hard thing it is to die!" You will father a brood of daughters who will hate you.

*Bitch*, you mutter at me, *bitch*.

It's only time that separates us, Daddy, only history.

At eight in the morning, the American volunteers bed down in the medieval castle of Figueras—a real castle, complete with moat and drawbridge and stone walls twenty feet thick. On the walls the men write "Mike Gallagher, Brooklyn, New York" and "Taki Pappas, Chicago" and "Spain will be the tomb of fascism" and "Long live the Popular Front."

Men who have grown up sleeping three, four, five to a bed in New York tenements lay tired heads easy in the laps of comrades. Jake can't sleep. His head on his boots; some guy from Chicago whose name he can't remember has made a pillow of his thigh. Jake isn't used to so much breathing, the smells of so many different men. I'm not like them, he thinks. I'll never be like them. They're the salt of the earth. I'm Little Lord-fucking-Fauntleroy.

The panic sets in again: They're going to give me a gun and expect me to shoot someone. And someone's going to be shooting back at me.

Yeah, well, Jake that's what you came here for, you volunteered to be a soldier.

Finally, he sleeps.

When they walk out into the late afternoon sunshine, the sky is so blue he cannot bear to look at it.

And then another train creeping south.

"Must be going two miles a fucking hour," one of the guys says.

After a few minutes, Jake says, "Ten."

"Huh?"

"Ten. We're going ten miles an hour."

"How do you figure that?"

"The distance between telephone poles, the number of poles passed in the space of a minute."

"Hey, I like this kid. You're a real brain."

Daddy, today I had lunch in Figueras. I ate a strange kind of ham that looked like uncooked bacon. In the image in my mind Figueras was a medieval town and the castle perched over it, squat and unmistakable, on the hill above. I realize now that the picture came from *The Story of Ferdinand*. Figueras is a city.

I looked up the word for castle in my dictionary: *castillo*. *Castillo*, that's an easy one. I asked in a travel agency, where there are brochures advertising package tours to the Costa Brava, Madrid, Paris, London. No, they didn't know of a castle. But one of their customers did. He speaks English. It's a gambling casino, he told me. Follow this road out of town, eight, nine kilometers. Turn right. You can't miss it. I'll see the signs, they say Casino. A universal word. Where in the states am I from? California, San Francisco. He'd seen pictures, it's a beautiful city, he hoped to go there someday. I smiled, said, You have a beautiful country, too.

I have to stop and rest before I walk to my car, which is parked two or three blocks away. Possibly illegally, I can't puzzle out the signs. There doesn't seem to be any such thing as disabled parking here. It's getting late, I'd better get going.

Daddy, I never found the castle. I drove around and around looking for it, kept asking, but no one else seemed to have ever heard of it. I should have known I'd be in trouble when he said *You can't miss it.* I gave up. I thought, if it's a casino now, it's probably been done over, they aren't going to let me go poking around. I used up the last of my film taking a few pictures of the place where I didn't find the thing I was looking for.

The thin, big-headed children run alongside the train and cry out, *"Pan, pan, un poco de pan, camarada."*

The villagers have no bread, but they have plenty of oranges. At every station where the train stops—and the train stops at every station it comes to—big-eyed strangers hold out oranges and call, *"¡Vivan los Americanos! ¡Vivan las Brigadas Internacionales!"* The juice from the oranges dribbles down Jake's chin and onto his shirt. How quickly you get filthy, from sleeping on the dirty floor of the train headed south, from the sticky juice of the Valencia oranges, from your own sweat and that of your *camarada.*

*¡Vivan los Americanos!*

*¡Viva la revolución!*

*¿Tienes pan?*

*¿Tienes tabaco para mi padre?*

The next morning they are served a liquid that is hot and bitter and called coffee. It is followed by a glass of cognac that leaves Jake fuzzy-headed for the rest of the day.

They sing, "John Henry," "Home on the Range," "Casey Jones," and of course, "The Internationale."

At Villanueva de la Jara, south of Madrid, where they are to receive basic training, a banner is strung across the plaza with a quote from *La Pasionaria*: "Better to die on your feet than live on your knees."

(Is it? Jake wonders.)

Prior military experience? None. Work experience? None. Ah, an intellectual. Welcome to Spain, Comrade. Here's your uniform.

Daddy, I look at the photograph of you in Spain, and you look lost in your clothes. I've read enough books, I know the uniforms were makeshift, women's ski pants even, hitched up with rope belts; or like matador pants reaching to just above the ankle. Daddy, you are a gawky twenty-year-old swimming in your uniform. You tried to grow a beard to make yourself look older but it came in as peachfuzz. A cigarette hangs out of the corner of your mouth, but you don't look tough, just silly.

I want to see you, but it's not you that I see. It's a dream, where everything melds together. I'm sitting in the dark of the Orson Welles in Cambridge or the Roxie in San Francisco. I'm in two places at once, watching *Ballad of a Soldier*, *Paths to Glory*, watching a movie of your life running in my head. Your part is played by Sal Mineo. The old guys like you, *You're all right, kid*. The grizzled factory worker, the hard-line old-timer who tosses his arm around your shoulder, he's played by Humphrey Bogart.

The men undress and climb into the river to bathe. Jake's only used to seeing the smooth young men in his gym class naked. A scar, fat and red, snakes up one man's leg, from ankle to thigh. One is covered from neck to ankles with thick black hair. Jake sees a Negro naked for the first time. He's surprised at the blackness of his penis; he'd assumed that, like the soles of their feet and the palms of their hands, it would be pale. More than a few of the men are bowlegged.

"What you gawking at, kid?" someone shouts to Jake, who blushes deep red.

The men train, using wooden broomsticks slung across their shoulders in the place of guns.

Finally, they are sent to the trenches. Here are rifles, *Mexicanskis*, made in the u.s., sent to the Czar—a hammer and sickle stamped over the Czarist eagle—sold to Mexico, donated by Mexico to the Spanish Republic. Here's 150

rounds of ammunition, all the Mills bombs you want, a needle bayonet. Come on, come on, get on the trucks, get on the
trucks. We need to be ready to move out the minute it's dark.

One of the commissars pleads with a higher-up, "Some of
these guys have never fired a gun before. You've got to let
them get off a few shots before you send them into the
trenches."

So, for the first time, Jake jams the heavy rifle against his
shoulder and aims for a tree across the *barranca*. He misses by
a good twenty yards.

Come on, come on, back on the trucks. Without headlights, a bitter-cold, moonless night, the trucks creep along in
blackness.

Two trucks packed with men take a wrong turn off the
Titulcia Road and drive behind enemy lines.

Two trucks, packed with men, take a wrong turn and disappear forever into the night.

How many days now in the trenches? Twenty-two.

To the tune of "The Red River Valley," the men sing:

> *There's a valley in Spain called Jarama*
> *It's a place that we all know too well,*
> *For 'tis there that we wasted our manhood*
> *And most of our old age as well.*

They carry out "revolutionary education." A man with a
bullhorn shouts across to the fascist trenches: "Spanish brothers! Conscripts forced against your will to fight! Republican
Spain, the democratically-elected government, embraces
you! Desert, and you will be welcomed into our ranks."

As the night wears on, the speeches about the workers and
the peasants and the volunteers pouring in from all over the
world are replaced by jeers about fascist fags and *la madre de
Franco*, and the doings of priests and nuns behind the locked
doors of convents.

Jake does not grumble. Not about the Lucky Strikes his sister sent that never arrived; not about the heat nor about the lice. He isn't a whiner and he isn't a quitter. He teaches the other men Spanish phrases and gives them haircuts. It's important, looking OK, or at least not too bad, for keeping up morale.

Every morning, they strip down and pick the lice off each other, squeezing the fat insects, bloated with blood, between thumb and forefinger till they pop.

The men sing:

*Waiting, waiting, waiting*
*Always fucking well wait-ing . . .*

For the rest of his life, Jake will not be able to rid himself of the suspicion that he has lice. His flesh will prickle until he has to drive across town to buy a bottle of Rid. He will wash his hair, his pubic hair, his body, with it.

Daddy, in classical physics, each particle of matter has a single history, a single path. But in current theory, each particle is assumed to follow every possible path. To find the probability that a certain particle passed through a certain point, one adds up the waves for particle histories that are not in real time, but in imaginary time—time expressed in imaginary numbers, numbers which when multiplied by themselves yield negative numbers. When you move into time expressed in imaginary numbers, the distinction between time and space collapses. That's what I came here for, to move into imaginary time, to see if by collapsing space, I could collapse time, too.

Maybe I have to imagine every possible history for you. I could begin all over again. I could look at that photograph of you taken on the day you graduated from college and see not awkwardness but fixity. I could imagine you as someone who found in the certainties of the American Communist Party of the thirties the same comforting certainty he found in mathematics, in engineering; who found a masculine world of right angles and bridges that could withstand so much stress the opposite of your mother's world of fluttering femininity.

Or I could imagine a Jake Etters who wanted to die, like I did when I was your age.

Maybe I have to imagine the histories that didn't happen; that your mother put her foot down: "No, we're not going to San Francisco. Jacques, you're going to get to go to Europe the summer after you graduate from college. We're going to Mexico." You never see the scaffolding collapse. Instead, you go to Mexico, you repeat your mother's sentiments, "I just don't understand how people can live like that." Jake, Jacques, the photograph's the same: you stand against the railing of the *Normandie*, the wind whips your clothing, your hair, it's only the look in the eyes that is different; you are not pretending. You are what you were meant become, a rich college boy traveling to Europe.

Or I have to imagine that your grandfather never left Germany. Instead of your fighting with the Lincolns, you become a loyal fascist. I imagine that you enlisted in the Condor Legion, flew the sortie that bombed the Lincolns at Brunete. On July 13, 1938, you marched through the streets of Berlin, past the throngs of cheering women and men, past the mothers who lean towards their children and take their chubby hands in their adult ones, showing them how to wave the red-and-black Nazi flag.

Or I could imagine that the Western democracies came to the aid of Republican Spain; that World War II never happened. Or I could imagine that you had a brief flirtation with communism, but didn't enlist in the Lincolns; you joined the Army, fought in the Pacific. After getting your doctorate in engineering, you worked for a while for an engineering firm, drifted away from the Party. Thinking you were smarter than any of your bosses, you left to found your own firm, and made millions. You never went to the party on Prospect Street, never met Eleanor McKenzie.

Can I imagine the square root of negative-1? Can I imagine there's no I?

Daddy, I have a bare skeleton of facts and artifacts. On June 15, 1937, you sailed from New York to Le Havre on board the *Normandie*; there are visas and embarkation stamps in purple ink on the back pages of your passport. I have the three photographs of you: one of you leaning on the ship's railing; one in which you are posed in your too-big uniform, with the other men of the brigade, a cigarette in the corner of your mouth; a fuzzy photo of you with some Spanish peasants, and I can barely make out the expression on your face. Daddy, I know that at Villanueva de la Jara there was a banner strung across the plaza: *It is better to die on your feet than to live on your knees.* I've read about it in books. It is a fact. What I don't know is whether you ever saw it. I don't know if you thought, *Is it?*

Today's vocabulary lesson: *coño*, cunt; *gazpacho*, vegetable soup; *fiambres*, corpse (literally, cold meat).

Jake's beard was growing thicker and the men at the *estado mayor* were taking a liking to him. Put a college boy from a fine family in a trench for a couple of months and what pretensions don't get scratched off when he scratches his lice bites will get washed off in the mud.

*Hey, college boy, you've got a degree in engineering, right? You're going to Madrid. They need an engineer, to talk about a bridge. Keep it quiet, you can't be too careful, those Trotskyite spies are everywhere.* The story passed to his comrades was that a reporter from a Detroit paper was in Madrid, wanted to do a story on a local boy in the fighting. So Jake goes off with an adjutant, a guy not much older than him.

"Vermont," the adjutant says. His name is Stan. "How about you?"

"Detroit."

"Your old man an auto worker?"

"No. Uh. Lawyer."

"Yeah?" Stan lets Jake sweat a bit in the silence. Then he smiles and says, "I'm a traitor to my class, too," and claps him on the back.

The two class-traitors walk arm-in-arm through the night-time streets of Madrid. The city is blacked out. The cars are allowed headlights so long as they are covered with blue paper. But there is hardly any gas, so only rarely does an arc of blue light cut through the darkness. Yet the streets are full. Some people whisper, some shout, no one speaks in a normal tone of voice. To walk in the dark with strangers so close, to hear the voices that could not be attached to any face coming through the thick night, so blue it is black. A white-skirted woman, only her skirt visible; or a hand caught by a ray of light slanting out a window.

"Jeez," says Stan. "This is neat."

The waiter in the restaurant asks, "What can I get you?"

"What have you got?"

The waiter shrugs and appears to be thinking. "Only garbanzos, Comrades," he says finally.

"Hey, Jake, what'd you say to garbanzos?"

Half an hour later, the waiter returns, smiling. He has managed to get some mule meat to add to the garbanzos, just for them. They chew and chew and chew.

They walk in darkness to a brothel. Jake loses his virginity in Madrid, in a brothel where a hand-lettered sign cautions the patrons "Remember, treat the women as comrades."

Like drinking a glass of water, Lenin had said. Jake shakes the woman's hand when she opens the door. The woman laughs, hands him a glass of harsh Spanish cognac and urges it down, and then another, and another. While the room is spinning around him, she takes off his pants and hoists up her own skirt and dispenses with the matter in about the time it takes to drink a glass of water.

Jake waits downstairs for Stan, and waits. The women give him more cognac and, finally, he falls fitfully asleep in a big armchair.

A grinning Stan shakes him awake. The sun is up. Jake wonders what Stan has been doing all this time. He wonders how with his head so foggy he will ever be able to talk with them about the bridge.

But at the office, they have coffee, real coffee, and after so many months of ersatz, it does the trick: Jake discusses metal fatigue and stresses with some comrades from Eastern Europe; he knows better than to ask where in Eastern Europe.

Madrid is a carnival, red flags and red-and-black flags flying everywhere. No one will take their money. *Tiempos Modernos* is still playing at the Capitol. Maybe they'll go tonight. They walk past tobacco shops with their signs that read *No hay tabaco* and the restaurants that stay open with the hand-lettered *No hay comida* in their windows. Black-bordered signs are pinned on doors, *Por mi padre, Por mi querido hermano, Por mi madre.*

They take a tram out to the National University, where the mathematics and engineering departments are in fascist hands. They walk along the sandbagged front and one of the comrades calls out to them, "Hey, come take a shot." Jake goes first; Stan waits next to him. It is like stepping up to the air guns at a carnival. Jake looks through the gun sights, takes a shot at movement—but only grazes a brick. A fascist rifle answers him.

"Close, huh?" Jake turns and says to the empty air.

Why do a dead man's clothes always look too big on him?

"We're moving out tonight."

"Says who?"

"Morrie, he was just up at the *estado mayor.*"

"I'll believe it when I fucking see it."

"We're finally fucking getting out of here. How long's it been?"

"Two fucking years."

"Hey, Jake? How long have we been in these here trenches?"

"137 days," Jake says.

March, march, march keep on a-marching. At first, the nervousness makes him giddy and he has to work to keep himself from smiling and looking goofy. But then, after the first ten miles, he is just tired, too tired to be scared. If you fall asleep on your feet the corporals will kick you awake. If the corporals fall asleep on their feet then the sergeants will kick them awake. If the sergeants fall asleep on their feet . . . See, it makes sense to have a chain of command.

Crouched on the field, waiting to attack, Jake gets the shakes. He gets the shakes bad: his teeth start chattering, chattering loud. One of the men shows him what to do. You put one hand on top of your head, the other under your chin, and hold your mouth shut. There you go, you're still scared, but at least you're not making that God-awful racket.

"Look at that sucker." The sun is a sucker, a fucking leech. A river in front of them is getting sucked up by it, the steam rising through the morning air. You sleep for a while in the hot sun, and when you wake your lips are cracked. You reach for your canteen, but then you remember that you drank all your water already.

Attack at noon. Move across a field of wheat. Suddenly black dots appear against the blue sky and then there's the hum of motors and there isn't even time to think, "The fucking Condors."

Men are crying for water and for first aid.

The earth is no longer beneath him and then it lands underneath him. Pain everywhere. Quick pats all over. No blood. Flex arms, legs. Nothing broken.

"Grab the grass!" someone is shouting into his ear. "Hold onto the grass!"

The force of the bombs is so great it's lifting them off the earth. A tree, a goddamn tree, roots and all, sailing through the air.

The sound, which is like thunder, parts, and in the few seconds' lull, he hears, "The Lord is my shepherd, I shall not want," and then those words are picked up and tossed around and broken apart and I just saw a leg fly past me in the air. Maybe the leg of the poor bastard who said, The Lord is my shepherd.

Jake doesn't pray, later he will be proud of himself for that. An atheist in a foxhole, so there.

Remember that song you sang, "Waiting, waiting, waiting, always fucking well waiting . . ." Well, boys, you aren't sitting around the Jarama Valley waiting anymore. Happy now?

Stench. Stench in the air, of the shit in his pants; stench of sulfur, dead comrades. Stink of burning: they've set the barley field next to this one on fire with incendiaries. Not so bad though: the smoke covers up the smell of the cold meat rotting in the hot sun of a Spanish afternoon.

Grab the grass, grab the grass. It's like a storm, just bullets instead of rain and the wind is death.

This is fighting the fascists? Lying here on an open field, getting killed? Somewhere, probably, refugees are getting out of a village, or some other battalion is cresting a ridge, because they're drawing fire. *Vivan los Lincolns*, the most heroic targets in all of Spain.

The planes have unloaded their bombs and become black dots and then disappeared. The smoke clears. Silence on the field of Brunete. Silence that can only mean death. Jake stands. *And I only am escaped alone to tell thee. Le Abraham Lincoln Brigade c'est moi.*

Bill stands up, and Stan—the other Stan—the shipyard worker from the Bronx. Everywhere, all across the field, men are rising up, everyone repeating the same actions, feeling their limbs all over: No, nothing broken. My arm's not ripped apart. I'm not going on the sheer ragged energy of the dying.

Are these ghosts? Are they dead, and is there really a here-after? What the fuck will Communists do in heaven?

In the distance, men from the Spanish division are running towards them. The Spanish comrades are shaking their heads, laughing. *Only seven dead. Impossible! How could you take that and lose so few men? We thought you were all gone. Here's water. Manuel, run back for the stretchers. How many wounded? Here's water and cigarettes and anise and don't cry, comrade, it's over, it's over.*

Did I get it right, Daddy? I know, I've had it easy, I've never even seen a dead body, I don't know the smells of death, of battle. I'm spoiled, Daddy, spoiled rotten. I only know what I've read in books, what I imagine.

Was it on that field that you ceased to be Jacques, your mother's son, and became Jake, the dead man who would father me?

When you came to Spain you went straight to Villanueva de la Jara, south of Madrid, then moved north. The route I take is the opposite of the one you took: you fight first at Jarama and Brunete, and then, as the Republic shrinks, you lurch back, north and east, to Aragon, Teruel, the Ebro River. I move south and west, reversing the order of your battles, your defeats.

Daddy, in a few days, when I am farther south, I will try to find the field where this battle was fought. I will keep asking everybody in my bad Spanish, using my tourist phrasebook. Everyone will be so kind to me. They will lay a hand on my shoulder, listen closely, try to puzzle out what I am saying.

"*En la guerra,*" I will say.

"*¿Qué?*"

"*En la guerra,*" I will repeat. Is it my bad Spanish they can't understand?

They will try to help me, but they will scarcely seem to

know there was a war fought here. It was a long, long time ago.

I'm standing in line at the bank, waiting to cash my travelers' checks. My ankles hurt. I feel queasy. I'm spending too much money. Four days down, six to go. I want to go home. I'm sick of having to climb these long flights of stairs to my rooms in cheap *pensiones*. I'm tired all the time. I want to see Matt. I get up to the window and I rip out one, two, three checks, sign them over. Only four left. There's always my credit card, I can slide it into a machine here, just like I can at home, push some buttons, and those big, brightly colored notes will slide out in return.

What did I come here for? This is crazy. Why didn't Matt talk me out of this? Here I am, with my tourist phrasebook. I can say, *¿Dónde está el baño?* and *¿Acepta Visa?* and I think I'm going to find some clue here?

Daddy, I want to do this right but I'm too pregnant, too tired, don't have money, don't have enough time. I keep meaning to buy more film, to write in my notebook, but I keep falling asleep instead.

Now I'm in Barcelona. It isn't the world that George Orwell described, the Barcelona where red flags and black flags flew everywhere; where every wall was scrawled with the hammer and sickle; where even the bootblacks had been collectivized and their boxes painted red and black.

What did I think? That in Spain time had stopped? That here I would find a clear answer—some things are worth dying for, emblazoned on the horizon?

This is a city, Daddy. It could be Milan or Rome or London or Frankfurt. A post-war miracle of steel and smog and cars. I can buy a Big Mac here. It doesn't matter at all that this war happened fifty years ago. I know, Daddy, if Britain and France and the u.s. had supported the Republic, if they'd stood up to Hitler, then maybe World War II would never have happened. But they didn't.

That doe-eyed Spanish boy sitting opposite me in this café, he wasn't even born, probably his parents weren't even born, when the war was fought. It's the faces of the old women, the old men, I should be searching. I'm middle-aged, Daddy. I'm middle-aged and you're dead.

On the way back to my car I pass a vendor selling crafts and cassette tapes from Nicaragua, the red and black of the FSLN flag. I stop and tell the two old men working there—try to tell them—that I'm a North American solidarity activist, but I'm not sure they understand me. I could say, *"El pueblo unido jamás será vencido."* I buy a wooden disc with an inlaid picture of a dove, a magnet on the back, made by a women's crafts cooperative in Esteli.

From Barcelona I drive south to Tarragona. This could be northern California: the mountains rising from the ocean, the palm trees, the great broad-leafed succulents, the brown hillsides.

This place is filled with history, but it's not the history that I'm looking for. It's history that's safely dead.

Tarragona was a Roman resort. I buy a postcard of the worn stone fountain that the Roman colonizers left behind. I go to the museum, stand before shards of Roman pottery sealed in a glass case. The woman whose hands shaped this pot, the woman who lifted it to her lips and drank water from it, the child who bumped against it and broke it—all of them are dead. Someday even this shard of pottery, and the hermetically sealed glass case that holds it, will have crumbled into dust.

Then I turn inland, heading for the Rio Ebro. I drive into the interior. I am driving backwards in time. You must have seen towns like this, Daddy, that seem hardly to have changed in a thousand years, the mottled yellow houses with the red roofs in the hills of northern Spain. I pass groves of olive trees with their silver leaves. I see the unbearable blue of the Spanish sky.

I stop in one of these yellowed towns clinging to the side of a hill. I want to eat, but it's two in the afternoon; everything's still closed. I'll wait, I wander around the town. The door to the church is unlocked, so I go inside. The rough-hewn pews, the scrubbed floorboards. The statues, with gazes turned heavenward and crude postures that read "piety," "devotion"—yet they move me. Some untrained hand carved these, determined to speak its truth.

The windows are high, barely admitting light. The air is dark, heavy with centuries of dust. I go outside, wander through the graveyard. Most of the inscriptions have worn away. There's a building off to the side, its door open.

Bones. Hundreds, thousands of them. White legs and white arms and delicate finger-bones and stumpy toe-bones, pelvises and skulls. White bones piled in disarray.

For a few seconds, I think of Cambodia. I think I have stumbled across some horror. But no, I remember reading about this, somewhere: that they dig up the bones from graveyards to make room for more of the dead, store them in ossuaries.

He does it, finally, five months after he comes to Spain. He squeezes the trigger, the bullet is fired, the body crumples. *God, it was me who did that. It really was, it was me.* He feels proud and giddy, like a kid at a fair; and then he throws up.

After that it's—well, it's never easy, just never as hard again.

No. Maybe that's wrong. Plenty of the men must have never killed at all, just stayed dug in trenches, their bullets shooting wide of the mark, shooting close to the mark but not quite close enough.

Later, Jake, you will stand on a hill and watch the clean Nationalist Army roll past in their green tanks, rows of them, with uniforms that are identical. These men are not outfitted in women's ski pants, they are not given thirty-year-old guns.

There are no old men in the brigades of the fascists, no men hiding a hand in their pockets because they are missing two fingers and are afraid they will get sent back home.

Two Greek-American brothers join the Lincolns, one named Hercules and the other named Pericles. "No shit," they were greeted wherever they went, "Hercules and Pericles. Eh, how about that?" "How the fuck can we lose, with Hercules and Pericles on our side, huh?"

Brunete to Aragon; Aragon to Teruel. He came in June, it's March now, a lifetime has passed. It's his turn to get it next, he knows it's his turn next. He's been in Spain too long, everyone who came over with him is dead. Dead or lucky, sent back home blinded or crippled.

Jake knows all about probability. He knows that if you toss a coin into the air, and it comes up heads, the chances are fifty-fifty on the next toss that it will come up heads. And fifty-fifty on the toss after that. And the toss after that. Even if it comes up heads a hundred, a thousand, a million times in a row, always the chances on the next toss are fifty-fifty.

He keeps telling himself, over and over again, that his chances of getting shot are just the same as they were the first day he went into battle. There's no such thing as your number being up. No such thing.

Now I'm standing on the banks of the Ebro. I thought it would be as broad as the Amazon, the Mississippi. It's an ordinary river, not nearly as wide as the Charles. Gray water bearing steadily towards a distant sea.

I walk along its banks, setting my right ankle down carefully with each step, scoping rocks, clumps of earth, worried about twisting my ankle. I read that in places in Spain where battles were fought, you can find dirt-encrusted metal buttons from military uniforms, leather belts, shell casings, pelvises bleached pale by the sun, rusted Mills bombs, old shoes, skulls. I walk along the banks of this river, looking for a fragment of you.

Today's vocabulary lesson: *maricones fascistas*, fascist fags; *quinta columna*, fifth column; *resistir es vencer*, to resist is to win.

Mostly it was boring, wasn't it, Jake? The sitting around, waiting to go into battle, the camps that were more like Hoovervilles, *chavolas*, lean-tos made of reeds and palm fronds that protected you from the sun but not from the flies and the thick heat.

They get pushed back to the Ebro. The fascists have bombed the bridge across the river. Lucky Jake knows how to swim, but these kids from Brooklyn, they sure as hell never got out to the country club for a dip on a hot summer afternoon. Jake's trying to tell them to trust the water, let themselves float, as long as you don't panic, the current will carry you across.

They don't believe him. "Look," he says, dives into the water, rolls on his back and floats, swims across, then swims back. "It's easy."

Here's a barrel, where the hell did that come from? Just hold on, the current's going downstream but eventually it'll carry you to the other side. Start hiking north, we'll meet up. But Manny gets panicky, as the water rushes him downstream, starts screaming "Help! Help!" and lets go.

Dubinsky's dog-paddling his way across. He gets short of breath, his arms are worn out. He thinks, Everybody's got to go sometime, why not now? Drowning, it wouldn't be so bad; it would sure as hell beat getting your guts shot apart. He let's go; he lets himself sink. His feet touch clay. He's in four feet of water. Four fucking feet! He wades ashore, laughing.

The last sentence of your manuscript reads, "I showed the men, most of whom didn't know how to swim, how to swim, and most of them made it across the Ebro."

What happened afterwards that you couldn't write?

Was it losing you couldn't put into words? Did you come here to cease to be your mother's precious Jacques, to purge the woman from your soul? Could you only speak of defeat in her tongue?

Stan, the shipyard worker from the Bronx, says, "I'm a fucking volunteer, aren't I? I can de-volunteer, can't I?"

"Quit bellyaching," someone else says.

"Bellyaching? Bellyaching? Hey, you know what? We're losing this fucking war. Can you guys get that through your thick fucking heads—"

"Shut up," Jake says. If it wasn't so hot, he'd make the effort to rouse himself and land a sock on his jaw.

The next morning, they spend an hour and a half sitting in the early morning sun listening to a commissar talk. How long do you men think the civilized world will watch the naked aggression of Hitler? (Someone sitting near Jake drawls: "I dunno. How lo-ong do you think they'll watch it?") The people of the world, who love freedom and democracy, are rallying to our cause . . .

Some of the men start scrawling FONIC on the walls, for Friends Of the Non-Intervention Committee. It's all a joke, come on, Jake, can't you take a joke?

Stan de-volunteers, or deserts, gets marched back a few days later, his head hanging, pus dripping from his left eye. He gets put on trial, sentenced to death, but his sentence is commuted to being sent to the front.

During the trial, Jake sits on the muddy ground, listening. He's afraid to look up, afraid he'll meet someone's eyes. But when he does steal a glance everyone is sitting, just like he is, staring at the ground or off into space.

"Our strength is not in fancy weapons. Our strength is the spirit of our men." That's what the commissar keeps saying.

The Brigade, the decimated Brigade, is to be integrated

with Spanish soldiers. When the conscripts from Alicante arrive, they are all so young, some only sixteen, at that age of boyhood when they look more like girls than men, their olive skin covered with soft down, their liquid eyes. One boy pulls a live rabbit from his cardboard suitcase.

When the Spanish soldiers are wounded they cry out *"¡Mamá! ¡Ay Mamá!"* The Americans call out "Ma! Ma!"

The Spanish boys have a mocking familiarity with death. When one of them accidentally blows himself up with a Mills bomb ("First time one of those ever worked," one of the Lincolns says), the boys from his village shrug and say, *"Pobre Pablito."*

That is what Jake yearns for: to understand that the beating of his heart counts for no more than the beating of any other heart, that only to his mama is he a precious, darling boy. He wants to be a cog in a wheel doing what needs to be done.

Late one night, Jake is alone with one of the boys in his *chavola*. He grabs the boys hand, unzips his own pants.

You are horny, but it is more than that. You need the boy to be a lightning rod for your repulsion, to draw that wild electricity from you and ground it into the dirt. Daddy, I know what you were thinking when you felt his groping mouth against you, *Cocksucker. Punk. Homosexuality is a product of a decadent society.* This boy's groping mouth was like the dysentery, the lice: something that would be left behind when you marched into the future, where the sun would always be shining.

Daddy, did you think, Within my own heart is lurking the desire for an end to the fighting, for clean sheets, a good night's sleep, the false peace of the past? And you were a loyal, developed Party member. If it's in your heart, how much more in the hearts of those conscripted for the fighting? How much more in the men who came to Spain full of idealism?

This is one of the times that people hardly speak about. I read, in a footnote, that towards the end of the war around fifty members of the International Brigades were shot for desertion. I know that anarchists and Trotskyists were killed by troops loyal to the Communist Party. (Daddy, you are sweating in the hot Spanish sun. In the Soviet Union, Left Oppositionists are being marched through the Siberian snow to their deaths, singing "The Internationale" as they tramp through the swirling snow to be shot. Some call out "Long Live Stalin" as the order to fire is given.)

Daddy, did you take the doe-eyed Spanish boy out and have him shot? Did you tell yourself it was because he was a fascist spy? Did you only dream you took the Spanish boy out and had him shot? Did you do it and tell yourself it was a dream?

Daddy, trust no one. You will father a race of daughters who will betray you. Fifty years from now, one of them will fly here on a jet plane; she will drive across those mountain passes you stumbled through. She will look down on you. She will imagine your life. She will understand you.

Trust no one, Daddy. They will all betray you.

Only the dead, safe in the Spanish earth, safe under the swirling waters of the fast-moving Ebro, only they can be trusted.

I'm tempted to forgive you, tempted to mourn for my father: for Jake Etters, who rode aboard the trucks that took a wrong turn and disappeared behind enemy lines; for my father taken out by a fascist sniper in Calle de la Luna de Madrid; who died in the swirling waters of the swiftly-moving Ebro; for my father, who was taken out and shot with a doe-eyed Spanish boy who was or was not a fascist spy. For my father, whose bones lie scattered with the bones of hundreds of others in a Spanish ossuary; his bones bleached white by the hot Spanish sun, lying under the unbearably blue Spanish sky.

For my poor father, who did not get to die, heroic in the Jarama Valley, who did not swirl under the muddy waters of the Ebro, who did not stop a bullet on the road to Huesca, for my father, who had to go on living for decades after his death.

Mourning, forgiveness are too easy. They aren't what I came here for.

The Internationals are to be repatriated. It's a last-ditch effort on the part of the Republic to get the fascists to withdraw their "volunteers."

*La Pasionaria* bids you farewell: "Mothers! Women! When the years pass by and the wounds of war are staunched, then speak to your children. Tell them of the International Brigades. . . . Comrades of the International Brigades! . . . You can go proudly. You are history. You are legend. . . . We shall not forget you. . ."

The Lincolns are grinning, they're getting the fuck out. The Spanish comrades stare glumly at the death that awaits them alone.

The men of the Thaelmann and Garibaldi Brigades, who have managed to get here from Nazi Germany and fascist Italy, have found out that the Soviet Union's not going to take them. They are supposed to return to their own countries and continue the struggle against fascism. Stalin knows: never trust a man who would sacrifice his life for yours. Flip a coin with death's head on either side into the air and the chances are one hundred percent it will always come up heads. (Comrade, what can I wish you but a clean wound straight to your heart, and take a few fascisti with you when you go.) The coin is spinning, spinning in the air as a German with fake papers, a blond among the black-haired Spaniards, flows with the refugees streaming into the south of France; it comes up heads, of course, heads, one night when the butt of a rifle bangs against the door of a French farmhouse. You are an exile from fascism, repatriated to the one country that opens its borders to you, the country of the dead.

Daddy, everything's muddy after that: your obituary said that you tried to keep fighting. Did you slip into a Spanish battalion and fight hand-to-hand in the last desperate days of Madrid, seeking, still desperately seeking, your death? Was that just a story? Were you one of the grinning guys, glad to be getting out?

I'm done. My time is up. My plane leaves from Paris in two days. It's mid-afternoon. I'm tired. I've rented a room. The landlady of the *pension* keeps looking at me. I'm an oddity in this small inland town, a woman tourist, alone. I open the window. The wood of the sill and frame are old, soft beneath my fingers. I raise the shade, pull open the white curtains.

The sun streams through the window. The dust motes dance in the air. The bare, scrubbed floorboards. The wardrobe. The iron bedstead, the white cotton sheets and heavy white cotton blankets. A crucifix on the wall above my bed, a picture of a doe-eyed Mary opposite.

I prop the pillows up behind me. The veins in my hands are thick now, and so blue they are almost purple; my body filling up with blood. Already, inside me, a primitive pump is beating: what exists before a heart.

I am leaving here, tomorrow. Here has become there; there, here. And then I will fly on that 747 and it will switch back, back to the way it's always been. Here, there. Now, the past.

The warmth of the rumpled pillow under my cheek, the saliva dried on my face: I've been asleep. The light has changed from unbearable blue to gray.

I sit up in bed. I feel a bit queasy. I lean over, and pull the box of salted crackers out of my satchel, nibble on a few. An afternoon breeze billows the sun-bleached muslin curtains.

I realize I've dreamed of my father. But I'm happy. One of my odd motionless dreams, a frozen image: Daddy, you were sitting in the Danish-modern chair where you always sat in our old house on River Street in Cambridge. You were sitting in that chair, wearing tan pants and a blue shirt. The shirt had a brown splotch half-way down on the left side (soy sauce, maybe?). The top two buttons were undone; I could see your gray chest hair. Your brown shoes had been kicked off, were lying on the floor next to you. You were wearing maroon socks. Your face was lined. Your gray hair was thin. That's all.

Daddy, for the first time I dreamed of you not as I saw you when I was a child. You weren't the troll under the bridge preying on the three billy goats gruff; you weren't the giant living at the top of the beanstalk in the clouds. In the dream, you looked at me, and I looked at you.

This is what I came here for. To lie alone in this room and watch the motes of dust in the shaft of light from the low afternoon sun, to dream this dream.

## COLOPHON

The interior of this book was designed by Nora Koch, set in Monotype Dante and Adobe Albertus types using Adobe Caslon Ornament dingbats. It was Smythe sewn for readability and durability.